CROSSHOUSE AT WAR

Love, loss and loyalty in a village at war

Jacqueline Heron Wray

ISBN: 978-1-9993610-8-2

This novel is entirely a work of fiction although some of the historical details and characters are factual. Persons named within the script are fictional and are the product of the author's imagination. Apart from those in the public domain, any similarity to persons past or living is coincidental. Representative of the era, the novel contains a small amount of strong language.

DEDICATION

To those who served in times of war, who stood firm in the face of danger, and whose courage shaped the freedoms we hold today.

We remember with gratitude.

We honour with pride.

We stand in thanks.

The author is proud to donate all royalties from the sale of CROSSHOUSE AT WAR to Erskine Veterans Charity, supporting their dedicated care for veterans and their families.

PREFACE

Erskine Veterans Charity is proud and honoured to support Crosshouse at War, a poignant tribute to the courage and resilience of a community shaped by two world wars.

War reshapes lives in ways both visible and unseen. With this book we encounter not only the bravery of soldiers who answered their nation's call, but also the steadfast spirit of families and neighbours who endured hardship with dignity. The story of Crosshouse reflects the shared experience of communities across our country, communities bound together by sacrifice, loyalty, and hope.

At Erskine, we are committed to supporting those who have served and those who stand beside them. This book serves as a powerful reminder that remembrance is a responsibility we all share.

The author has preserved these important stories and ensured that the legacy of service and community spirit lives on.

Susan C M Hamilton

Communications Officer

ERSKINE
Veterans Charity

CONTENTS

ACKNOWLEDGMENTS

Weaving Through the History of Crosshouse by Charles Hannah and Jimmy Stewart is courtesy of Sadie McHarg (née Stewart).

The following provided memories and stories of life in Crosshouse during World War Two:

Gordon Walker

Matt Dorrans

Archie Johnstone

Stephen Crawford

Martha Law

Billy Arnott

Nancy Fleming

Pete Heywood

James Heron

The Forgotten Battle by Patrick Macgill

Loos 1915 - The Unwanted Battle by Gordon Corrigan (2018, Sharpe Books)

http://www.secretscotland.org.uk

https://www.bbc.co.uk/bitesize/guides/z4n4jxs/revision/

The Daily Express

Grateful thanks to Jean Murphy and Holly Heron for their beta reading skills, and finally to my husband Mike for his continued support, patience and understanding.

PART 1

CHAPTER ONE

Maggie, 1915

The glimmering warmth of candlelight bounced from the glossy black range and back into the room, creating a rosy glow. The range – a huge presence in a small room – was the very heart of the cottage. Maggie often thought that her Jim was a bit like that range: solid and trustworthy, and something which she absolutely could not do without. She took great pleasure in polishing the cast iron fire surround with blacklead every day. Once she had cleared out the ashes and re-set the fire, she buffed up the steel trims with wire wool until they shone. She had done this every day since her marriage to Jim almost 21 years ago. Maggie had been in service before her marriage, cleaning other people's ranges, setting other people's fires. When she got one of her own, she was overwhelmingly proud and had never taken it or Jim for granted.

Maggie looked over at the small stack of dishes beside the sink. Jim had, as he always did, brought water in from the street pump before he went to the pub for a well-earned pint after a day down the pit.

Maggie had always worried about Jim working in the coal mine; accidents were an almost daily occurrence, but now she was grateful that he was a miner. He needn't feel guilty about the *Britons: Lord Kitchener Wants You. Join Your Country's Army! God Save The King* posters which had sprung up all over the country. He was fighting this war deep underground; it had always been dangerous work, but never more vital that it was now.

Maggie groaned under the weight of the kettle as she lifted it from the range, heavy even before it was full of water. She teetered towards the shallow sink in the corner of the room using a hand-knitted cloth to protect her hands from the heat emanating from the handle. After tipping most of the scalding liquid over the mismatched crockery which lay awaiting its fate, she filled the teapot which was ready and waiting on the wooden work top beside it. She had done this so many times she knew exactly how much water to leave in the bottom of the kettle to fill the teapot almost to the top. Scooping up the washing soda that was in a chipped bowl by the sink, she added it to the water and sloshed it around with a wooden spoon before letting the dishes steep for a minute or two until she could risk her rough, red, workworn hands going in to wash them. After years of housework, she could withstand hot water, but even she drew the line at dabbling in almost boiling temperatures.

As usual, not a scrap of food had been left on the mis-matched plates. Dinner tonight had been potatoes with a small knob of butter, plenty of salt and pepper, a potato scone, and a glass of creamy milk.

Maggie's sister Jean worked as a dairy maid at one of the numerous farms dotted around Crosshouse and Knockentiber. About once a week she would visit to swap snippets of gossip and news, and she always brought a bit of butter and a few eggs.

'Did I tell you that the dairymaid is getting married?' Maggie shook her head.

'Well, Effie the dairymaid is gettin' wed to Archie, the ploughman's son.' Jean folded her arms tightly beneath her ample bosom.

'Next week if you please, they say there is no point in waiting when there is a war on. Of course I smiled and nodded to keep them happy, but I will get my knittin' needles oot jist the same.' She touched her nose with her index finger.

Maggie had become adept at making a little go a very long way. The shops were always half empty. Individuals with money travelled far and wide buying up supplies, leaving the likes of Maggie to make do with what was left. Villagers complained bitterly about it while they queued at the Co-op.

'Mr Asquith needs tae do something aboot it, it's just no fair. We are being left with nothing while the rich folk have full bellies and full pantries.'

Maggie looked towards the range where Chrissy was sitting on a wooden stool warming her toes in front of the glowing orange embers, a calm quiet scene which Maggie drank in as she sipped from her cup, feeling as much warmth from gazing at her daughter as she did from the hot, watery tea. In the quiet of the moment, she allowed herself to imagine what the boys were doing. *Where were they? Did they have enough to eat? Were they warm enough?* She refused to allow herself to ask the question, *Will they come home safe?* Betty, James's wife, had received a letter just the other week, but Maggie hadn't heard from John or Billy for weeks now.

Chrissy was avidly reading a book by the soft glow of the oil lamp perched on the broad mantle shelf, curling her toes in the colourful rag rug which Maggie had made several years ago. Each piece of cloth held cherished memories: clothes that had once been worn by her boys, by her mother and sister, handed down and worn out, but still serviceable when cut up into strips and woven into sack cloth.

Maggie was so proud of her daughter; she did well in school and loved to read. The teacher had remarked more than once to Maggie that he was very impressed with Chrissy's reading skills and penmanship.

'Did you weed the vegetable patch this afternoon, Chrissy?'

Her daughter didn't look up.

'Chrissy, put that book down. I'm talking to you. Did you get the weeding done?'

'Sorry, Mammy, aye I did, and I have nearly finished the scarf I am knitting to send to James, then I will start one for Billy. Sally's finished the socks she has been knitting, but I think her mammy helped her. She says she didn't, but some of the rows and stitches look different to me! Sally is always telling fibs.'

Maggie laughed at this observation. Her daughter was wise beyond her eleven years and had an astute sense of fairness in all things to do with school.

'Did I tell you that Jessie fell in the drill hall when we were marching and doing our exercises? She landed on her wrist and you should have heard her yelling. The teacher threatened her with the belt if she didn't haud her wheesht and stop making such a racket. He told her she needed to be brave like our soldiers.'

'Quite right, too,' said Maggie, which pleased Chrissy no end.

'Can we go to the pictures on Saturday, Mammy... please? I will help Dad to lift the onions and dig up the potatoes, and I will run over to the farm to save Auntie Jean coming over with the eggs and butter. Oh, do you think she might even have some cheese this week?'

'Take a breath, lassie, you will be doing all those things whether we go to the pictures or not,' said Maggie, trying to be stern but failing miserably. And don't think for a minute that I don't know what you are doing. Bedtime, miss, and no more reading the night.'

'Och, Mammy, can I just finish this chapter? I wish I could go to Avonlea and be friends with Anne Shirley and Gilbert Blythe.'

'I'll tell you what, you can go to bed and dream about them!' laughed Maggie. 'Make the book last more than a few days for a change – you are never away from that library.'

'It's freezing through in the bedroom, Mam. It's so cosy here ... just half an hour longer, please?'

Maggie looked into her daughter's earnest shining eyes and her heart melted. If truth be told, since the boys had been posted who-knew-where, Chrissy had kept her sane, and she relished their time together and wanted to keep her close by for company whenever she could. Why had James and Billy volunteered? Now John was talking about joining up before he was forced to; he was still only seventeen, but his eighteenth birthday was looming fast.

Maggie had been conscious of John's reaction when his big brothers marched out of the village in their uniforms. His face illuminated with elation and pride. Bunting and flags were flapping and swaying in the breeze. A pipe band drummed up feelings of invincibility and patriotism. There was so much cheering and waving as she watched her boys who were dressed up as men. Her lads who would be expected to fight like men and, if necessary, die like men. John had danced with enthusiasm, hardly able to contain his excitement as all the brave young men in the battalion disappeared into the distance, leaving Maggie feeling like she had lost something which she could never get back. Her heart felt like a block of ice which could shatter into tiny pieces at the slightest provocation, never to be made whole again. Fat wet tears had tumbled down her face that day and every night since.

'Right, how about another half hour by the fire and... a cup of cocoa?'

'Ocht, Mam, you are the best mam ever! I bet Anne Shirley and Marilla Cuthbert would love you as much as I do,' she said absently as she stuck her nose back into the idyllic world of *Anne of Green Gables*, the juxtaposition of Anne's world and Chrissy's as wide as the ocean which divided them.

CHAPTER TWO

1915

Jim was long gone by the time Chrissy was ready to leave for school.

'Here's a piece 'n' jam for play time,' Maggie said.

Chrissy eyed the bread and jam wrapped in brown paper with disdain.

'Jam again?' She rolled her eyes dramatically, making Maggie smirk.

'Aye, jam again, and you should be thankful to have a piece to eat at all. I've picked some apples, so I'm going to make jelly, that's if the store has any sugar. Take an apple too, and run or you will be late.'

'Cheerio, Mammy, see you later,' Chrissy said and she was off, skipping her way to school with not a care in the world.

Maggie wasted no time. She pulled on her coat, fixed her hat firmly on top of her head, grabbed the list she had scribbled earlier, and made her way to the village shops.

The Co-op was managed by Andrew Fisher's grandson. The villagers were immensely proud that a Crosshouse boy was the Prime Minister of Australia; it gave many of the young village lads ambition they had been lacking, and they dared to hope for a better future for themselves, as did some of the girls, too. As war progressed, women were taking on roles that had previously been male dominated. Not only that, but they were doing them well. Although Emmeline Pankhurst and her militant suffragette campaign had been put on hold for the duration of the war, the way women had stepped up and got on with the most demanding and physical jobs had not gone unnoticed and gave substance to the motto, *Deeds not Words.*

Maggie stood outside the Co-op and looked in the window, tutted loudly, and shook her head so hard that her hat almost fell off. Housewives were continually being reminded about the wheat shortage. *Eat less bread and beat the U Boats.* She had become quite a dab hand at making potato bread and scones. Thankfully they never seemed to be short of potatoes, living in the country and growing their own.

Closing her eyes for a moment, Maggie recalled looking into the co-operative store window just over a year ago. It had been packed with things she could barely afford, but they were there, and she had often saved for treats.

She remembered gazing longingly at the packets of custard creams and Bourbon biscuits and wondering what they would taste like. She had tried digestive biscuits once when the shop was selling cheap bags of broken biscuits and had marvelled at the crumbly grainy texture. Shop-bought biscuits were a rare extravagance. Maggie had inherited her mother's gift for baking – her mother's shortbread recipe took some beating and was always a welcome indulgence.

The shop window, once vibrant with bottles of pickles, jams, teas and coffees, now looked empty and bare.

Maggie pushed the door open making the bell jingle its shrill tune, announcing her arrival. She tutted again when she noticed her beetroot-stained fingers.

Inside, the aroma of paraffin and flour clung to the wooden floor and walls. The shelves were sparsely stocked with tins of condensed milk, soap bars wrapped in brown paper, and jars of barley, lentils, split peas, oatmeal and salt. At the far end there was a jar only a quarter full of tea next to one half full of cocoa.

Her spirits lifted when she spotted a few small paper cones filled with sugar and she was glad she had got there early enough to buy some. She hoped that she would be able to buy some tea. The days of a spoonful for each person and one for the pot were long gone. A chalkboard near the counter read:

Donations for Belgian relief Still Welcome

Crosshouse Co-op Reading Room:

Next Lecture 'Women and the War Effort'

Thursday, 7pm

'Good morning, Mrs Barnes, what can I do for you today?' asked Mr Fisher.

'Well, I am pleased to see you have some sugar and tea left, and it hasn't been bought up by the rich folk in Kilmarnock.'

'I know, but my hands are tied – until they introduce rationing, it's first come, first served.'

'Fine, I ken Mr Fisher, it canny come soon enough for me and the rest of the village.'

The other women in the shop nodded and agreed with her.

'Hear, hear, Mrs Barnes, it's just no fair, is it? I was just saying the other day... oh no, listen, the church bell just tolled once.'

A hush fell over the shop.

'That means a telegram has arrived.'

'That'll be the post from Kilmarnock. God help whoever it's for.'

'Aye, Mr Fisher, God help them indeed.'

Just for a moment the shop became a sanctuary, half lit, half hopeful, holding its breath.

CHAPTER THREE

James, Diary Entry 1915

"I saw some rats running from under the dead men's greatcoats, enormous rats, fat with human flesh. My heart pounded as we edged towards one of the bodies. His helmet had rolled off. The man displayed a grimacing face, stripped of flesh; the skull bare, the eyes devoured and from the yawning mouth leapt a rat."

Unknown

Today is the 25th September 1915. My whole being is totally preoccupied and exhausted merely by willing myself to hack it, to survive, to do what is expected of me and to do it well.

Last night was long, cold, and busy as usual.

Stand-to arms lasted until it got dark, and then we cracked on with duties and jobs too dangerous to attempt in daylight. We often work through the night until dawn and the morning stand-to.

We repaired parapets, spied on the Huns' defences, moved guns into position, got supplies, improved and repaired trenches ... the list is endless.

There are detailed ammunition, ration and water parties. Groups of us are sent to go and get daily supplies from the wagon lines. Can you believe the water is often fetched in old petrol cans? Our tea tastes horrible, but ocht, it is warm and wet, and we are glad of it most of the time. Nothing can beat our snifter of rum in the mornings. It fair warms us up and steadies the nerves.

The horses, donkeys and mules, big gentle beasts, plod through the mud carrying the bulk of the supplies. I often wonder if they know what is going on ... are they as scared as me? We have dogs and cats trained as ratters. Cheeky wee devils at times, they fairly entertain us with their shenanigans.

Some of the dogs have helped us to lay cables for the telephones and power, and we even have a canary to warn us when the poisonous gas is on its way. Dogs and pigeons carry messages too. We could not do what we do every day without them. Suddenly I can hear *All things bright and beautiful, all creatures great and small* playing in my head. It makes me smile.

The wiring parties work all night, repairing or rebuilding our own wire barricades as well as using sappers to cut through Gerry's, making it easier for us to break through when the time comes to attack, slithering on our bellies through the mud, our faces camouflaged with dirt trying not to make a sound, heading out to cut away at their barbed wire barriers. Some of us were instructed to head towards the sap head listening posts. It was strange listening to the brusque unfamiliar German accents, wondering what they were saying. Were they talking about us? Were they feeling the same as we were, frightened, alone and far from home?

Aye, the trenches came alive at night. Gerry sent up flares which lit up the sky with a peculiar powdery-green light and then fired machine guns out over no man's land at any sign of movement. All we could do was to stay very still under the greenish haze, hunker down and hope for the best.

We do the same to them, mind you.

During the day it is different. Loads of us complain of boredom, aye, boredom, can you believe it? Not one soul can be seen above the trench. Nothing to see in no man's land in daylight hours. We check our guns, our equipment and uniforms; we eat, we talk, we look forward to letters from home. We try to ignore the flies, the mud, the noises, and catch 40 winks, yearning for sweet dreams however short-lived.

The officers and NCOs carry out regular inspections, amongst other things checking our feet for signs of trench foot, which is rife. (I have seen men's feet looking like huge ripe juicy red tomatoes once their boots come off. I remember last winter many of the lads lost toes, even feet, because of frostbite and gangrene.)

We must wear our uniforms properly, no slacking, and rightly so in my opinion: standards and discipline need to be maintained. Without standards, regulations and rules we would fall apart. We have an incentive to comply: to avoid being assigned the title of sanitary personnel. Sanitary personnel are responsible for clearing out and maintaining the latrines. I would'nae wish that on ma worst enemy...well, unless he's a Gerry, of course.

We get rotated from the front every week, thank God. We spend no more than six days, sometimes only four, in the fire trench, which, being our first line of resistance, is full-on and the most dangerous. Behind that trench is the support trench, and behind that is the reserve trench. All three are connected by communication trenches, criss-crossing so that we never need to poke our heads above the parapet. The support trench is where the kitchens and dressing stations are. In the dressing stations, our wounds get cleaned and dressed, but they often get infected and suppurated. Festering stinking wounds, dribbling with green pus. The flies love it.

When our turn comes to go back behind the line, we are thankful to have survived another stint at the front. Knowing that back there, we can sleep, have a wash, get clean clothes, and sleep a bit more is like paradise compared to the front.

We are usually knee-deep in mud, deeper in places if there are no duck boards. The sludge beneath our feet is a curious thick blend of yellowish chalky clay, rat excrement, dirt, and God only knows what else. I hate that mud almost as much as the rats seem to revel in it as they dart and scramble about, bellies fat from feasting on human flesh. There are flies everywhere, swarms of them, as well as fleas and lice.

Some of the Tommies and Jocks, that's what we are called, say that they enjoy military life. They like the camaraderie, the beer, the cigarette and rum rations. They even enjoy the meals, mostly tins of bully beef, pea soup with horse meat and horrible loathsome hard biscuits. Those hard little bastards crack and break the teeth of many a lad but aren't so bad if you grind them up and mix them with a bit of jam if you are lucky enough to have any.

It is grand to get letters and parcels from home. Socks, scarves, chocolate, jam and cakes. When we are billeted, we visit the estaminets which are all over the place; these are cafés set up in the local people's front rooms where we can buy food or a dram for a halfpenny, have a laugh and try to forget where we are.

When we go over the top, we take our iron rations, tins containing tea, sugar, meat, cheese and those bloody biscuits, enough to last us a day or so in case we get stranded.

I remember one young lad, he looked about 15, when he experienced life on the front line for the first time.

Shocked, he cried out: 'Is it always like this?'

'Only on Saturday nights,' was the reply he got. Aye, we have to keep some sort of sense of humour, don't we?

Just last week, the chaplain said in his service that by next Sunday many of us would have ceased to exist. Cheery, eh? But straight to the point. The officers know that this is not going to be an easy battle, well, not for us, anyway. For a start, we are going to use gas for the first time; Gerry beat us to it last April at Ypres, causing an uproar. The Hun was called evil and underhand for using it, but now our cylinders are at the ready along the trench, sauce for the goose... sauce for the gander. Looking out towards no man's land we can see Tower Bridge, well, that is what we call it. A landmark which we have tried in vain to destroy. Gerry has a vantage point from up there with views out towards our front line and beyond. Our artillery has also tried to blast through the 100-foot-deep coils of barbed wire on the German lines, but the soldiers firing the guns lack the experience to cut through it completely. On top of that, the Huns have prime positions on top of the slag heaps which are dotted about. We know the officers are expecting the worst. There are 14 motor ambulances and 17 ambulance trains ready and waiting for us to fill them.

We know that the soldiers on the other side are mostly young, frightened lads just like us. Mental, really, when you think about it, pure and utter madness.

We had a violent thunderstorm the night before last which has not helped our situation one-bit, torrential rain, soaking into our permanently damp great coats. The hems soaked up the clay and rainwater and clung to us, so heavy, making movement and sleep almost impossible.

This morning, some of us seem to be sleeping standing up, others are tucked into any available nook or crannie. I hear someone in the latrine vomiting as if he will turn himself inside out. The sight and smell of sheer terror is unmistakeable, surrounding us like an invisible cloak. Fear is seeping into every orifice, every pore, every nerve.

"The Big Push" they are calling it. I just hope I can push hard enough. We must make our way towards Loos and capture the trenches that Gerry has been holding for a long time now. We are going to release gas and smoke intermittently. We do not have enough gas, so we are hoping to fool Gerry into wearing his gas mask by releasing smoke in the hope that he will not know the difference. The masks are vile things to wear, really disorientating, I can nae see or hear properly when I'm wearing mine. It has been nicknamed by some captain as "the googly-eyed bugger with the tit", very apt and descriptive. Frightsome looking things, but they save our lives.

At midnight last night we were told that wind conditions were favourable and that the attack will go ahead as planned, so here we are.

The lads who are going to release the gas are wearing arm bands. The bands will prove they are not shirkers. Why? Shirkers are shot. We have been told in no uncertain terms that once zero hour comes and we go over the top, anyone trying to retreat will be shot.

CHAPTER FOUR

Maggie, 1915

It had been a hot and hard day. The copper boiler in the communal washhouse had been put to good use as always on a Thursday. Maggie's hands were red raw from the hot water, washing soap, and all the scrubbing and pounding.

Thank goodness it's a nice day. I will get everything air dried outside, she thought and tried not to focus on the ironing and mending that would follow. Chrissy had often helped her with the washing during the school holidays, but since she had heard of the poor wee soul who had lost his life just over a month ago, Maggie had forbidden it. News had come from the village of Springside, telling them about a lad who had climbed up to the stove when his mother wasn't looking. He had fallen into the boiling water and died of his burns in hospital. Maggie shuddered and hugged her waist, feeling quite sick at the thought, and wiped away a bead of sweat that was trickling down her forehead.

She had just finished hanging the clothes out to dry when Chrissy came skipping along the lane. The bow was long gone from her hair and was now in a pocket, Maggie supposed. Her daughter was beaming from ear to ear; she jumped and clapped and looked fit to burst.

'Guess what's on at the pictures next week, Mum?'

Maggie put her fingers on her chin and drummed them for a few seconds. Then she threw her hands into the air and shrugged her shoulders.

'I don't know, the latest newsreels, I expect.'

Chrissy exhaled loudly and rolled her big brown eyes at her mother.

'I give up – why don't you tell me?' Maggie replied, also rolling her eyes dramatically.

'Charlie Chaplin, Mum! Can you believe it? I don't know which film, but Agnes Gemmel told me, and she knows everything. Her mum is taking her next Friday. Can we go too, Mum, please? *Please?*'

'I think a night out is just the ticket, pet lamb. I'll ask your dad if he can spare an hour or two and we can all go together. How about that?'

Chrissy ran and jumped into her mother's arms and screeched.

'Can we make some puff candy to take with us?' Chrissy asked and bit her bottom lip.

'Aye, we might even be able to buy some aniseed balls from the sweetie shop on John Finnie Street if they have any.'

Chrissy whooped and danced. 'I am the luckiest girl in the whole wide world! I bet Anne Shirley hasn't seen Charlie Chaplin and I'm sure she hasn't got this book.' She held up a book about Florence Nightingale. 'I just got this out the library. Can I wear my dress?'

'Slow down, I can hardly keep up with your blethering! Yes you can, you look a proper picture in it, just don't get sweeties stuck to it.'

The dress in question was a hand-me-down from Maggie's friend in town. Her daughter had gone to America to be a nanny. She often sent food parcels and the occasional hand-me-downs from her employers for her little sister. They were then passed to Maggie for Chrissy after she had outgrown them. Even though they were well worn, they had been cared for and were like nothing that could be found in Ayrshire.

Chrissies eyes shone. She thought about what she would say to Agnes when she got back to school. She wasn't a naturally boastful little girl, but Agnes had not mentioned sweeties or dresses. This was just too good to be true, and it would be one in the eye for cry-baby Jessie too.

*

'Mum, Mum, wake up!' Chrissy called out at the top of her voice.

Maggie awoke with a start. She sat bolt upright, her breathing shallow. 'What's wrong, Chrissy, are you hurt?'

Chrissy skipped into the bedroom, swinging her arms.

'It's tonight, Mum, Charlie Chaplin! Aren't you excited? Dad was before he went to Aunt Jean's to see if she managed to get any eggs and cheese, and if she has, this will be the best day ever!'

'You frightened the life out of me, lassie.' Maggie slumped back onto her pillow and moaned. That girl would be the death of her; she rarely had a chance to lie in, but today being Saturday, she had been hoping for an extra half hour.

'I'm going to the end of the road to wait for Dad to come back, he might give me a wee nibble of cheese. Oh, there is a letter for you behind the clock. John said I should give it to you when we get back from the pictures, but I'm scared I'll forget. Cheerio.'

And with that she disappeared, running as fast as her legs could carry her.

Maggie dressed quickly but her feet felt like lead as she walked towards the mantlepiece.

She saw it immediately, tucked inconspicuously behind the clock. She knew she should wait until Jim came back, but she just couldn't resist the temptation to open the envelope to read what was inside. Would the contents confirm what she already suspected?

Just as she was opening the envelope, Jim strolled in, closely followed by Chrissy who was carrying a can of milk and a lump of cheese. Jim had wisely taken charge of the eggs. He looked at Maggie's face and the penny dropped instantly. He knew exactly what the envelope contained – John had discussed it with him and he had reluctantly given him his blessing. He remembered when he had been fighting the Boers and the feeling of relief when it ended in 1902. He had lost so many friends and comrades, many to typhoid fever rather than the enemy. More than 22,000 men were lost in total. He was only 28 when it ended, but he had felt much older.

Jim turned his treasured brass snuff box round and round in his hands. It was engraved with his initials, JTB – James Thomas Barnes. It was the perfect size to fit in his pocket when he was in the mine, the contents more than welcome. He considered his father's pocket watch too precious to use unless it was a special occasion, but he sported it today in readiness for the night out at the pictures. He remained silent until Maggie had read the letter. Her hands flew to her mouth, and she fell back onto her thread worn armchair.

'Don't fret love, we knew this was coming, it's just a bit sooner than expected.'

'A bit sooner? Almost a year, you mean! He's just a bit of a boy! What was he thinking?'

'I expect because his pals were going, he wanted to go too.'

Maggie stared at her husband incredulously.

'You knew? You *knew?* Did he talk to you about it? Why didn't you talk some sense into the boy? He's young for his age. I just don't see how he will cope! You've watched the newsreels haven't you, is that what you want for him?

Her big brown eyes that could still make Jim go weak at the knees even after all these years shimmered as she fought to hold back the tears that were waiting in line for their turn to tumble down her cheeks.

'Chrissy, run to the store, pet lamb, see if they have any bread to go with our cheese, there's a good lass.'

Chrissy was bursting with energy and relished the thought of a run to the shops. She hoped she would meet some pals to remind them she was going to the pictures that night. She placed the Florence Nightingale book she had picked up to read carefully on the table beside the oil lamp. She always treated her library books with the utmost respect, terrified that something might happen to spoil one and then she wouldn't be allowed to borrow any more. The idea was unthinkable. She hadn't noticed her mother's tears; she was way too excited.

Jim took Maggie in his arms and tried to explain that John going to fight for King and country had been inevitable.

'All three of our boys, Jim, three of them! Nancy along the road still has her boy at home. It's not fair!'

Jim let go and stepped back from her.

'Listen to yourself, Maggie. You know that boy is exempt. We have been so lucky – we have four healthy weans, our boys are brave and proud to be fighting the Hun. It's how we brought them up! You should be proud, too.'

Maggie stared at him. 'Let's not spoil today for Chrissy. What's done is done. I know you are right, but my heart hurts, Jim, it really hurts.'

She turned on her heel and went out to fetch water for the kettle as Jim lit his pipe and puffed. She looked back over her shoulder, and they gazed at each other. She saw Jim's eyes glisten and knew no more words were necessary.

CHAPTER FIVE

James, Diary Entry 1915

I glance along the trench towards my brother Bill standing on the fire step. His eyes catch mine and the horror of what is about to happen is etched into his face, that familiar face which today is almost unrecognisable as my fun-loving wee brother I have shared my life with. Will we also be sharing our last hours on earth together here at Loos? Our mither's face flashes into my mind's eye. For a fleeting moment I wonder what she has been doing – has she been knitting more socks for us? Chrissy has been knitting too, sending us notes and news from home. Would my mum and dad receive a letter in the coming weeks informing them that her sons are not coming home? I hoped at least one of us would survive for her sake. An image of my father returning from the Boer War in 1902 also flashes into my head. I remember the sheer elation of seeing him again, my dad, the war hero ... Would that be me? What *is* a war hero anyway?

Some of us are crying, some praying, many gazing at photos of loved ones knowing that it might well be the last time they will see their faces. I recollect the look of love and surprise on my Betty's sweet face when she opened the door and saw me standing on the doorstep. My leave had been arranged at such short notice that I didn't have time to write to her, to let her know that I was coming home. What a sight I must have been, mud and clay clinging to my uniform, lousy, rancid and stinking to high heaven. She didn't seem to mind though.

She filled the tin bath for me, stoking up the range to get enough warm water for a good soak, blethering the whole time, asking questions ten to the dozen. Her laughter and chatter enveloped me and made me feel safe and loved. The pleasure I felt in that bath in front of the fire, the feeling of clean warm water lapping over my legs and red swollen feet is almost indescribable.

I enjoyed the sensation of warm water trickling down my face as she poured it over my head from a large enamel jug. I will never forget that bath.

She even managed to clean up my uniform quite a bit. How she managed that, I don't know.

I had six days leave in total, but two of those had been used up travelling. I think I mostly slept while I was home. I thoroughly enjoyed the home cooking, hot food, fresh milk and butter and tea that didnae taste like petrol. To lie in a clean fresh bed with a soft pillow and with no fear, no shells, guns or rats was like a dream come true. A braw dream from which I didn't want to wake up.

I can hear the whistle blowing; this is it. In a strange way I am relieved ... the waiting and wondering has been agony. I am lucky enough to have a ladder; some of the boys will need to scramble up and over the parapets as best as they can. It is confusing and chaotic. The sound of artillery, explosions, shouting, machine guns is relentless. The wind has changed direction; we are being gassed with our own stuff. It is hell on earth, unbelievable chaos. The lad beside me has had half his head blown off. Many of the boys have already removed their masks, not realising that the gas meant for Gerry is now assaulting us with its deadly noxious fumes. An obviously unprejudiced wind is wafting our own stuff right back at us. Lads are coughing, vomiting, all the while getting shot and blown to bits. Carnage, pure and simple, slaughter, confusion and carnage.

Suddenly and unexpectedly, I hear the strains of the regimental march *Blue Bonnets over the Border*, the instantly recognisable and uplifting sound of the bagpipes that has kept us marching even when we were dog-tired and weary, when our feet were throbbing with pain, when we thought we could not take another step. The tune fills my ears, bringing with it a sense of purpose and clarity to my jumbled brain. As if by magic, we are united once more, marching together to *Blue Bonnets over the Border* towards the enemy, even though seconds before every basic instinct in our bodies had been telling us not to.

We had got to Loos well ahead of the reserves who had been kept too far back. The hand-to-hand fighting had started. We desperately needed more men. Gerry was on top of the slag heaps taking his pick, mowing us down swiftly and easily. Eventually the 21st London Division arrived, but the Tommies were exhausted, they had marched all day and night to reach the front only to be sent straight into battle, poor devils.

No man's land is ironically strewn with men. Disembowelled men. Bits of men. Bodies hanging from the barbed wire. Blood, so much blood, body parts of what just hours and minutes before had been sons, brothers, husbands and fathers. Talking, laughing, praying, and weeping beings who had battled forwards and towards what so many knew was certain death in the name of serving King and country.

I know that those of us fortunate enough to survive this massacre can expect to spend countless nights clearing the bodies. Dragging what had been our friends or what is left of them into shell holes, laying a light covering of earth on top of them, removing identity discs and any belongings ready to send home to loved ones. Recording each name vigilantly and with reverence.

I am still here. I hold my shaking hand out in front of me. I touch my face; it feels rough and gritty. I taste the salty metallic tang of blood on my tongue. *Is it mine?* The pain coursing through my body is excruciating. Bill ... where is Billy?

CHAPTER SIX

Billy, Diary Entry 1915

James is looking at me. I stare back at him, hoping that somehow he will be able to read my mind, and yet also hoping that he can't. Does that make sense? I want him to know that I love him. I haven't ever said that to him out loud. We don't do that where I come from – it's a given. I think about Crosshouse, much like Loos, a small mining community, close knit, but a place where coal-ingrained men with calloused hands don't go around hugging and telling folk that they love them. The village where I grew up, where my mam and dad are now with my wee brother John and wee sister Chrissy. I can picture them, sitting by the range, and wish I was there with them.

Dad told us stories about the Boer War, funny stories, heroic stories that bear no resemblance to this hell on earth I have found myself in.

James and I would play soldiers when we were small, using sticks as rifles and folded newspaper as helmets. We would occasionally let John join in, creating a fitting low rank for him. James was always the senior rank because he was the oldest. We always won the war, returning home with muddy, grazed knees, tired and hungry after a day play fighting an invisible enemy. Victorious against all odds. We would tell Mum every wee detail about the battle that day. Tales of one- upmanship. Who had been the bravest, who had had the best battle plan. Mum had heard it all before, but she smiled and frowned, making the appropriate noises in all the right places while she ruffled our hair and hurried us along to wash our hands before sitting down to eat.

If I am being honest, part of me imagined that that was what it would be like when I signed up to fight for King and country. There was no doubt in my mind that we would win.

James and I marched off to fight the enemy in our shiny smart uniforms, almost deafened by loud cheers as the villagers waved us off enthusiastically with flags and smiles. The pipe band stirred up feelings of patriotism to the point that I thought I might burst with pride to be part of it.

That was until I caught sight of my mum's face. I have never seen her look like that before. Her expression chilled me to the bone, but I did not know why… until now.

Loos has been attacked by and is now being held by German troops. The terrain is flat apart from slag heaps and colliery towers. The lifting gear by the main pit stands about 150 feet tall. We call it Tower Bridge. I can see it clearly in the distance as we wait.

The whistle is blowing; it is time, I look towards James, but he is no longer there.

*

I wake up.

Where the hell am I now? I try to move my legs. They are on fire, and ache like no ache I have ever felt before. I try to open my eyes, but they are stuck shut. There is a strange smell; it's like carbolic soap, meths and surgical spirit, an overpowering but undoubtedly clean smell.

Somewhere nearby I hear the crash of metal hitting something hard. I jump. My whole-body aches and I am suddenly very scared. *What's happening?* Memories of the trenches slither into my mind, like a venomous serpent. My memory has, up until now, mercifully blocked out where I had been, what I had heard, the carnage I had witnessed. I try to scream but nothing happens. I can't seem to make a noise. No one can hear me … except … yes, they can. And they have. I hear a woman's voice say softly:

'Billy, it's alright, I'm here.'

I feel a hand squeeze my shoulder.

'Doctor will be here soon, and we will get you some more morphine. Try to take a sip of water.'

I feel something cold press against my lips. Water begins to trickle down my chin. I start to gulp at the liquid, suddenly aware how dry my mouth is.

'Where am I?'

'You are in a military hospital in Belgium, Billy. You are safe.'

I feel numb and confused. *Why can't I remember getting here? Why can't I remember what has happened to me?*

A hush descends. I hear footsteps approaching.

'It's the doctor to see you, Billy.'

I wait in silence.

'Remove the bandages from his eyes, Nurse.'

The command is curt and to the point.

I can feel the nurse peel away layer after layer of the cloth that has been wound around my head and over my eyes. Finally, it has gone. I open my eyes and see nothing except a vague shaft of light to my left.

'I can't see!' I feel panic rising in me again; I start screaming out: 'I cannae see! I can nae bloody see!'

Again, the touch of a hand on my shoulder and a soothing voice, but I can't hear what is being said above the shouting. I want the shouting to stop, but it won't.

'More morphine, Nurse. The dose is in his chart.'

I hear lighter footsteps scuttle away.

After an injection and having my eyes bathed, the doctor returns.

'Hello, Doctor. I can see some shadows in my left eye,' I whisper.

'Champion news, old boy, that's what we like to hear. Nothing in your right?'

'No, nothing at all.'

He touches my face and pulls at my right eyelid. He shines a light in first the left eye, then the right, then back again.

'The good news, old chap, is that I believe you have a strong chance of recovering some vision in the left eye. I'm afraid the right one has had it; it is badly burned and ulcerated. Do you remember anything about the battle?'

'No …' *Why won't my mouth move properly? Why are my words mushy?*

'There is no easy way of telling you this so let's get it over with. You caught a blast; you have lost your right arm and your right leg. There was some internal bleeding, but we seem to have fixed that. You also have extensive burns to your hand and face, and your jaw caught some shrapnel. You will be here for some time until we can transport you safely back to Blighty.'

'I'm from Scotland. Can I go there? Does my mother know what's happened to me?'

'One step at a time. Yes, your commanding officer has written to your family. I'm not sure how long it is taking for post to get back home.'

Events are coming back to me. I remember looking at James just before we went over, but he disappeared.

'Any news of my brother?' my voice croaks.

''Fraid not, old boy, but that's not to say he's not in a field hospital in France. Chin up!'

Chin up, says he. *What bloody chin?* I've been blown to pieces, I'm half blind, no one knows where my brother is ... at that moment, I want to die. I don't want to live like this. I'm certain of that. I'll be called one of the lucky ones no doubt. I tuck what used to be my chin into my chest and weep.

CHAPTER SEVEN

Maggie, 1915

Chrissy and Maggie spent an hour making puff candy. Maggie watched her daughter's face when she added the baking soda to the bubbling syrupy mixture. It seemed to double in size and fizzed as if it had a life of its own. It never failed to make her eyes pop.

'Now, Chrissy, what have I told you before?'

'It's very hot, Mum, so hot that if I touch it, it will stick to my skin and peel it off, and I won't even be able to turn the pages of a book.'

Maggie nodded and frowned, wondering if she had overdone things with her warnings.

'What time will we catch the bus, Mum?'

'Go and ask your dad, I'm busy – he's through there, smoking like a lum.'

'Ma teacher says it's not lum, it's chimney. I like how she talks. I want to talk like that one day.'

Maggie laughed out loud at her button-bright little girl.

'I'll give you chimney! It's no' that long ago we used to send weans younger than you up the lum, sorry, the *chimney* to clean them so just you mind your manners, Miss! You and your *I want to talk like that!*'

*

Chrissy was unable to sit still. She bounced on her seat and was chattering ten to the dozen until, much to her annoyance, she spotted one of her classmates on the same bus. Cry-baby Jessie! Not only that but Jessie had the coveted front seat.

She had hoped that this would be her treat and only *her* treat. She consoled herself with three things: she had a big bag of puff candy, they were going to buy a quarter of aniseed balls, and Dad had promised chips on the way home.

Chrissy thought about pretending that she hadn't seen her school friend beckoning when suddenly Jessie appeared at her side.

'Do you want to come and sit beside me and pretend to drive the bus? Ma mammy doesn't mind moving.' Jessie's eyes gleamed.

'Ooooh, I'd love that!' All her previous thoughts were now forgotten. 'Can I, Mum? Can I take some puff candy too?'

'Of course you can, pet lamb, but leave enough for the pictures.'

The girls giggled as they swayed, exaggerating the seesaw movements as the bus trundled along the bumpy road. Once safely seated, they began chattering ten to the dozen whilst checking out the passing fields full of cattle and waiting expectantly for their first glimpse of Kilmarnock in the distance.

During the journey it had been agreed they would all sit together in the theatre. The girls were ecstatic. What tales they would have to tell teacher, and the whole class, on Monday!

The girls held hands and jumped off the bus, whooping with delight. The sweet shop was only a short distance away and they ran ahead to look in the window. Although there were much fewer sweet treats on display than there had been before the war, it was still a sight and smell to behold. The heady sugary sweetness of boiled fruit drops, toffees, caramels, liquorish and, of course, chocolate filled their nostrils when the door swung open.

Chrissy and Jessie stood quite still for a moment or two, taking in every inch of the vision before them. Glass jars bejewelled with sweets all colours of the rainbow stood to attention on the wooden shelves. They followed the adults into the shop and held their hands over their mouths to stop themselves from crying out with pure joy.

'Guess what?'

'What?' said Chrissy, her head tilted to the side in anticipation.

'My mammy has just bought Fry's peppermint creams – a whole quarter!'

Chrissy thought that the statement "a whole quarter" sounded odd but chose not to say anything in case it jeopardised her chances of getting one.

'Jessie, this day could not get any better, could it?'

Jessie nodded enthusiastically as they held hands and skipped towards the King's Theatre.

Chrissy thought the theatre was magical, like nothing else on earth. Plush red seats with gold painted arms sat in neat rows sloping down from the back of the theatre to the front. Matching velvet curtains trimmed with gold hung majestically across the stage. People dressed in their Sunday best and soldiers in uniform swarmed like ants up and down the aisles as they were shown to their seats by usherettes dressed in tailored suits and pill box hats in the richest of greens, also trimmed with gold braid and adorned with gold buttons.

'Which would you rather be: divinely beautiful, dazzlingly clever or angelically good?' Chrissy whispered to Jessie.

Jessie stared at her new best friend with a bewildered expression on her face.

'What are you talking about, Chrissy?'

'That's a question Anne Shirley asks Matthew when she's on her way to Green Gables. Haven't you read it?'

'No, I haven't. It sounds kind of sissy, though.'

'Oh no, Jessie, you *must* read it. Being here has made me think about it. I think I would like to be clever and beautiful. I mean, the usherettes are beautiful, but I bet they are clever too, don't you think?'

Before Jessie could reply, the pianist started to play *It's a Long Way to Tipperary,* and the hubbub of what seemed like a million different conversations fell silent before voices were raised again, this time singing in unison.

Chrissy gazed at the fancy wall lights and promised herself that she would have lights just like them in her bedroom when she grew up.

Keep The Home Fires Burning was played next; men allowed tears to flow freely, safe in the knowledge that they would not be seen in the now dim light. Mothers, sister and sweethearts reached for handkerchiefs, some sobbing openly.

Soon the curtains separated, unwrapping the vast white screen. It shimmered, making its presence felt through a haze of tobacco smoke.

Then, just like magic, flickering images appeared in front of the multitude of eyes focused directly on it.

Pathe Animated Gazette, Chrissy read out loud and was immediately shushed by her mother.

Soldiers trudged wearily, knee-deep in mud, while horses pulled carts carrying the wounded and artillery. Ambulances trundled across makeshift roads. Some of the men looked directly at the lens, smiling, waving and smoking cigarettes.

Then there were scenes of a hospital ward, nurses in crisp, white aprons and caps, men sitting in wheelchairs, lying on beds, hobbling on crutches, bandages on every part of the body imaginable.

'I think you need to be clever to be a nurse, don't you Jessie?' Chrissy whispered.

'Aye, I think you do. Ma big cousin is a nurse in Glasgow,' Jessie answered, without taking her eyes off the screen as she munched on some sweets.

'Is she really? That's what I want to be! I've read all about Florence Nightingale, you know.' Chrissy was so glad that Jessie was with her. She would ask her lots of questions when the picture finished.

'Chrissy, Jessie, haud yer wheesht, I can hardly hear the music, now be quiet the pair of ye!' Maggie settled back into her seat and scrutinised the figures flickering on the screen.

The camera zoomed onto a man recumbent in bed. He had a bandage around his right eye; his right pyjama sleeve was pinned up and he had a cage under his bedclothes. On the locker beside his bed stood a glass of water, a spittoon and a biscuit tin.

Maggie gasped. Her hand flew to her wide-open mouth, and she thought she was going to dissolve and disappear through the chair.

'Jim!' she elbowed her husband sharply, not taking her eyes off the screen. 'Jim! Look!'

By the time Jim had reacted, the picture before them was showing scenes from the trenches.

'It was Billy! I swear on my mother's life, I just know it was Billy!'

'There now, Maggie, how could you possibly tell with all the bandages? It could have been anyone. Calm down, lass, and have a sip of ginger beer.'

'I know it was him, he definitely had the look of Billy about him and …' she paused, '… he had my biscuit tin beside him, the one I got a few Christmases ago. I tell you, it was him, I just know it.'

CHAPTER EIGHT

Billy, 1917

His journey had been a long and harrowing one. Billy vaguely remembered lying in a furrow full of muddy water and being dragged about 300 yards towards the Regimental Aid post where basic first aid was carried out. He would have been given a tetanus injection for blessed pain relief; he remembered the procedure having been there a couple of times before. The walking wounded were returned to duty immediately, but he knew his injuries were way too severe for him to be on active duty again.

He learned much later that he had then been stretchered out to an Advanced Dressing Station in a bunker further back and then on to the Main Dressing Station to be made fit for transportation to the Casualty Clearing Station located about a mile behind the ADS.

He had woken up in a hospital full of men like himself who were maimed and disfigured; it had been horrific, and he wished more than once that he had died a quick death on the battlefield. He endured numerous facial surgeries and while travelling along the long road to recovery, he discovered the unique camaraderie that developed between the men who had been thrown together, and the encouragement from mentors who had already been through or who were further through the process than he was. It went beyond mere friendship and created a safe feeling of solidarity between them.

And now, here he was, back in Ayrshire.

He had known the Dick Institute as a space to enjoy art and culture. He'd always appreciated art, and he loved to sketch, draw and even paint, but the institute was now some sort of hospital – it was really quite surreal.

One thing he did know: he did not want visitors, not under any circumstances. He needed to get his head around his reworked face and lack of limbs before he could even begin to allow others to try to come to terms with it all.

The nurses were wonderful. They sat and talked, they wrote letters dictated by those who couldn't write for whatever reason, they laughed and joked, telling tales of local goings on, romances, stern sisters, with Sister Reid being the worst by all accounts, and seemingly hard-hearted doctors.

The grounds around the institute weren't vast, but they were green and open. Where there had been flower beds, vegetables were growing and being tended to by any man who was able to. The air was fresh and clean, and it was peaceful apart from the odd rumble of a motorised vehicle or the clip-clop and clatter of a horse-drawn cart as locals went about their business.

'Are you ready to go back in, Billy? They will be serving afternoon tea soon. I know you love your tea and scones.'

Billy knew her as Nurse Brownlee, but wished he could call her Vera. He also wished he could hold her in his arms and kiss her passionately. He knew it would never happen; she seemed to love each of her patients unconditionally. No wonder most of them fell in love with her. He had accepted that he would live a life of solitude, or one with his parents. He was unsure as to which option would be the worst-case scenario. Could he work? What would he do?

'Will Dr Durnie be coming around this afternoon?' Billy asked, and smirked as Vera flushed bright red.

He'd noticed how Vera's pretty face lit up whenever she saw Dr Charles Durnie, a tall, well built, sandy-haired boy of a man. He seemed to be oblivious of the fairer sex and focused only on his patients.

She stood behind him during ward rounds, as close as was decently possible. She watched his limbs move beneath his white coat and imagined his arms around her, holding her tightly, telling her she was the only girl for him. Then she would blink and be back in the room, surrounded by mentally and physically scarred young men who hung on to the young doctor's every word. Most of them who had made it to the Dick Institute were past the worst of their horrendous ordeals, but it was never taken for granted; infections had a way of taking hold and doing their worst. Hence the fastidious use of disinfectants and stringent cleanliness protocols.

When the ward round was over, Billy beckoned to Nurse Brownlee.

'Now is your chance! He's writing up notes over there, all by himself. Sister has rushed off somewhere. Go and talk to him.'

'I don't know what you mean, Mr Barnes, really! You need to concentrate on your recovery, not on me.'

The look in her eyes and the pink bloom on her cheeks denied everything she had just said. She flitted around a few beds before heading in the direction of the rugged doctor.

What could she say? She felt her hands start to tingle, and her knees weakened slightly. She took a deep breath, smiled tentatively and plucked up the courage to speak.

Being this close to him, she found it difficult to resist touching his arm, anything to make him notice her.

'Doctor, I just wanted to remind you that the boy in bed six is waiting for his discharge papers.'

Without looking up from the chart he was holding, he replied: 'I am well aware of that fact, Nurse. Can't you see I am in the middle of something?'

Vera felt humiliated. Why had she said something so stupid? She knew he wasn't the forgetful type, and she also knew he had been working all night at the infirmary. She bit her lip and tried not to cry. What on earth was wrong with her? Normally she took everything in her stride; many of the doctors spoke very harshly, especially to nursing staff, and she let that slide like water off a duck's back, but this? This was different.

Aware that she was still standing there, he looked up and noticed her glistening eyes staring at him. Charles Durnie was not a thoughtless or unkind man, but he was physically and mentally exhausted. Last night had been truly awful: several young women had been admitted following an explosion at Ardeer Munitions Factory. Working with TNT had caused their skin and hair to be tinged yellow, and now that skin had burned, extensively so. Some were missing limbs and most had been taken straight to the mortuary. He knew what he had witnessed would stay with him forever.

As soon as he saw her face, his heart melted. 'Thank you, Nurse Brownlee.' He stopped mid-sentence; for the first time in his life, he could not think of what else to say.

He had not only noticed this caring and compassionate young woman who competently carried out her duties – he also happened to think she was attractive. Her uniform was always neat and tidy, her silver buckled belt sat snugly around her tiny waist, and her rich brunette curls were just visible when they escaped from the confines of her cap, something that always seemed to happen when Sister Reid was around, causing her to reprimand Vera severely and loudly.

'Nurse Brownlee, I will not have your hair compromising the wounds of any man in my care! Go and attend to it at once!'

Idiot, he thought to himself. *Stupid idiot*, but his face disclosed nothing of what he was thinking.

'Shall I pinch a buttered scone from the kitchen and leave it with a cup of tea in the duty room when you have finished here?'

'That is kind of you, Nurse Brownlee, that would be most welcome.' He smiled at her. She was convinced that he would be able to hear her heart now pounding in her chest.

'Nurse Brownlee, I have been looking everywhere for you.'

Vera waited for the onslaught. She had long suspected that Sister Reid was holding a vendetta against her. She was constantly on her back, telling her off for the least little thing. True, she was cold and brusque with all of her nurses, but Vera felt that where she was concerned, it was calculated and relentless.

'The sluice is dirty and untidy. Please attend to it at once, Nurse Brownlee.'

Vera's eyebrows shot up as she stood to attention.

'I was about to start a dressing round, Sister. Could one of the auxiliary nurses attend to it?'

'Nurse Brownlee, how dare you question me! I have asked you to do it! *I* will attend to the dressings.'

'Yes, Sister.' Her voice was hardly more than a whisper. To have been belittled like that in front of Dr Durnie was just about the last straw. She felt like crying, but she was damned if she would give that woman the satisfaction. Vera entirely understood that discipline in the nursing profession was vital, just as it was for the armed forces, but not all sisters – or matrons for that matter – had such an antagonistic manner. Some were even compassionate.

'Oh, and Nurse Brownlee, I am one staff nurse short this weekend. I know you were due to have Saturday off, but I have put you on night duty. It's written on the off-duty chart. I just updated it.'

*

Vera attacked the sluice room with an unfamiliar aggression. Not only was the slop-hopper and the deep ceramic sink spotless, she was releasing months of pent-up anger with each bed pan she scrubbed. Her anger finally dissipated when she flushed the cistern for the final time before standing back to admire her work.

She was exhausted by the time she had finished, but the room was gleaming from top to bottom and looked brand new.

As she worked, she thought about what had just happened.

Had Sister heard her making plans with Jean to go to the pictures on Saturday night? Had she done this deliberately to upset her?

This wasn't the first time the two women had locked horns. If off-duty had to be changed at the last minute, Vera had noticed that it was always hers that changed – and never for the better.

'If it happens again, I'm going to challenge her. I swear I am! Sister or no Sister, she is a human being just like me.'

*

Vera complained about Sister Reid to her mother on her last day off.

'You knew what you were getting into, my girl. I did try to warn you!'

'Mother, just once would you take my side, see my point of view?'

The outburst from her daughter was rare and unexpected.

'Vera, you don't know anything about Sister Reid, do you? You don't know what she may be coping with in her private life. From what you tell me, with the hours she works, she doesn't have one. Didn't you tell me that she never seems to take a day off?'

Vera huffed, blowing a curl from her forehead.

'Yes, I suppose so, but we are *all* overworked and tired.'

'All the more reason to be more understanding. At least you come home once in a while and get spoilt while you are here. You have us to sound off to. It truly sounds like Sister Reid has nowhere and no one from what you have told me. She may be a sister, but she is also a human being.'

'I'm still going to challenge her,' Vera muttered obstinately as she went upstairs to bed.

CHAPTER NINE

1917

'Chrissy, have you thought about what you would like to do when you leave school?' Chrissy's teacher smiled and invited her to sit down.

'Yes, Miss, I have imagined all sorts of jobs I would like to do, but now I know for certain. I want to be a nurse. I feel that I really *need* to be a nurse. I just can't explain it.'

'There is no need for explanation, Chrissy; it is called a vocation. Do you know what is involved in becoming a nurse?'

'I have tried to find out about it in the library, but there wasn't much information available. I was wondering if I should go to Kilmarnock Infirmary to get more information about what it's like to be a nurse.'

'I can help you, Chrissy. If you are serious about nursing, there is a path you must take, but it won't be an easy one. You'd start as a probationer, usually in a hospital. Kilmarnock Infirmary has an excellent nurses' training school. You'd be under the eye of the matron, Mary Morrison, who will expect you to be neat, obedient and tireless. They don't take kindly to slackness.'

'I don't mind hard work, you know I don't, Miss.' Chrissy's eyes were sparkling and her cheeks flushed with excitement.

'After a year or so, if you've proved yourself, you might be accepted into proper training. That's two or three years, usually unpaid, with lectures on anatomy, hygiene and how to care for wounds and fevers. You'll learn to bandage, to bathe, to comfort. You will see things that will break your heart and strengthen it too. It's not just skill, it's character. They want women who can keep their heads when others are losing theirs. And in wartime, that's no small thing.'

Chrissy nodded earnestly.

'You'd need references, perhaps from me, or the minister, and a bit of money to get started. Most hospitals offer board and lodging, and provide uniforms. You will need a good pair of boots and a strong constitution; it's a case of strict discipline and long hours. But I'll tell you this: if you've got the calling and the grit, nursing's one of the noblest things a woman can do. You'd be serving not just the sick, but the country itself.'

Chrissy's chin lowered to her chest, and she looked at her feet, not sure how to respond.

'How much money would I need in the beginning?' Her voice was almost a whisper.

'The amount varies; you may be eligible for support from the church or some other charitable group.'

'My family needs me. My brothers are at the front, my dad is ill and my mum is working so hard. She works in Ardeer Munitions Factory now. I had hoped I could work in the hospital and stay at home.'

'I'm sorry, Chrissy, that would be out of the question. Living in the nurses' home isn't just about convenience – it's about discipline and supervision. It allows Matron to enforce curfews and to monitor behaviour. I know this because my sister is a nurse. You will be expected to work 12-hour shifts as well as attend lectures and study on top of that.'

Chrissy had been overjoyed that her beloved teacher thought that she was capable of such achievement. She wasn't at all daunted by the schedule and expectations, but now she felt as deflated as a punctured balloon. Her feet felt like lead and she felt foolish for the first time in her short life. How could she have imagined that she could fulfil her dream? It hadn't occurred to her that the work would be unpaid. Her mammy and da were looking forward to her contributing to the family purse, plus they needed her at home. Who would look after Dad when Mammy was working long shifts in the factory?

Disappointment descended upon her and lay there heavily, followed by a hefty veil of realisation. She felt that she had the weight of the world on her young shoulders, but she decided there and then not to relay any of this conversation to her parents; it would make them feel sad and helpless. She also knew her circumstances could not and would not change, so why upset them?

She hardly saw her mammy these days with her working long shifts in the factory, and ever since she had read the telegram informing them that James had been killed in action, her mother had changed. She rarely smiled, her heart was weighed down by a deep intrusive and gnawing sadness. Her father was no longer fit to work down the mine. He was a shadow of the man he had been just a year ago; it was almost as if he had lost the will to live.

When her mum thought she saw Billy on the big screen at the pictures, it was as if something had smashed through the wall of sadness, she had built around her and ignited a raging fire in her belly. Maggie just had to find out, and she didn't care who thought she was wasting her time. She worked tirelessly, finding out the name of the hospital used in the film, contacting the regiment and anyone else who might be able to help until at last she found someone who could confirm that it had indeed been her son up there on that big screen. And all because of an old but distinctive biscuit tin!

She developed a new lease of life after finding out Billy was alive. Injured, but still alive. John was still missing in action, but she would never give up hope that he would come home safely.

Maggie read the letters from Billy repeatedly. She knew he was badly wounded but did not know to what extent; he rarely mentioned his injuries, and when he did, it was only to say that things were getting better and that he was getting stronger every day.

The therapy and support Billy was receiving in the hospital was slowly but surely liquefying the rock-hard stone of despair deep inside him. He knew James was dead, and, at first, he wished he was too, but his eyesight had returned in his one good eye and there was talk of an artificial leg. Plus, now he was back in Ayrshire. He knew he should be grateful; it was difficult but no longer impossible for him to feel a slither of gratitude.

He enjoyed the comradeship in the hospital; he even recognised a few faces although not many recognised him. Days were spent enduring rigorous therapies, playing cards and dominos and reading the newspapers. Those who could walk pushed those who couldn't out into the grounds. Packages from home were compared and shared. Banter was plentiful and sometimes a bit saucy; they always made sure none of the nurses were in earshot before telling their jokes. Especially Sister. Once you had "that" look from the formidable woman, you did not risk being on the receiving end of it again. Even the crustiest of doctors avoided it at all costs.

Billy wrote to his mother and said he was not ready to see anyone yet and that he would let her know when the time was right. He hoped she would understand.

One thing he was sure of – he did not want to see his little sister until he was certain he could cope with her reaction. He barely recognised himself in the mirror; the reconstruction he had received at Aldershot had made a difference, but he knew that his face had changed almost beyond recognition. Billy was sure Chrissy would be shocked when she saw him; how couldn't she be? He needed to know that his parents would prepare her for their first meeting and that it would be handled delicately.

*

Maggie walked into the house and flopped on the nearest chair.

Jim was sitting by the range, puffing on his pipe and warming his toes. Maggie noticed that one of his socks needed mending and made a mental note to do it after next wash day. She also noticed the light from the oil lamp reflected on the gleaming range. Chrissy was almost as adept at cleaning it as she was herself. However, she couldn't think about it now: she felt like she had been dipped in an icy bucket of water and then wrung out to within an inch of her life.

Jim looked up and smiled weakly at his wife. He had a healthy-looking rosy glow when he sat there in front of the glowing embers, his thick head of hair now more white than black. As if reading her mind, he got up slowly and pointed to the chair.

'Come and sit here, hen, warm yourself up. I've filled the kettle, cup of tea coming up shortly. We've saved some pie and tatties for you, and Chrissy has been tidying up. She went to bed ages ago. She has worked hard in the garden the day and she got some news about a job. I'm sworn to secrecy though.' He let out a throaty laugh that immediately turned into a rattling chesty cough.

Maggie shuffled to the big armchair and gratefully sank into the cushioned seat still warm from her husband's slight body. She unlaced her sturdy black shoes, kicked them off and then placed them by the oven.

'Bless that wean, my wee pet lamb, she is so grown up these days, and I've never heard her complaining once about all the jobs she must do now.'

Jim brewed the tea exactly as Maggie did, warming the pot, one spoonful per person, but not "one for the pot" now that tea was so scarce. He handed a cup of the steaming hot liquid to his wife then gestured to the clock on the mantlepiece.

'There's something up there you might be interested in.'

'I can't be bothered moving. I think I'll just sleep here the night.' She sighed then yawned loudly.

Jim reached over and picked up the open envelope.

'This came for us the day.'

Maggie's hands shook until she realised it wasn't a telegram. Her shoulders relaxed and she began to breathe normally again.

'Is it from oor Billy?'

'Just read it, wummin,' he grinned, while gripping the shaft of the pipe between his teeth.

The paper shook in Maggie's trembling hands She had grown to loath receiving mail ever since the telegram had arrived saying James had been killed in action, and another to say that John was missing in action. She had developed a mistrust of anything being delivered to her door and handled envelopes as cautiously as she would TNT at work.

'He is ready to see us, thank God! He wants to see us at last!'

A frenzy of garbled words poured out faster than Jim could comprehend.

'I will need to save some of the rations. I will bake shortbread ... there is a jar of bramble jelly in the pantry, I've been saving it. Will you go and ask Jean if she can spare anything? Chrissy has just finished knitting another pair of socks, so I will take them too, oh, and cigarettes...'

'Maggie, drink your tea, eat your supper and go to bed. We can get things sorted oot the morn.'

'Aye, right you are, Jim, right you are.'

She would sleep soundly tonight.

CHAPTER TEN

Billy, 1917

Fluffy soft clouds bounced above the chimney pots on London Road while the sunbeams played hide and seek in and around them. The walk from the bus station had been slow, but pleasant. They walked past what they still tended to call the Corn Exchange and reminisced.

'Ma mam and da remember when the Corn Exchange was opened back in 1863. I think it was a posh do by all accounts. Kilmarnock Brass Ensemble played during the interval. Now look at it, not a barley sack in sight! Do you remember going to a concert there when it became a theatre? That was when we were winchin'. Ah, those were the days, Jim,' Maggie sighed.

'We were not winchin', it was after oor Chrissy was born, wummin. With four weans you certainly couldnae say we were just winchin'.' Jim huffed, pleased to have remembered something his wife had forgotten.

Maggie flushed.

'I remember now. I think all the kissing and cuddling that went oan on the way back hame made it feel like we were still winchin'.'

They were both out of breath after walking up the hill towards the Dick Institute. When they entered the grounds, Maggie spotted an empty bench not too far from the entrance and thankfully sat down, nodding at other families who looked as if they were also waiting for visiting time to begin. The give-away being baskets stuffed with brown paper packages, tins and books –some even had fruit!

'Do you remember when this place opened?' Maggie asked a pipe-puffing Jim, smartly dressed in his Sunday best and sporting his best cap. Maggie brushed an imaginary fleck of dust from Jim's shoulder and then continued to cradle her basket, grateful for something to hang on to.

'Here we go again ... no, I can nae remember.'

'I remember it even if you don't, Jim. It was back in 1901. James Dick's wife opened it. I remember seeing her photo in the *Kilmarnock Standard*. It said the Dick Institute was built in memory of his brother, Robert; he got the money to build it from a gold mine or something. Imagine that – a real gold mine!'

'You'd *need* a gold mine to build the likes of this,' he quipped and poked his finger into one of the paper packages.

Maggie slapped him playfully.

'Oh no you don't, at least not until we get inside. Just the other week I read in *The Standard* that this is one of the biggest auxiliary hospitals in the country. All the books and museum pieces that were once on display here have been stored safely just so boys like oor Billy can come here to get better. I think that is just great, don't you?' Maggie looked wistful and continued: 'Anyway, I remember her hat – it was the biggest and most beautiful...'

Just then, there was some movement; the people who had been sitting on benches closer to the pillared entrance stood up and walked towards the double doors.

Jim breathed a sigh of relief; he had not relished a full description of what Mrs Dick had been wearing that day.

He and Maggie climbed the steps that led up to the entrance of the magnificent and imposing building.

The square-tiled floor of the stairwell was spotlessly clean. The polished wood panelled walls were bathed in sunlight, making them shine, and the banister which ran alongside the imposing stone staircase gleamed like a conker straight out of its shell.

Looking up, Maggie could see the gallery, piended roof and the magnificent dome, seemingly floating high above the entrance. Any other time she would have been mightily impressed, but she only had one thing on her mind: Billy.

After speaking to a rather stern looking nurse, Jim and Maggie waited to be directed to the correct ward.

'Is this your first visit, Mr and Mrs Barnes?' The nurse sounded kinder than she looked.

'Aye, I mean, yes, it is, Nurse. This day has been a long time coming.'

'Come with me, please.' The nurse led them to a small room just off the corridor.

'Please take a seat,' she said and beckoned them towards two bentwood chairs situated next to a large sash window.

'William was severely injured. Life changingly so. He told me that he hasn't been forthcoming about his injuries with you – he was trying to spare your feelings. That said, he is anxious that his appearance may shock you.'

She paused and inhaled deeply.

'William has lost his right arm and his right leg, though thankfully below the knee. He is also blind in one eye and is still recovering from extensive burns and shrapnel wounds to his jaw. He was fortunate in that he was operated on by Harrold Gillies, a talented plastic surgeon who works in Cambridge Military Hospital. He is a very lucky young man.'

Maggie and Jim looked at one another in silence, grateful for the chairs and the privacy.

'*Lucky?* How can you say he is lucky?' Maggie choked back a sob.

'Mrs Barnes, I must tell you that your son almost gave up the will to live. He was melancholy to such an extent that he wouldn't eat or talk for an extremely long time. It has taken a lot of patience and effort on William's part to overcome his despondency, but he has done it. He is glad to be alive, and you must be too.'

Maggie allowed the sob lodged firmly in her throat to escape. Her shoulders shook as she bent forward, holding her head in her hands.

Jim, chin trembling, gazed into space. He knew he dare not look at Maggie or he might disgrace himself and weep in front of this complete stranger.

Maggie took her well-worn embroidered handkerchief out of her pocket and dabbed at the salty beads of despair relentlessly coursing down her face.

'I understand how you must be feeling. I don't want to sound harsh, but you must pull yourself together, Mrs Barnes. There is a WC next door. Go in, wash your face and put on a brave front. A reaction like this, however natural, could have a severely detrimental effect on your son.'

'Billy ... his name is Billy.'

Without acknowledging this small outburst, the nurse went on.

'Billy,' she hesitated, 'is a very brave boy. He has overcome so many obstacles and he has shown great courage. We are all very proud of his resolve and I know you will be too.'

'We *are* very proud,' Maggie said, and sat up, thrusting her jaw forward, suddenly in defence mode. 'I have already lost one boy and I don't know where my youngest is. I am proud of Billy ... fit to burst proud!'

The nurse had hoped for this reaction. She had had this conversation more times that she could remember. She had seen every reaction in the book, some overwhelming, some underwhelming; she couldn't make up her mind what was worse.

When Maggie reappeared, she looked composed. Jim winked at her, and they walked together towards the dayroom to be reunited with their precious boy

*

Mum and Dad have taken my injuries in their stride. You could have knocked me doon wi' a feather. They blethered, shared and reminisced almost as if nothing had happened to me. Mum looked glassy-eyed at times, but I had been worried that she would scream, faint or run for the hills. Faither shook my hand and said great to see you, son, great to see you, in his usual understated way. Mum asked, 'When can Chrissy visit? She really wants to see her big brother again.'

'How will she cope, Mam; I'm not the big brother she remembers, am I?' I replied.

'Yes, you are, Billy, just missing a few bits here and there.' And then we laughed nervous laughs, hoping she was right.

I woke up on the day of Chrissy's visit feeling nervous. My wee sister, seeing me like this ... I hated the thought, but I so longed to see my Chrissy, to give her a hug, to reassure her that I was still me. But *was* I still me? I knew

I had changed in ways no one else could understand unless they had been blown to smithereens by a shell, unless they had seen the horrific sights I had seen. I would'nae wish it on ma worst enemy.

I spotted Chrissy as soon as she arrived. I couldn't believe the young lady walking towards me with Mum and Dad was really my sister, my baby sister. She was tall, much taller than I remembered, and her hair was shining like a brand-new shilling, peeping out from under her stylish hat. My wee sister! She looked so grown up!

I swallowed, and bit what was left of my lip.

Before I could say anything, she launched herself into my arms ... or rather, my arm!

'Billy, oh Billy, where have you been! We have missed you so much.'

'I'm right here, Chrissy, right here, and I'm going nowhere anytime soon.' I cried for the first time in weeks.

'I brought you socks; I knitted them myself,' she preened. 'You only have one foot so they will last you twice as long.' She raised her eyebrows and tilted her head to one side.

I knew in that instant that she was looking beyond my injuries and disfigurements. She could see *me*, Billy. I thought I would burst with happiness.

'Now, Gran has sent shortbread. I made jam tarts and puff candy.' She placed a well-worn Peak Freans biscuit tin on my locker.

'It would be good manners to share, Billy.'

Billy laughed out loud; this normality had knocked him for six, so unexpected but oh so welcome.

'Help yourself, wee Chrissy, I know you will anyway.'

Maggie hurriedly brushed away a stray tear. She looked at Jim, and they shared a smile of relief and gratitude.

The nurse was right, thought Maggie, *Billy is lucky, and so are we.*

*

Vera approached the family and asked if anyone would like a cup of tea.

'That would be lovely, Nurse, it will help him wash down some of these.' Maggie nodded towards the now open tin of home-baked goodies

'Billy is a model patient, Mrs Barnes; he has been helping some of our new arrivals to settle in. He's a natural! I don't know what we will do without him when he goes home. He has given hope to some of the boys who'd all but given up.'

Jim, Maggie and Chrissy looked at each other, beaming from ear to ear.

'We are very proud of him, hen, I mean, Nurse,' said Maggie, forgetting herself.

'Would you like tea, young lady, or would you prefer milk?'

'Tea, please,' answered Chrissy somewhat indignantly. 'I am fifteen, nearly sixteen, well, in six months I will be.'

Vera thought the bright young girl seemed much younger than that, and suddenly she felt ancient at the ripe old age of twenty. She knew that she and her colleagues were older than their birth years. This vocation, as some called it, meant dealing with emotions, sights, smells and daily challenges that most young women could not begin to imagine.

Her thoughts drifted to Charles; they were now Charles and Vera. They had walked out twice now, the first time for afternoon tea. It had been stinted and overly polite at first, but once they'd relaxed it was obvious to both of them that there was definitely a spark of something between them. After the second meeting, she couldn't imagine her life without him. She hoped and prayed that he felt the same about her.

Charles was walking towards Billy and his family, and Vera thought her heart would burst when she saw him smiling, even if it wasn't directed at her

'Before you leave, I would like to have a word with you both,' he said, looking at Maggie.

'You too, Billy,' Jim said.

'We can talk in my office.'

'Nae bother, Doctor. Should we be worried?'

'Absolutely not, Mr Barnes, quite the opposite. Take your time – I hear that tea is on the way.'

Charles looked directly at Vera and smiled, and her heart skipped a beat.

*

Jim, Maggie and Billy were sitting in the doctor's office. Maggie was twiddling her thumbs nervously, but Jim and Billy appeared to be quite relaxed.

'I hope oor Chrissy isn't making a nuisance of herself out there. Are you sure the nurse won't mind showing her round the place?'

'Not at all, she was asking some very relevant questions, and she seems to be genuinely interested in what goes on here. Nurse will show her around within limits, you understand, but now let's get down to business. As you know, Billy was operated on by Dr Gillies in Cambridge Military Hospital in Aldershot. Dr Gillies offers places to men who have been patients, young men he feels could contribute and find purpose helping others who have experienced similar wounds and trauma.'

Jim and Maggie sat transfixed, hanging on to every word the doctor said. Billy had been given an inkling of what was coming and so remained calm.

'Dr Gillies needs veterans who can become counsellors to new patients, who can really understand what they are going through. In other words, they help the new patients to cope by offering moral support by sharing their experiences, by encouraging them to persevere and cope with multiple surgeries.'

He now looked at Billy.

'You know what it's like, don't you, Billy, that long recovery process? And yours isn't over yet.'

'Aye, I do that, Doctor,' Billy answered quietly.

'There are training programmes, and we know that you are gifted when it comes to art, Billy. We have seen some of your sketches; that talent could be put to good use in the designing and making of prosthetic masks and such like.

'There are also roles to be filled in helping with administrative tasks, photography and public awareness. Let's put it this way – you would never be bored.' Charles laughed.

'Are you saying that you want Billy to go and work with this Doctor Gillies?'

'That is exactly what I am saying, Mr Barnes.'

'Count me in, Doctor! I don't see how I can go back to the village like this, and I like the idea of being useful, helping boys like me.'

Maggie gasped.

'Are you sure, son? It's a long way away.'

'I've been further, Ma. I'll be able to visit. Maybe you could come a visit me when I'm settled.' He offered her a lopsided grin.

'I'm afraid I need to cut this short. I will get the ball rolling; there is a lot to do before we get to that stage. I will write to a member of the team, and we will take it from there. For what it's worth, Billy, I think you are doing the right thing. You won't regret it.'

CHAPTER ELEVEN

Vera, 1918

When she read the words written on the sheet of paper she was holding in her hand, Vera gasped out loud; her cheeks became flushed and tears trickled down her face.

'What's wrong, Vera? Is it bad news?' Her colleague and friend Jean frowned, genuinely concerned.

'It's nothing really,' Vera whispered as she tried to compose herself before the night sister did her rounds. The letter had been burning a hole in her pocket all evening, but now she was glad that she had decided to keep it until now, to open in the gloomy night light.

'What is it then?' Jean squinted and folded her arms in frustration.

'It's a letter from Charles, Dr Durnie.'

'I know who Charles is,' Jean said, and cleared her throat and smoothed her apron.

'And what is the good Dr Durnie saying to make you react like this?' Then her hands flew up towards her mouth. 'He doesn't want to see you again!' Then she gulped, colour draining from her face.

'He's married, isn't he, he's married, he couldn't tell you to your face, so he wrote you a letter! Oh Vera, come and sit down. I'll fetch some tea.'

Vera looked at Jean, who was known to be melodramatic, tears still absconding from the assembly in her eyes.

'No, I don't need to sit down, well, maybe I do, I don't know!'

'Sit down anyway, I'll get the tea, and you can tell me about it. If you want to that is?' Jean added, knowing she wouldn't settle until she found out.

Just then Sister Reid walked towards them.

'What is going on here? Nurse Brownlee, when did you last check on Mr Robertson? He looked agitated when I walked past his bed. Go and see to him at once! Nurse Cairns, what are you doing here? You should be carrying out rounds in ward two.'

Jean was about to explain that she was having her break but thought better of it when she spotted Sister's stern expression.

'Yes, Sister,' Jean answered as meekly as she could muster as Vera skuttled up the ward towards her agitated patient.

Jean was also agitated; now she would need to wait until morning to find out what had caused her dear friend to react in such a way. Always one to drink from the side of the cup that was half empty, Jean decided that it must be bad news and began to make plans to cheer her bereft friend.

Muttering under her breath, she made her way along the corridor.

'Night Sister Reid is always picking on us ... just last week she told me off for fidgeting during the ward round, then she said my hospital corners weren't neat enough and made me make the beds again,' Jean fumed.

'Old hag!' But she looked forward to having a good old moan about her when she and Vera could catch up.

The nurses at large assumed that Mima Reid was nothing but a bitter old maid who knew nothing about carrying a torch for someone or about having fun.

Little did they know that Mima knew so much more than they could ever have imagined. Underneath the cast iron exterior housing a heart seemly made from stone lay a woman who had loved and lost, who was carrying secrets deep inside her, secrets that weighed her down almost as if she was carrying a heavy chain with links made from despair and heartbreak in equal measure. It held her in its python-like grip and refused to release the pressure on her body for an instant.

Mima had two secrets that she dared not share with another living soul.

Mima marched onto the ward and announced that she was going on her rounds and then she would be occupied in the duty room for a short time.

She noticed her nurses sigh with relief when they answered, 'Yes, Sister,' in unison.

Mima sat in her chair and pulled it closer to the desk. Now that she was alone with the door safely closed, she allowed tears to run down her face, but hastily dabbed at them with her handkerchief; she did not want to emerge with a blotchy red face.

She had received news today about her sister who was a patient in Ailsa, the Ayrshire District Asylum.

Lizzy had been unwell for some time now, constantly tired, complaining of headaches, forgetfulness. Mima had hoped that it may have been as a result of a recent infection and that her sister's febrile temperature had been the cause. Her doctor had been wonderful: he had visited the family, helped in any way he could, but Lizzy's daughter, who was still living at home, had no longer been able to cope with her mother's "mounting madness", as she called it.

Lizzy had taken to making up bizarre stories; some sounded plausible enough to anyone who didn't know her, others were peculiar beyond belief, which the family found to be increasingly distressing.

'I've had twenty husbands, you know, one of them was a prince. He had so much money; he bought me jewels almost every day.'

'Right, you are, Mother, so where are these jewels then?'

'How dare you call me mother! I am Princess Arabella of Peru! My subjects adore me, and don't you forget it, and I am going to live forever, you didn't know that, did you? I have enough jewels and money to share with everyone!'

What upset and embarrassed her daughter most was her mother's lack of inhibitions. The postman hadn't known where to look when she had spoken to him suggestively and started to remove her clothes. It had been the last straw.

Mima had only scraped the surface of psychiatric nursing, but something was niggling at her like a rat gnawing at her brain. Today her worst fears had been confirmed. She had travelled to Ailsa that morning to speak to her sister's doctor.

'Please, sit down, Miss Reid.'

Once Mima was seated, the doctor sat behind the enormous oak desk. He shuffled the pile of papers in front of him before speaking again.

'Miss Reid, I know you are a nurse, and that you have suspected your sister is suffering from pre-senile dementia, but I have to tell you that the condition that Elizabeth is suffering from is general paralysis of the insane, sometimes called paralytic dementia. It is caused by syphilis.'

Mima whispered the word at the same time.

'Patients often have delusional thoughts, often melancholic, paranoid or delusional. We have performed several tests, and I am afraid there is no doubt.'

'Her husband served in both Boer wars. He died in Ladysmith before the last one ended ... from an infection, we were told.'

'That could certainly explain how your sister contracted the disease – her husband was infected when he came home on leave, perhaps. We will never be sure...'

'I am positive, Doctor, that my sister is a good woman, clean living and loyal. I don't want to hear another word about it.'

'I understand, Miss Reid. As you know there is no cure, and her condition will continue to deteriorate. I am so sorry.'

Mima made her way back to Kilmarnock to rest before her night duty, the chain surrounding her just that bit longer and heavier than it had been before.

'There but for the grace of God go I,' she pondered.

Lizzy was one of the few people who knew about her guilty secret.

'Oh no, what if she starts talking about it!' Mima's heart rate quickened and she gasped for breath. 'Calm down,' she told herself. 'Who would believe her now?' This selfish thought made her eyes sting with tears.

'My poor Lizzy! To end up like this after all she has done for me.'

Mima allowed her secret treasured memory to come to life inside her head. Her handsome soldier, her fiancé. They had consummated their love, sweetly, tenderly and passionately before he went off to war. They had gazed at each other, neither one of them wishing to look away, they whispered plans, what they would do when the war was over, where they would live, how many children they would have, but he never came back.

Mima knew after her first bout of morning sickness that she was pregnant. She was terrified and knew without a doubt that her parents would disown her.

Lizzy had stepped in and taken control. She'd arranged for Mima to stay with a relative of her husband's. Mima would work for them on their farm until the baby was born. They knew of a childless couple who would adopt the baby, no questions asked.

And so, it had been. Mima thought of her son every day; she wept on his birthday every year. She tried not to think of his baby sweet head covered with soft downy dark hair, his blue eyes as they fixed on her with complete innocence vulnerability and trust. The pain of leaving him with those strangers had not diminished one bit with the passing years and she knew the heartbreak would remain with her until the day she died.

She overheard some of her nurses' whisper when they thought she was out of earshot.

'I've seen more emotion in one of those bricks out there! She has no idea about what it is to be young, to be in love. I'd feel sorry for her if she wasn't so unpleasant.'

Mima's thoughts turned to Tennyson's poem: *'Tis better to have loved and lost, than never to have loved at all.*

I mean no disrespect Mr Tennyson, but I'm not sure I can agree with you there, thought Mima as the chain crushed the breath from her chest.

CHAPTER TWELVE

Vera 1918

Standing by her bedroom window, Vera hopped from one foot to another as she watched carriages and the odd car go by. She could see the Dick Institute across the street on the left. The sun was shining although the air was crisp: a perfect Autumn afternoon. The leaves were all shades of brown, orange, yellow and maroon. Vera watched as some floated earthwards to congregate as a multicoloured carpet on the pavement.

Glancing towards her dressing table, she saw her gloves and hatpins ready for the afternoon out. Her letter was nestled beside them. That letter, the one Jean had suspected was bad news, had actually been Charles asking for permission to visit her parents.

She had escaped to her room for a while. Her mother was flitting around downstairs, removing invisible flecks of dust from the perfectly polished furniture and fiddling with the flower arrangement on the hall table.

Her father was reading his newspaper in the study. She had left him muttering to himself about developments at the front, puffs of smoke rising above his red leather wingback chair.

Vera had chosen a sensibly warm outfit from her now sparse wardrobe. Her hat was on the stand in the hall. She had only managed to drink a cup of tea this morning. Her stomach was churning and, most unfortunately, making some rather peculiar noises she hoped would go away sooner rather than later.

She loved her mother dearly, but she just had to escape the barrage of questions, proclamations and what she deemed to be words of wisdom.

'Do you know anything about his family?'

Vera had told her parents more than once that Charles had one brother and two sisters.

'You know, Vera, I had almost given up hope of you ever getting married! You're not getting any younger. So many young men have lost their lives and the rest are at the front ... it's all just too awful for words!'

'He hasn't asked me yet. He might have asked to meet you both to see if we are suitable – have you thought of that?'

'Don't be so silly, Vera! You are my one and only child, I just want you to be happy, I want you to have a family of your own someday. I wish we had been blessed with more children, but it just wasn't to be, you know...'

'Mother, please, yes, I do know, now I need to go and fetch my handbag from my room.'

'Is that what you are planning to wear? Shouldn't you wear a dress?'

'Yes, this is what I will be wearing. I don't have much choice now, do I?' Vera tried not to sound annoyed. 'It's chilly outside. We'll be going for a walk in the Kay Park, and then on somewhere for afternoon tea. I don't want to feel cold now, do I?'

'Do you really need to work tonight? It's too bad!'

'We've been over this, Mother; the off-duty is prepared well in advance, and a couple of the girls are sick with flu. Sister Reid says we must pull together and do what we can and that is exactly what I intend to do.'

'Keep your voice down, Vera, your father is reading his newspaper, and you know how upset the news can make him.'

Vera sighed and started to climb the wide wooden staircase while her mother muttered something about being glad she did not have sons to worry about like some of her heartbroken friends.

Once in her room, Vera watched a beam of watery sunlight as it skimmed over her hatpins, making them glisten and gleam.

She looked in the mirror and smoothed her hands over the chestnut locks piled on top of her head. She looked taller with this style, her hair was usually flattened under her nursing cap. Although not a vain girl, she was pleased with what she saw.

The doorbell rang, making her turn on her heel and head for her bedroom door. She was halfway down the stairs when she saw her mother open the front door and gasp with glee.

'Dr Durnie, how do you do? Please come in.'

Charles shook her hand and replied: 'How do you do, Mrs Brownlee? What a beautiful home you have,' he added while looking from side to side. 'And please, call me Charles.'

Mrs Brownlee smiled and flushed ever so slightly. She was immediately taken by the handsome young man standing in her hall. Some leaves had blown in through the open door, and she frowned at them with displeasure.

Just then, Vera's father opened the door to his study. He came out and introduced himself, and gave Charles a reassuringly firm handshake.

'Come through, Charles, we can have some tea before you walk out.'

'That would be very welcome, Mr Brownlee. It's rather chilly out there although I haven't come very far,' he laughed.

'Ah, Vera, there you are. Charles is here,' her mother said needlessly.

'Before we have tea, could I have a word with you alone, Mr Brownlee?' asked Charles.

Vera's father held the study door ajar and gestured that Charles should follow him in.

'Of course, we don't want to get caught up with making tea now, do we!' It was a statement rather than a question.

Vera and her mother made their way to the kitchen. Mrs Brownlee once had a daily help, but the girl was now working as a conductress on Glasgow trams. Vera's mum was not a natural in the kitchen, but fortunately Vera could follow recipes in the *Bread and Baking* and *Win-The-War* cookery books and seemed to have the natural aptitude her mother lacked, and so working with the available rations she had rustled up a modest but tasty looking spread.

The two women looked at each other and without speaking they hugged each other tightly.

'Oh Mother, I can hardly breathe! I love Charles more than I can say. What if he wants to talk to father about something else?'

'No need to worry about that! I saw the gleam in his eye: it was unmistakable. His face lit up when he saw you on the staircase.'

'Really? Did it really?' Vera hugged herself.

Just then, the two men appeared in the hall.

Vera looked at Charles. He walked towards her and took her hand.

'Vera, I have just asked for your father's permission to marry you, and he granted it, so ...'

Charles got down on one knee.

'Vera, would you do me the honour of becoming my wife?'

'Yes, of course, my darling, of course I will!'

'That's settled then! We must make arrangements! It won't be the sort of wedding I would have wanted for my daughter before the war, but we need to cut our cloth, so to speak. The sooner the better,' Mr Brownlee said, his voice full of emotion.

Everyone agreed, but Vera suddenly spoke up.

'Will I need to leave nursing once I am married? What about my work?'

'Oh Vera, why would you want to work once you are married?' Her mother sounded incredulous

'My work is important, vital even, Mother! I thought you understood?'

Charles spoke up.

'You will be able to continue working, Vera, at least for the duration of the war...'

'Which may be over soon if newspaper reports can be believed,' Vera's father added.

'Tea, everyone; we can discuss it over tea.'

'Good idea, Mother, let's have tea.'

CHAPTER THIRTEEN

Vera, 1918

Vera was enveloped in her husband's strong arms. They lay together in silence except for the sound of their breathing.

Their wedding day had been perfect. Quiet, understated, but perfect. She hadn't known such a feeling of total happiness in her life before ... that was, until tonight.

They had chosen a small hotel on the island of Arran for their honeymoon. Both had delightful memories of childhood holidays there and so it seemed like the perfect choice.

It was said that Arran was like Scotland in miniature: hills, glens, Goat Fell, secluded beaches ... it even had castles, mostly ruins but Brodick Castle was occupied by Lady Mary Louise Douglas-Hamilton.

They booked into the hotel, both of them feeling shy about using the new titles of Dr and Mrs Durnie.

Vera had felt the need to remove both gloves when they signed the register, to show off her brand-new gleaming gold wedding band. She was also wearing her engagement ring. It had once belonged to Charles's grandmother; a beautiful ring made from a trilogy of sparkling diamonds.

They self-consciously left in the afternoon to walk along the beach and take in the wonderful sea air in the shadow of Goat Fell. Turning a corner, they found themselves in a tiny cove and realised that they were completely alone. Charles took Vera's hand and led her to a dimple of sand surrounded by tall grass on three sides like a horseshoe.

He pulled her down onto the sand and kissed her passionately. Vera became giddy and pressed herself against her husband's broad chest. Charles moved his hand under her blouse and covered her right breast with his hand.

Vera could hardly breathe; the longing she felt was so unexpected. They had kissed and fondled each other before, but it had been nothing like this.

Vera felt her body sink into the soft white sand as she melted under his touch. Charles was breathing heavily as he caressed her. He pulled away from her and gazed into her eyes, her soft blue eyes that now shone with love for him. He didn't think he could ever be this happy if he lived for ever.

The sound of children's playful voices carried by the wind reached their ears.

Charles stood up and offered his hand help her to her feet.

'I love you more than life itself, Vera! You are my world and always will be.'

Vera looked into his brown eyes and said nothing. There was nothing to be said. She reached out and kissed him passionately.

'Let's go back and have dinner. I am very tired; it has been quite a day. I have a new nightgown; I can't wait to change and go to bed.'

Charles gasped and looked at his wife with amazement.

'Vera Durnie, you have shocked me to my core! I can't think what you are implying!'

'Charles Durnie, don't disappoint me on today of all days!' she replied seriously.

Now on their feet, they held hands and looked at each other, both knowing that this was just the start of their life together and that it would be wonderful.

*

'Are you happy, wife?'

'What do you think, husband?'

'I need you to tell me, Vera, was it...'

Vera placed a finger over his lips

'I have never been so happy. I can't believe this is real. We are meant to be together – listen ... our heart is beating in unison.'

Charles laughed. 'My darling wife, our heart, don't you mean *hearts*?'

'No, Charles,' she replied, suddenly very serious, 'I mean our *heart*. They are moulded together, yours and mine, forever. If you hurt, I hurt. If you are happy, I am happy. We will share everything from now on.'

'I wouldn't have it any other way,' he murmured into her ear.

Vera could feel his desire rising and rolled towards him, kissing his face, neck and chest passionately. He pulled her on top of him and grasped her tightly around the waist.

'Your new nightgown is crumpled on the floor, I hope you realise?'

'What nightgown?' she whispered as their bodies melted together, connected as one.

CHAPTER FOURTEEN

Chrissy, 1920

Aiming the beam of torchlight towards an aisle in the stalls, Chrissy gritted her teeth, puffed out her lower lip and blew upwards. The group of boys nudged each other and sniggered. One of them doffed his cap and bowed.

'Ma pal wants tae ken whit time ye finish?'

'I told you lot last week, and the week before that, when I finish is my business, now for crying out loud, sit up and shut up!'

'Ooo, you're breaking his heart!' the boy said and theatrically held his cap to his chest.

'You heard the lassie,' said a man sitting behind them, clenching his teeth on the pipe hanging out of his mouth. 'If she disnae throw you lot oot, then I will. *Alf's Button* is aboot tae stert. Wheesht!'

The boys sniggered again, but this time they stayed quiet.

'Is there a bit o' trouble here, Miss Barnes?'

Her boss, Senga, who was five feet ten inches tall, stood beside her and raised her shoulders whilst eyeing the boys intently.

Satisfied that they were ensconced in their seats and that they had settled down, Chrissy replied, 'Nothing I can't handle, Mrs Wood.'

'That's ma girl, one more wrong word from them and they will be oot on their ears.'

Chrissy was mortified; she certainly didn't want her boss thinking she wasn't up to the job. Generally, people were well behaved, jovial and ready for a laugh, but no trouble.

She stood at the back of the cinema waiting for the news reel to start, feeling hot under the collar. Those annoying boys! Every week they went through the same repertoire. She tugged at the collar of her uniform as if trying to let steam escape.

What my brothers would give to have a night at the pictures! What did they give! James and John sacrificed their lives; Billy, half his body.

This was the fourth week in a row she had been harassed by them, and she was not at all amused.

'Aisle nine, please,' said two young women rushing in.

'This way,' Chrissy whispered as she ushered them to their seats with a beam of light.

She had just returned to her place when a woman asked for directions to the WC. By the time Chrissy had returned, the feature film had started and a hush had descended over the theatre apart from the odd bit of sweetie paper rustling. The incident with the boys was forgotten, for now.

'See you the morrow. I need to get back – my mam is finishing early tonight. She's been on night shifts for the last week. I think everything is done and ready for tomorrow.'

'Right-o, Chrissy, see you the morrow and thanks, lass, you always go above and beyond, unlike some.' Segna nodded towards the projectionist in his booth. 'I wouldn't like to tell you how many cups o' tea he's swallowed this night!'

Exhausted, Chrissy headed for the rear exit. The night was still and dark, and the moon was full, showering beams of light into the street. She was quite happy walking alone at night; she thought she could take care of herself better than most. She had grown up with three brothers, and that alone had stood her in good stead, although she now realised that being much younger and being a girl meant that they let her win most play fights. Oh, how she missed them, especially Billy. They had a special bond and were friends as well as brother and sister. He had always looked out for her at school. *Hopefully he will be able to come up for a visit soon*, she thought, remembering proudly his achievements

As she rounded the corner and started to walk along King Street, she noticed several groups of people here and there, a few courting couples in doorways. She tried not to look at them but couldn't help wondering what it would be like to have a boyfriend.

She crossed the street, heading for the bus station. She suddenly felt that she was being followed. Looking over her shoulder, she saw nothing but an empty street, so when a voice called out, she visibly jumped.

'Miss, hello, Miss, can I speak to you for a minute?'

Chrissy swung round and saw the young man who had been at the pictures earlier with his two rowdy pals, only now he was alone.

'I take it you want to apologise?' Without waiting for a reply, she went on: 'If you ask me, it's the other two who should be doing that. I had you down as the quiet one.' Her fast and sharp retort made him take a step backwards.

'I wanted to give you this.' The boy handed her a small box of sweets, identical to the ones sold at the cinema.

'Why?' she asked, softer this time but not without a hint of impatience: she did not want to miss her bus.

'I wanted to apologise for ma pals. They were out of order – you have a job to do, and you don't need folk like them making it harder for you.'

Chrissy reached out towards him, noticing his strong arms, his clean-shaven face, the softness of his eyes. She took the sweets.

'Thank you... em?'

'Bob, Bob Ramsay.'

'Thank you, Bob Ramsay. I'm Chrissy Barnes, pleased to meet you, I think!'

They smiled at one another.

'They were teasing me. The short one is my brother, he's only thirteen. The one with the cap and the mouth works beside me at the farm; he's only got one arm, but you'd be amazed at the things he can do, more than able bodied folk half the time. I've been trying to pluck up the courage to ask you out. I see you almost every week, in fact. I can hardly concentrate on the picture because I am looking around trying to see where you are.'

Chrissy flushed. She was glad of the dim light. She wasn't sure how to respond. Nervously she replied, 'Oh, I hadn't noticed that he was missing a limb! He's got such a cheeky face and attitude.'

'Aye, and my wee brother is ... what can I say? ... a typical wee brother. He torments the life oot o' me.'

They walked together towards the bus station.

'Did you serve, Bob? Were you in the army?'

'No, but I wasn't a conchie, a conscientious objector ... I'd never do that. They reckoned that the work I did on the farm was too important. Said I needed to keep working to put food on our tables. The U-boats were trying to starve us into submission. Well, we didn't let them!' he said proudly. 'I still work long and hard on the farm. I've nothing to be ashamed of.'

He frowned and she could see him poke his tongue against his cheek as he exhaled. He looked genuinely hurt; it was obvious that he was proud of the service he provided for his country. Her eyes became dewy, and she fiddled with the buttons of her jacket.

'Bob, I am so sorry, I didn't mean to be rude. I'm tired ... it's been a hard day...'

'Made harder by me and the boys!' he smirked as they reached the bus station.

'Do you think we could go for a walk sometime? I mean, only if you want to? I'd suggest a film, but I expect you've seen enough of those lately.' He scraped his hand through his hair and bit on his bottom lip as he gazed at her, waiting for her reply.

'A walk sounds just fine, Bob Ramsay. I have a day off next Thursday ... or there's always Sunday afternoon?'

'Sunday afternoon would be perfect.' He was smiling from ear to ear and seemed unable to keep still.

'I live in Crosshouse: it's small, but there are some lovely walks along the burn or down towards the Milton Mill.'

'I can borrow ma pal's bike and cycle over to meet you. Where would be the best place, do you think?' The words poured from his mouth like water from a fountain.

'Meet me on the bridge, opposite the Carmel Stores at two o'clock.'

A shrill whistle pierced through the night air.

'I need to go; the bus is ready to leave.'

Chrissy nimbly jumped onto the bus and turned to wave.

'You won't forget, will you, Chrissy? Two o'clock Sunday!' As soon as the bus pulled away, he allowed himself a whoop of delight; he wanted to jump for joy, but there were way too many people standing around to do that.

As he walked out of the station, his heart was beating so fast he wanted to run and scream from the rooftops that this was a dream come true. He had never felt happier in his life. *I saw you months ago, Chrissy, and as soon as I did, I knew you were the girl for me. I did, I really did.*

*

On her way home, Chrissy took a detour past the chip shop. She opened the door and was hit by a wall of warm steamy air dripping with the aroma of fish and freshly cooked chips. Her mouth became moist with saliva almost immediately as she waited her turn to be served.

'Hello, Chrissy hen, what can I do you for?' This was the standard greeting from Geordie.

'Three bags of chips and a pickled egg, please Geordie.'

'Coming right up. How is your mammy and dad? Keepin' well I hope?'

'Mum is fine, Dad, not so much – he has good days and bad days, but he's still smiling, he manages a walk to the bridge every so often to catch up with his cronies to have a blether and a smoke, but mostly they come to visit him for a game of dominos.'

Her dad's cough had become much worse recently, the hacking fits causing him to become breathless and double over in pain, and when he hawked the phlegm was speckled with blood. Her mum was always changing the bedclothes; he drenched the bed sheets with sweat almost every night now.

Neighbours whispered to each other about how thin he looked and how sunken his eyes had become while smiling cheerily and calling out: 'You're lookin' grand, Jim!'

He could barely walk the length of himself without gasping for breath. He was such a proud man, he had worked until it was physically impossible for him to carry on when the doctor said he had to call it a day. He could tell by their expressions that the neighbours didn't mean a word of what they were saying. He could see for himself in the mirror that he was a mere shadow of the man he had been even a few short months ago. He was glad that they weren't dishing out sympathy by the shovel load though; he knew he couldn't stomach that. The lies were better.

'Tell him I'm asking for him. Is the pickled egg for your ma?'

'Aye, it is, you know us too well, Geordie.'

'Here's a pickled onion for your dad – the vinegar in that should chase away a few germs. What do you say?'

Chrissy thanked him and took her newspaper wrapped chips from his outstretched hands. She sniffed deeply.

'I can't wait to get this home! Thanks for the pickle, Geordie.'

'Be sure and tell your dad to come and see me any time, will you lass?'

'I will,' she answered and stepped out onto the pavement and made her way home.

*

Placing the newspaper package on the table, Chrissy turned back towards the front door, took off her coat and hung it on the hook. She popped her hat on top of a small chest of drawers and cried out: 'Let's get the kettle on! I brought chips!'

The fire in the range was burning brightly. The range itself was gleaming and glowing, although not as brightly as it had done in years gone by. She walked to the large kettle and was relieved to find that it was half full. She didn't feel like going out for water at this time of night.

Placing the kettle on top of the range, she called out again: 'Come on, the chips will get cold!'

'Wheesht, lass, your dad has just gone to bed, he's really tired the night. He heard you call out, but he's no hungry, though he's hardly eaten all day.'

'I'll go in and see him, take him a drink or something.'

'Leave him be, he'll feel a lot better the morrow if he gets a decent night's sleep.'

Reluctantly, Chrissy walked over to the wooden table and slid the oil lamp over to one side. She peeled the paper parcel open, releasing the delicious aroma captured within.

'Take a look at the kettle, see if the water is boiling. I've put the tea leaves into the pot.'

'I'll get the salt and a couple of cups. Is there any milk left?'

'A wee bit, I don't think it's on the turn just yet. Don't forget the sugar, lass, will you?'

Soon they were sitting with a paper full of chips each, warm and cosy by the soft orange glow from the range and the flickering oil lamp. Chrissy pushed off her shoes and twiddled her toes in the warm air.

She spied the small stool her dad had made for her when she was little; it was sitting to the right of the great black range, with an ash tray on it and her dad's pipe. He tended to use it as a foot stool these days as he sat in his chair puffing and coughing, toasting his feet while resting them on top of the solid little stool.

What happy memories that little piece of furniture held, deeply intertwined within the woodgrain and underneath countless layers of polish.

'Remember me sitting on that?' she nodded towards the stool, 'reading my books, begging to stay up for five more minutes.'

'Aye I do that. You and your books; you wanted to be Anne Shirley, I seem to remember, that is until you fancied yourself as Florence Nightingale.'

'Aye I did, Mam. I think I could have made a good nurse.'

'I'm sure you would lass, and I'm sorry that you didn't get the chance. I spoke to your teacher, you know, just before you left school, and she told me how much it meant to you. I hate that you were disappointed like that.'

'The smell of the vinegar on that pickled onion is making my eyes water,' Chrissy sniffed, and wiped her face with the back of her hand, taken aback by this disclosure. She thought about being a nurse all the time, and read any text books she could lay her hands on, but being an usherette wasn't all that bad, and the timing never seemed to be right to revisit her dream, and now... well, Bob could be a definite spanner in the works. She felt something profound, something she could not name when she had looked into his eyes tonight. It was like being swallowed whole and enveloped by a golden bubble of happiness. The feeling had taken her completely by surprise, but now she wanted more of it.

They finished the chips; Dad's portion, too, but saved the picked egg and pickled onion for him.

'Now, how about a biscuit. I have a few left.'

Maggie got up to fetch her treasured tin from the pantry.

'There is something different about you tonight, Chrissy, I canna put my finger on it, but you're glowing.'

'Away wi' ye, Mum, it's the fire that's glowing, no me.'

'No,' Maggie persisted, 'you've got a sparkle in your eyes – you look like you are about tae burst into song.'

'I can nae keep a secret from you, can I, Mammy? Right, I'll tell you, I met a boy tonight. He asked me out and I said yes. I'm meeting him here on Sunday afternoon.'

'Ah kent it! I just knew there was something different about you the night! What does he look like?'

'Oh Mum, he's tall, he has brown hair, well, I think it's brown, it was dark when he walked me to the bus station. He has sparkling, smiling eyes, he looks strong and he's a farmer, proud to be keeping the country fed. And when I looked into his eyes, I felt lightheaded.'

Maggie looked at her daughter; she had never seen her look so happy, so full of life, and by comparison she had never seen her man, her Jim, look so sad and tired of life. He had said so tonight after a strenuous bout of coughing, his handkerchief spattered with bright red blood. He'd looked at it and shaken his head.

'I've had enough of this pain, hen; I've had enough o' everything. I just want to go to sleep and never wake up. I'm sorry, hen, but it's how I feel.'

'Ocht, Jim, things will be better in the morning. We're planning to go and visit oor Billy, don't forget.'

'Don't, Maggie, please don't, you ken as well as I do that I will never see Billy again, but maybe soon I will be with oor James and John.'

CHAPTER FIFTEEN

Maggie, 1920

For the third night in a row, Maggie had slept on her chair in front of the range. She propped her feet up on Chrissy's stool and covered her legs and body with blankets.

She just couldn't lie beside Jim. His sweating had become so profuse, she thought that if she got drenched that she would end up with pneumonia. Plus, he coughed almost all night. She could still hear him and went to his side when he was particularly bad. The feeling of helplessness was overwhelming. Watching the man she loved with all her heart suffer and wither away in front of her eyes was almost unbearable.

She remembered when they were first married. Queen Victoria was on the throne. Jim had rescued her from the domestic service she had hated with a passion and given her a home of her very own, *their* very own. In those early days they had gone to bed when the sun set and got up when it rose again. Lying in bed together in the early days had felt a bit wicked. Maggie still felt that the feeling, the one she had when she lay next to her husband, was just too good to be true. She could never have imagined the feeling of being connected so exclusively, so passionately. She hoped other married couples felt the way she and Jim did. They were like two halves of one body; if he hurt, she hurt, and vice versa. When they had welcomed their first born, James, it had been the icing on the cake. She marvelled at every movement and every little noise he made. Then Billy came along. She had worried that she might not feel the same about her second baby, but when he arrived safe and well, she was thankful, her heart brimming with love for him. And then they had been blessed with John. When Chrissy had arrived several years later, she thought Jim would burst with pride; he loved his boys unconditionally, but he wanted them to grow up to be strong and self-sufficient, whereas with

Chrissy, he wanted to wrap her up store her away somewhere and protect her from the whole wide world.

It had come as a shock to him when his daughter had other ideas. She was strong, feisty, and very much had a mind of her own. She figured she could not only do what her brothers did, but that she could do it better, and as time went by, he came to believe it himself. She was the apple of his eye. Maggie had admitted to feeling a bit jealous of their closeness. This had shocked him to the core.

'My Maggie! I love you; you have given me four beautiful weans! I love them more than life itself, but Maggie, I love you more, so much more!'

This had brought tears to her eyes. Her rufty-tufty man, a miner, a veteran, saying words like that had taken her breath away.

It was quiet: no coughing, no Chrissy shuffling about in the upstairs room, no birds chirping their sweet morning chorus to welcome a new day, just silence apart from the crackling of the shiny black coal she had placed on the fading orange embers in the range. It must be early, but she needed to move. Her whole body had become stiff and sore.

Maggie reached for the kettle and gave it a shake. It was almost empty. Wrapping a well-worn shawl around her shoulders, she made her way to the water pump in the street.

I'll get more later, she thought. *I'll just fill the kettle for now.*

Although summer was not officially over, the early morning air was chilly and her breath hung in the air in soft luminescent clouds. Dew drops hung precariously from the pump, dropping to the ground as soon as she touched the handle.

When she returned to the living room, the coal had caught and the flames looked promising as they danced in the grate. Heat was not quite forthcoming, but she knew from years of experience that it was not far away.

'I feel like my life is over,' she spoke to the flames, now showing off their colour and the heights they could reach in a spectacular fashion.

'I have brought four children into this world. One is dead, one missing in action, lying dead somewhere in France, one is maimed, half the man he was, and for what? And as for Chrissy, it sounds like she has met her future husband. I just don't see where I fit in any more except to look after Jim, and I know in my heart of hearts that he doesn't have long for this world. I admit it, I didn't want to, but I admit it, my darlin' man is very sick. He's in pain, he's had enough.'

The flames continued their merry dance, at least bringing her warmth if not comfort.

'I'm fine now, lass, oh how I love you, Maggie. Look after Chrissy, not that she will need it, visit Billy and hug him for me, and don't worry about James and John. I can see them now; they're smiling, lass. I can't tell you how much better I feel, remember that.'

Maggie swung round, almost falling over in her desperation to reach out to her husband.

'Jim, oh Jim, you're feeling better? Thank God!'

She was still alone in the room, but she had heard Jim talking to her, telling her he felt better. She froze, unable to speak or move.

Look after Chrissy, visit Billy, I can see James and John, they're smiling ... what did that mean?

Maggie felt as if someone or something had punched her hard in the gut. The words she had just heard formed a chain around her throat making it impossible for her to speak.

She managed to walk slowly towards the bedroom door and reluctantly stepped inside. Relief flooded her body when she looked at her husband's face. Jim was asleep, in a deep peaceful sleep; he was not sweating, he was smiling.

The feeling of relief now escaped from every pore in her body, preventing her from putting one foot in front of the other, but she knew she must reach the bed.

'Jim ...' she took his hand; it was icy cold. She felt his usually fevered brow, also icy cold.

'Jim, no, oh please no! Don't leave me! What will I do without you?'

She began to sob quietly. The pain that developed in her head was so sudden and severe, she thought it might split in two. She reached for some water just as Chrissy came into the room. She knew instantly that her father was dead.

'Mum, Mammy, please don't! He's not in pain anymore. He wouldn't want you to be this upset, please, Mum!'

Chrissy took her mother in her arms and rocked her like a baby until she became silent.

'I know that, lass, he spoke to me. I know he's going to be just fine, and I know that he is with James and John. They are all together, and they're happy.'

PART 2

CHAPTER SIXTEEN

WW2

Chrissy, 1939

"I believe it is peace in our time."

Neville Chamberlain, 30th September 1938

Chrissy propped herself up on the wooden shaft of her mop and tucked a stray curl of hair behind her ear. The stringy grey mop head splayed out under her weight in the tin pail full of hot water at her feet. Steam rose and wafted across the now clean kitchen floor, filling the room with the aroma of carbolic soap.

Rex popped his scruffy head around the door and put a muddy paw up onto the back doorstep.

'Look at you, away ye go, get out that back door right now! I don't want to clean this floor again before Mum arrives.'

Rex looked at her adoringly with doleful eyes and dutifully did as he was told, heading for a sunny spot in the small back garden next to the pig pail.

Looking through to the living room, Chrissy could see her youngest son, Jack, asleep on the couch. The collar of his blue and white stripy pyjamas poked up over the crocheted blanket covering the thin but sturdy little body. The cushion under his head looked damp, but his breathing was steady and quiet; he looked so innocent and peaceful. Her heart filled with love for him, and she felt tears sting her eyes as she wondered what the future would bring for him. Everyone thought war was inevitable – hadn't there been preparations for months? The newspapers were full of stories about Adolf Hitler. The Prime Minister had visited Herr Hitler in his mountain lair at Berchtesgaden – Chrissy remembered the news reels showing the German people waving Union Jacks and swastika flags calling out, 'Heil Chamberlain!' But two days ago, Germany had invaded Poland.

Chrissy had felt sick to her stomach when she read that Sir Nevile Henderson, British Ambassador to Germany, had handed an ultimatum to German foreign minister Joachim von Ribbentrop saying that unless the British government received "satisfactory assurances" that Germany would withdraw the troops from Poland, "His Majesty's Government will without hesitation fulfil their obligation to Poland." Just last night the Prime Minister had informed the House of Commons that Britain had not yet received a reply from Germany.

Chrissy glanced at the beautifully polished mantle clock as it ticked steadily and rhythmically, oblivious to her anxiety. Dust motes danced and swayed in the beam of sunlight that was streaming into the room.

She threw the contents of the pail over the back step, which made Rex jump and shift his position, and then gave it a quick swish over with the mop before propping it up against the wall to dry in the sun. Wiping her hands on the back of her flowery pinny, she walked slowly into the house straight towards the wireless which sat next to the sideboard in the living room and turned it on to warm up. She treasured the Bakelite wireless and felt very fortunate that she and Bob had one. It was her pride and joy. She always felt a sense of satisfaction and pride when she splashed out tuppence for a copy of the *Radio Times*.

Jack was still fast asleep on the couch. She gently smoothed his soft brown hair, then walked into the kitchen, picked up the kettle and stepped towards the sink, looking out the window towards the fields and the burn as she filled it. She paused for a moment to take in the tranquil scene before her. The sun was shining and managed to dodge most of the fluffy white clouds as they drifted by. She spotted some children paddling in the burn and heard squeals of delight in the distance: *fishing for beardies or eels no doubt*, she thought.

Everything seemed so peaceful and normal. She hoped Jack would be well enough to go out and play with them again soon; he just could not seem to shake off this infection, and couldn't even be bothered with *Children's Hour* on the wireless yesterday. He was rarely sick so this bout of illness had surprised her. Thank goodness Katie had managed to avoid getting it ... John, too, though he was almost a man, but he would always be her first born wean. The thought of him being sent to fight for King and country sat like huge nugget of lead in her chest, causing her to stop breathing when she allowed it to. She had vivid memories of what her brothers had endured, and of the ultimate sacrifice two of them had made. The thought of it all happening again, after the Great War, the war to end all wars, was inconceivable.

It had been some time now since Public Information leaflets had started being distributed, things you needed to know if war should come. Now it seemed inevitable.

*

Maggie Barnes puffed and panted as she walked through the Boo'in, a narrow alleyway and a shortcut to her daughter's house. She saw a couple of small boys playing with marbles on the pavement outside the fish and chip shop, their bare knees gritty from kneeling on the ground. They were wearing grey shorts held up with braces. She noticed shiny patches on their rear ends where they had been sliding and scuffing along on their behinds. She hoped they weren't Sunday best shorts, or they would probably both get a leathering for spoiling them. Both wore black sandshoes over grey socks which were wrinkled around their bony ankles. She turned right onto Main Road, walking past Montgomery's Buildings and the post office. Passing the pub opposite the village shop, she stopped for a moment to look at the burn, or Carmel Water to give it its Sunday name, flowing gently and steadily under the bridge, its babbling and rippling soothing her frayed nerves. Maggie crossed to the other side and walked towards Irvine Road where Chrissy lived. It was unusually quiet.

She walked around to the back of Chrissy's house and looked over fields towards the bowling green. It was a pretty sight especially on a day like this. She opened the bright green back door after giving her customary seven knocks.

Stumbling into the kitchen, she dropped her heavy message bag on the floor before placing a biscuit tin beside the tea pot. She always took pride in her appearance, especially on a Sunday when she wore her matching coat and hat.

'Hello, Mum!' Chrissy called out. 'Have you been rushing about as usual?'

'Aye, hen, I hiv that. I had to wait for the shortbread to bake, and then I nearly had kittens when I couldnae find my lucky tin to put it in, then just as I was leaving Mrs Smith came to the door with a big pail of tatties, they're in a paper poke in ma bag. I kept a few for ma self.'

'Thanks, Mam.' Chrissy picked up the bag of potatoes and set it by the sink where a puddle of water immediately soaked into the brown paper bag causing it to split open and allowing the earth-covered potatoes to scatter over the clean wooden surface.

'And this will go in the sideboard, right at the back, or it will just disappear like that.' Chrissy snapped her fingers as she pointed at the biscuit tin sitting on the kitchen table.

Chrissy nodded in the direction of a large green moquette armchair. The arm covers and antimacassars had been freshly laundered and carefully ironed; she took great pride in keeping her home neat as a new pin.

'Go and sit through there, Mum, you look done in. Is your chest tight again? Have you remembered to take your pills?'

'Stop fussing, Chrissy. How is ma wee man the day?' Maggie was now whispering with concern.

'Ocht, over the worst now... I hope. He's cooler now and he has been drinking more, so that's a good sign.'

This was posed as a question rather than a statement. She needed reassurance; Jack had been sick much longer than he had ever been before. Other than the odd cold, he had always been a happy and healthy boy, complaining of nothing more than the odd scrape or cut.

Chrissy placed the kettle onto the cooker and lit the gas with a match before turning towards the pantry.

'It'll be boiling in no time, and thanks for the shortbread, Mum.' Chrissy indicated towards the rather bashed well-worn, clock-shaped tin on the table. Picking up the large brown tea pot which always sat beside the cooker, she took off the woollen cosy and lid, and looked inside: it was empty. She walked over to the cream- and green-painted cabinet which sat against the wall opposite the cooker and opened the hinged fold-down door, creating an instant surface to place the pot on. The tea caddy was in the glass-fronted cupboard above.

She warmed the pot and put in one spoonful of leaves fer herself, one for Mum and one for Bob. She hoped he would be able to get away from the farm on time. She added the ubiquitous one for the pot.

'I wish Bob would hurry up.' Chrissy tucked her hair behind her ears and wiped her brow with the back of her hand. Just as she spoke his name, Bob appeared in his stockinged feet, smoking a cigarette, hands caked with dried mud.

'Ma boots are on the back step,' he grinned at Chrissy as he took off his cap and hung it on the hook on the back of the door.

'I can't stay long, mind; there's loads to do before the cows need to be miked again.'

'Quick, turn the wireless up, it's nearly quarter past eleven!'

Maggie was sitting on the chair, gripping her cup and saucer so tightly that her knuckles shone white beneath her wrinkled skin. Chrissy was standing behind the couch, leaning on its sturdy back for support, bending over to stroke Jack's head as he began to stir from his deep slumber. Bob stayed in the doorway between the kitchen and the living room to avoid letting his mucky dungarees come into contact with the furniture.

"This morning the British Ambassador in Berlin handed the German Government a final note stating that, unless we heard from them by 11o'clock that they were prepared at once to withdraw their troops from Poland, a state of war would exist between us.

I have to tell you now that no such undertaking has been received, and that consequently this country is at war with Germany."

Hearing the words they had been dreading spoken out loud chilled them to the bone.

'Oh, dear God,' Chrissy whispered involuntarily as tears streamed down her face. She was sitting on the couch by Jack's feet, and instinctively she scooped him up into her arms and hugged him. The smell of Vick filled her nostrils. He squirmed a little and looked up at her, blinking, his top lip faintly tinged orange from slurping the Lucozade she had splashed out on to help make him better.

"You can imagine what a bitter blow it is to me that all my long struggle to win peace has failed. Yet I cannot believe that there is anything more or anything different that I could have done and that would have been more successful."

Maggie sat very still. She looked at Bob and Chrissy's pale faces as they listened to the rest of the broadcast.

'Not again! Oh please, not again!' she whispered.

CHAPTER SEVENTEEN

Chrissy, 1939

Posters started to appear all over the village:

ALWAYS CARRY YOUR GAS MASK;

DON'T WASTE FOOD;

EAT NATIONAL WHOLEMEAL BREAD;

WATCH OUT FOR POISON GAS.

Chrissy had read somewhere that the tops of some pillar boxes had been painted with a gas-sensitive paint that changed colour if liquid gas landed on it, but she supposed that might only be in London; she certainly hadn't noticed anything locally.

The coat and hat hooks in the lobby now sported cardboard boxes hanging by a length of string. Inside were the gas masks they had been told never to leave the house without. Chrissy thought they were creepy looking – even the pre-school masks made to look like Micky Mouse and Donald Duck looked sinister in her opinion.

But, for now, not much had changed; life seemed to be carrying on much as it had before the war had begun. They had been following blackout regulations since1st September. Chrissy and Bob, along with the rest of the nation, had a selection of heavy curtains and wooden blackout screens that Bob had made to fit some of their windows and doors. The Air Ministry were expecting night-time bomb attacks and urged the public to make it as difficult as possible for the enemy to find British cities, towns and villages. Chrissy hated how dark it was at night: the streetlamps had been switched off and although she could hear the rumble of buses going past the house, the slotted covers over the headlights meant she could barely see them unless there was a full moon.

Jack had been back at school for a few weeks now, but he was still very pale and lethargic. Usually, he was up with the larks while his brother was constantly threatened with a wet flannel in the face to get him out of bed. Katie had reached the age where she preferred to rise early to get into the bathroom first to take care of her ablutions without interruption. Chrissy suspected there might be a boy somewhere on the horizon but was keeping it to herself for now.

As usual, Bob was long gone; he usually had a cup of tea and some porridge before setting off for the farm and returned mid-morning for some eggs straight from the chickens and fried potatoes before the afternoon work started.

The toilet flushed and the sound of the cistern high on the wall filling with water gurgled throughout the house. Katie was humming to herself as she got ready for her shift at Scottish Aviation Ltd in Prestwick. At this time of year, no one spent any longer getting washed and dressed than they could help; winter was fast approaching and the house was cold. Chrissy made sure there was a warm bright fire burning in the living room first thing every morning. She usually laid coats on the floor next to the hearth on cold days, along with hats, scarves and gloves. She had done it since they were small and knew she would probably continue doing so until they left home!

'Boys, are you up yet? John, come on get up or you will be late. Jack where are you?'

Silence was the loud reply, so there was nothing else for it. Chrissy climbed the stairs, threatening John with a wet flannel as she wiped her cold nose on the handkerchief which was always kept in the pocket of her pinny.

'Right, I'll count to three!'

John groaned and pulled the bedclothes up around his head, wishing he could become invisible or just have at least five more minutes in his cosy bed.

Chrissy looked over at Jack. Her little boy was flushed, his mouth partially open, and he was having difficulty in swallowing. He tried to speak but couldn't.

'Oh, my poor wee lad, have you got a sore throat?' She tried to remain calm. She had never seen him like this before.

Jack nodded and put his hand on the left side of his neck which Chrissy could now see was swollen.

'Stay where you are, Jack. John, get up now. I need you to run to the doctor's.'

The sternness in his mother's voice jolted John into a state of wide awareness. He was remarkably close to his little brother; they fought and argued, of course, but there was a deep love between them which was obvious to anyone who saw them together.

'Right-o, Mam,' said John as he sprang to his feet, all thoughts of sleep gone. 'What shall I say?'

'Tell him that Jack has taken a turn for the worse ... he has a sore throat, he's burning up and he's having difficulty swallowing – hurry up!'

John quickly pulled on his clothes before running downstairs and out the front door.

John always felt ill at ease when he was near the doctor's surgery, which was thankfully rare. He stood on the front doorstep of the doctor's house, moving his weight from one foot to the other. He rang the bell, and the door was quickly answered by the doctor's wife, Mrs Durnie.

John knew his mum paid her money every month without fail yet although his brother was extremely sick, like his mum, he still managed to feel guilty about bothering the doctor.

Mrs Durnie opened the large front door with a loud creak. She smiled warmly at John and noted immediately that the boy was extremely anxious as he twirled his cap round and round in his hands.

'Come in. It's John, isn't it? I'll be right back, wait here for a moment.' She spoke softly, her voice reassuring.

Standing in the dimly lit hall, John looked at the large wooden staircase straight ahead of him. On his right stood a fireplace where an assortment of papers and kindling lay in the grate, waiting to be lit. To the left of the fireplace stood a dark, wooden half-moon shaped table, on top of which sat a Bakelite telephone. The telephone had a tray which was half out and half in, containing what looked like a small notebook and there was a pencil sticking out of it.

Vera Durnie returned to the hallway through a door that led the rest of the house. After listening carefully to what John said, she ushered him towards the waiting room. Twisting the shiny brass handle, she pushed the dark, heavy door open. It creaked almost as loudly as the front door had done.

Three heads looked up in unison when John walked quietly into the hushed interior. All three nodded in recognition, muttering good morning.

The waiting room had a red tiled floor and several wooden chairs along one wall, some of which were occupied. There was also a well-worn dark brown leather Chesterfield sofa against the far wall, which patients only sat on if necessary; one reason being most were intimidated by it, the other being it was extremely difficult to get out of. Once bitten, twice shy.

The ceiling was high and sported ornate cornicing. The bay window was dressed in cream-coloured lace curtains hanging over the lower panes. Blackout screens were propped up against the wall waiting for their night duty to begin. In front of the window a round oak table held a copy of yesterday's well-thumbed newspaper, an ashtray and a rather unruly looking aspidistra.

Centre stage stood an imposing marble fireplace which looked as if there had not been a fire lit in it for years.

Vera Durnie wrote the details John gave her about Jack in her notebook. She knew that Chrissy Ramsay was level-headed and not one to panic, so she couldn't help the feeling of deep concern settling in her chest. She would pass on the message as soon as Charles was free. This would not wait until after morning surgery.

Vera's experience as a qualified nurse allowed her to assist her husband with minor procedures, but she also acted as receptionist and telephonist. Mostly, she was his listening ear, his sounding block and his best friend.

Just then, the consulting room door opened; a patient came out carrying a glass medicine bottle, thanking the doctor profusely whilst apologising for bothering him at the same time. Vera walked with the patient to the front door, wished her good day, then turned on her heel to face her husband.

He looks so tired, she thought. Her husband had been called out in the middle of the night to a complicated delivery which had required forceps and chloroform. Thankfully, the mother was recovering, but the baby had died.

She and Charles had seen more than their fair share of death and tragedy, but they were always deeply affected by it and shared a deep empathy with the families and the community. Charles smiled warmly at his wife. A fire burned brightly in the grate; Charles liked a cosy room for his patients in the winter months. It gave a warm, amber glow to the dark, polished furniture and what had once been his father's green leather chair standing proudly behind his desk in the bay window.

A wooden sphygmomanometer case and a stethoscope sat side by side on the left of the desk. A Victorian brass ink stand, which had also belonged to his father, and blotting paper were in the centre, and on the right side sat some wooden filing boxes containing buff-coloured Lloyd George envelopes housing patients notes beside a heavy black telephone. Charles always kept a glass jar filled with boiled sweets, which were getting more and more difficult to come by, in the middle right-hand drawer, to reward children for being well behaved. He loved children and wished he and Vera had been blessed with a child of their own, but alas, it was not to be.

There were two chairs with hard round seats and bentwood backs in front of the desk. To the right of the window was an examination couch. It was extremely heavy and consisted of leather-covered horsehair on a solid wooden adjustable frame. Next to the couch, on the left, stood a cream metal trolley with glass shelves and a drawer which held bandages, an assortment of white enamel kidney dishes, glass syringes, a patella hammer, a Pinard stethoscope and a small square tray of assorted instruments. A metal screen on wheels, furnished with soft green fabric, sat against the wall at the foot of the couch, beside which stood a wooden coat and hat stand.

'Charles, John Ramsay is in the waiting room. His mother is extremely worried about young Jack; sounds like it could be quinsy throat to me?' She reeled off the signs and symptoms John had described.

'Ah, I had hoped he would be getting better by now; he hasn't recovered fully from his last infection. I agree, it does sound like quinsy. Tell the boy I will be there as soon as I can and tell the other patients they can either wait or come back again later.'

Charles donned his coat and hat, grabbed his leather Gladstone bag, and made his way out to his trusty Austin 10 which was parked in the driveway.

Vera dutifully and competently checked the bag three times a day to make sure that Charles had everything he required for almost every eventuality, keeping it replenished and neat.

'I may call in on Mrs Donnelly on the way back, just to make sure she is coping. I know the midwife will be going in, but it won't hurt to pay a visit.'

Vera looked at her husband and smiled.

'No, it won't,' she agreed, knowing wild horses could not keep him away from that poor family today. She watched him walk to the car, smiled and shook her head. Charles was ruggedly handsome. He had played rugby during his university days in Glasgow, resulting in a slightly crooked nose. His sandy-coloured hair was usually unruly, and his necktie was mostly pulled off-centre. Vera made sure he was well turned out first thing every morning: clean white shirt, polished shoes, neatly folded handkerchief in his breast pocket, but within a matter of hours he looked as unkempt as a child who had been playing football with his friends in the playground, but Vera knew that she would not want him any other way.

*

Chrissy had been busy while John was gone. Partly because it helped prevent her worrying too much, and partly because it would never do to have the doctor coming into a messy house. Firstly, she gave Jack a cool drink of water, but he had only managed to swallow a few sips. She tenderly sponged his hot little brow and dressed him in clean pyjamas before changing his damp pillowcase for a fresh clean one and plumping up the pillow inside. Casting an eye over the counterpane to make sure it was clean too, she then made John's bed and generally tidied up the bedroom. Finally, she had wiped round the bathroom and put out a clean towel so that the doctor could wash his hands. The soap had seen better days, but it would have to do; it had been difficult to get hold of lately although rationing hadn't started yet.

A firm knock on the door caused her to jump up and run downstairs. She could see the outline of Dr Durnie's hat through the frosted glass pane at the top of the green door. She removed her pinny and tucked her hair behind her ears before opening it to let him in.

'Come in, Doctor, this way,' said Chrissy nervously as she led the way upstairs.

Charles followed and called out gently to Jack as he entered the room.

'Good morning, young man. I hear you are causing a bit of trouble, eh?' he smiled.

Charles immediately noted that the child had a fever; he only needed to use his thermometer to find out by how much the child's temperature was raised.

'Now this will be cold, Jack, you be a brave boy,' Charles said kindly as he reached for his stethoscope and gently listened to the child's heart and lungs. Jack's breathing was laboured and shallow, and his pulse was racing.

Jack lay, not moving, just crying softly. Droplets of drool escaped from his mouth onto the clean pillowcase.

'Try to have a sip of water for me, Jack,' Charles coaxed.

The child did as he was bid, but he spluttered and choked as most of the liquid dribbled down his chin. His huge brown eyes looked earnestly at the doctor as he tried but failed to swallow more than one mouthful. Salt-laced tears welled up and started to trickle down his hot little cheeks again. Charles tried to examine his throat and tonsils, but Jack's throat had almost closed over.

'Right-o, Jack, I will be back shortly. I just need to speak to your mummy for a moment.'

Outside the bedroom door Charles looked gravely at Chrissy.

'I am afraid Jack will need to go into hospital; he has a quinsy throat. Normally I would have expected this a few days after his last infection, but for one reason or another it has chosen to manifest now. I am afraid it really has taken a tight hold; he has a large abscess on one of his tonsils. He must go to hospital as soon as possible. Wrap him in a blanket for now and I will take him in my car.'

Chrissy gasped and her eyes filled with tears. 'Oh no… but I have been looking after him, I really have! He's had his cod liver oil, his malt and orange juice, he never goes out without being wrapped up, a hot water bottle at night…'

'Mrs Ramsay, please stop. There is nothing you could have done to prevent this. As I said, normally it would happen a few days after a bout of tonsillitis, in this case, however, an infection has been lying dormant and has chosen to raise its ugly head. This is not your fault.'

*

Chrissy's cheeks looked dewy and rosy as the light from the fire bounced off them. Rex was slumbering and snoring peacefully by her feet. He stuck to her like glue these days. He seemed to know she needed another presence beside her, but not one that would interfere with her thoughts and memories. A quiet reassuring presence. She stared into the flames, mesmerised by the variations in shape, size and colour, all so similar but oh so different, each one flickering and crackling against the other, tumbling around exuding energy. A piece of coal tumbled onto the hearth closely followed by another which fell on top of the well-worn hearth rug. She sat transfixed and watched it smoulder and smoke as it melted into the wool. She made no attempt to grab it with the fire tongs and throw it back into the grate; she wished it was on her chest, sinking through her skin down into her icy heart where it would burn right through her and end this blackness that enveloped her.

The rest of the room was very dark: the blackout blinds and curtains were secured in place as usual, but Chrissy hadn't bothered to switch on any lights; she couldn't see the point.

An acrid scorched odour rose from the hearth rug and stirred something inside her just as Rex nuzzled her knee with some urgency as if to say, *Come on, Mam, sort this out.*

She slowly stood up, dealt with the offending ember and rubbed at the black mark on the rug with her foot.

What was the point of anything anymore? Only God knew where John was. He had joined the RAF and after his first leave, communication had been scarce to non-existent. Katie had moved to her cousin's in Monkton. It made more sense for her to live near to her workplace, and she had made lots of new friends in the area. Chrissy was glad she had gone, but suspected her daughter would still be at home if her mother spoke more than two words to her on a daily basis. Bob was so busy, she hardly saw him these days and she had decided she liked it that way. Sitting alone she could close her eyes and think about Jack. She could allow herself the luxury of re-living every moment of his short life from the day he had been born upstairs in the bed she still shared with Bob until his last moments on earth, lying in a starched white envelope of sheets in Kilmarnock Infirmary. The hushed disinfected environment where she had felt so out of place, so useless, so frightened. The nurses in their immaculate uniforms exuded efficiency and calm.

She would never forget arriving at the hospital, waiting outside the ward. The hygienic smell seemed to overwhelm her; she could hardly breathe, it was so heavy and pungent. She re-lived over and over again being ushered into the duty room and being told that Jack had passed away. Bob had tried to comfort her, but she did not want to be touched, she did not want to listen. She did not care that Bob needed comfort and support too, and she did not want the tea offered so sympathetically. Something, somewhere inside her had died too. Chrissy didn't know what it was, she only knew that it was gone. She couldn't remember how she got home that day, she couldn't even remember how long ago it had been. A day? A week? A month? A lifetime.

She rarely went out other than to the store for her rations.

Queues were the order of the day, and she despised the enforced false companionship they created. She was obliged to listen to sympathetic words of comfort, which, although well-meant, washed over her like an icy mountain waterfall, chilling her to her very core. A constant reminder that Jack was no longer with her.

If only she had taken him to the doctor sooner, if only she had noticed the decline in his general health. 'It's not your fault,' Dr Durnie had said, but Chrissy was convinced that it was, and the guilt slowly gnawed at the parts of her that grief had not yet reached and devoured.

The minister had been a regular visitor. His calm reassuring voice tried to get through to Chrissy, to reach the part of her that had died when her son did. How could she tell him that she found it so hard to believe in a God who could allow the suffering and death of a young child who had had his whole life ahead of him? Now, she would never see him grow, get married, have children of his own. His bright radiating light had been snuffed out and would never shine again. She was not just heart-broken: her heart was nothing more than a block of solid ice, so solid her husband feared it might never melt. He had said as much, as had Katie, but Chrissy didn't care.

*

Vera Durnie cycled away from the Co-op. The basket hanging from the handlebars was only half full as was the usual state of affairs these days. Afternoon surgery would be starting soon; she had to get back in time and certainly before Charles had finished his house calls.

Suddenly, she became aware of a woman walking towards her, crossing the road right in front of her.

Vera niftily swerved around the woman, ramming her front wheel into the kerb in the process. She stood astride the bike; her highly polished brown lace-up shoes had a firm grip of the ground beneath her. She looked elegant as ever in a green tweed suit, cream blouse and a brown hat worn at a jaunty angle showing off her bright natural curls. Although she was now in her forties, she was proud of the fact that she did not have a single grey hair.

Chrissy jumped back onto the pavement; her eyes immediately filled with big salty tears that immediately trickled down her face only to congregate again under her chin.

Vera propped her bicycle against a nearby wall and put her arm around Chrissy's shoulders. She removed a beautifully embroidered handkerchief from her pocket and handed it to the distressed woman by her side.

'I am so very sorry, Mrs Ramsay, are you hurt?' she asked kindly. She had been hoping for a chance to speak to Chrissy since the minister had asked for her advice about how they could help but hadn't expected to almost run her over in the process.

Chrissy couldn't bring herself to speak. Now that her tears had stared to flow, she could not and did not want to stop them.

'I'll walk you home. Put your shopping in my basket. I need to pass your house to get home so it's no bother. I won't take no for an answer.'

Vera reached for her bicycle and watched as Chrissy did exactly as she had been told.

She pushed the bicycle across the road towards the shops on the bridge and headed for Irvine Road. She could hear a bunch of local boys talking animatedly as they tried to catch eels in the burn. She could tell that Chrissy had heard them too and her heart ached for her. She knew what it was like to lose babies, three in total, each loss harder to bear than the last. How often had she looked at mothers and babies over the years with an indescribable yearning so omnipresent and agonising? She let out a long, low sigh.

As they walked, Vera deliberately did not talk about Jack. Instead, she kept her tone light.

'I've been meaning to call on you, Mrs Ramsay … may I call you Chrissy? We go back a long way you know,' she smiled. 'I have a proposition for you; would you mind if I came in for a moment?'

Chrissy started blinking rapidly, and she felt her knees shake. What could the doctor's wife want with her?

'Of course, here we are, come in, you will need to take me as you find me, though.' She cleared her throat and rubbed the back of her neck where a red patch appeared.

Vera smiled warmly. 'Lead the way, I'm right behind you. I'll carry your shopping while you put the kettle on.'

CHAPTER EIGHTEEN

Chrissy, 1941

Chrissy reached into the back of the sideboard to fetch the good *china* tea set and arranged some shortbread onto a plate. Rex watched her intently and cocked his head to one side hoping for a crumb, which was not forthcoming. Chrissy refused to be drawn by his puppy dog eyes this time.

'Out you go boy, you have a bone in the garden. I'll need all my wits about me for this.' *What could she want with me?* She chewed on her lower lip and tucked an imaginary stray curl behind her ear.

Rex obediently did as he was bid; he was such a good dog. Chrissy couldn't believe that so many folks had their pets put to sleep after the government had distributed pamphlets from the National Air Raid Precautions Animals Committee. They advised the people of Britain to send or take household animals into the country before things got bad. The pamphlet had ended with: *If you cannot place them in the care of neighbours, it really is kindest to have them destroyed.* The same advice was printed in most newspapers and was broadcast by the BBC on the wireless.

Each time she heard it, she shuddered with disbelief and thanked God that she lived in the country. What a terrible decision city dweller had had to make! She had long decided that even if she lived in the heart of London, she could not part with Rex and, so far, they were managing fine. She had recently read about a woman being fined for feeding crumbs of stale bread to the birds. She knew she must be careful and respectful of the rules, but the little dog was and always would be part of the family.

Her hands trembled as she carried the tray of tea and biscuits into the living room and placed it on a table she had unfolded before placing a lace cover on it in readiness.

'Did you hear about poor Mr Bole?'

Chrissy looked quizzically at her visitor and said she hadn't.

'An incendiary bomb landed in his back garden the other night. The poor man had to get out of bed and try to put the fire out in his shirt tails. The whole time he was moaning about the damage that had been done to his carrots!' Vera grinned.

'Oh my, no, I hadn't heard and nor has Bob unless he

forgot to tell me. He is so busy on the farm. We are digging for victory in our garden, but Bob is digging on a massive scale as you will be aware. Every day he gives thanks for the Scottish Women's Land Army – he says they couldn't cope without them. Such a worthwhile thing, being in the Land Army, don't you think?'

'I certainly do. In fact, I'm glad you brought it up. I know you have been knitting and sewing for the Women's Voluntary Service and the Women's Rural, but I wondered if you would consider something else?'

Chrissy stopped mid-sip and stared at her guest. She could knit and sew from home – she didn't need to connect with anyone unless she had to. Her mother was worried about her; she had told her so more than once. Was she behind this intervention, she wondered with more than a bit of annoyance. Why couldn't her mother just leave her alone?

'Such as, Mrs Durnie?' Chrissy replied with more than a hint of suspicion.

Vera settled back into her seat. 'I love the colour of your sofa, such a fetching shade of green.'

Chrissy soaked up the compliment and relaxed a little.

'Dr Durnie has a brother who lives just outside London. As you know, the reports are grim, and my heart goes out to those people, especially those in the East End, and reading between the lines we aren't hearing half of what is going on down there. Dr Durnie's brother and his wife have a son, Martin. He's eleven and it has been agreed that he will come to live with us for a while. We met the boy not long before the war – he's delightful, blonde hair and blue eyes, just like his mother.'

Chrissy had stopped breathing; for a moment she thought Mrs Durnie was going to suggest that the boy should come and live here in this house, Jack's house. She exhaled a sigh of relief and put down her quivering cup and saucer. The teaspoon fell to the floor with a soft clunk.

'You may not be aware of the additional duties Dr Durnie has had to undertake. All general practitioners not working for the armed forces have been required to adapt to the new challenges and conditions brought about by the war. He is involved with care in Kilmarnock Infirmary as well as surgeries in neighbouring villages and beyond. As you know, I am a trained nurse and assist where and when I can but now that we will have a child living with us it will be increasingly difficult.'

'I see,' said Chrissy although she did not entirely understand what the doctor's wife was getting at.

'I remember when your brother Billy was a patient of mine. I also remember how you took his injuries in your stride, how interested you were in our work and ...'

She paused.

'I need help, Chrissy.' She omitted the word *desperately*, which was how she felt. 'We have the huge vegetable plot to contend with, clinic notes to update, ordering supplies, cleaning and more patients than ever. The Women's Institute depend on the extra vegetables for food parcels, and they make jam using our fruit.'

Vera's usually calm voice began to quaver a little. She had been feeling so tired lately. The "change of life" did that, though. She hadn't thought twice about agreeing to her nephew coming to stay, but it had to be said, it did roughen the edges of what had once been the clockwork smooth running of the household and surgery.

Chrissy picked up her cup again, glad of the prop. In other words, she wants me to be a skivvy and look after the vegetable plot, she thought. I can do that. Chrissy had been aware that she was crying less, engaging in chores that had been neglected for so long, but the guilt she felt by being almost normal again weighed heavily on her shoulders.

'I am proposing basic training. I want to teach you about the equipment we use, how to order supplies, how to sterilise instruments, that sort of thing.

You could also mentor Martin, my nephew, when he arrives. His mother tells me that he is keen to learn what he can about gardening and how to look after chickens. But the mentoring would be secondary to your clinical work.'

Chrissy sat stock-still, bolt upright in her chair. She looked at Mrs Durnie as if she had horns growing out of her pretty hat.

'Me? You want me do all that?' Had she heard her correctly?

Vera leaned forward and placed her hands in her lap and smiled a genuinely warm smile.

'Mrs Ramsay, Chrissy, you are one of the most knowledgeable ladies in the village. It hasn't gone unnoticed how well read you are. You learn quickly, you have experience in many things, and your presence as a stalwart, a source of advice and encouragement in the village has been sorely missed of late.'

Chrissy's mouth fell open, and she flushed red with embarrassment, but she did not cry, for the first time in forever she did not cry after having a conversation with someone.

'Do you really think I am up to it?'

'No, I know with absolute certainty that you will excel in your duties. Your attention to detail is second to none, and I remember how you interacted with the soldiers in the Dick Institute when you came to visit your brother Billy. You're a natural born nurse!'

Chrissy flushed again, not sure what to say.

'I will need to discuss it with Bob; he'll be back later tonight.'

'Of course. Come over to the house on Monday, say, ten o'clock. That will give you time talk it over with Bob and think it through.'

Vera rose and formally shook Chrissy's hand. She really wanted to hug this woman who was a shadow of the woman she had been. She truly *did* need a second pair of hands, but she was also determined to be instrumental in helping Chrissy to find herself again, not to forget the past, but to once again look to the future.

*

'Have you been talking to Mrs Durnie about me by any chance?' Chrissy asked Maggie.

'I don't even remember the last time I saw her; you know I never bother the doctor. Why do you ask?'

'Have you been talking to the minister about me then?'

'Chrissy, what is this aboot? Has something happened?'

'As a matter of fact, aye, something has happened. Mrs Durnie offered me a job. She says she remembers me when I visited oor Billy in the hospital, and that I was a "natural", but the more I think about it, she was just feeling sorry for me, and I do not want pity, nothing can bring Jack back to me, and no one will convince me that if I couldn't have acted sooner. My wee boy would be coming home from school any minute now, bursting to tell me all his news. But he's gone, Mam, and I will never see him again, and the pain is unbearable at times. There's a lead weight in my heart that will be with me forever.'

'Come and sit-down, lass, I want to talk to you.'

'You've been doing way too much talking to all and sundry if you ask me! You're always interfering, and giving your opinions – I don't need it!'

'I know I haven't talked much about my work during the last war. I always thought it was best forgotten. Did you know there was an Ardeer village? It was called Ardeer Square. They demolished it a while back – it even had its own bank and a dentist! It was one of the world's largest explosives factories. I don't know if it still is. It even had its own battalion attached to it. Folk still remembered the massive explosions in 1887 and 1913. Did ye ken that some houses in Irvine had their windaes blown oot by the blast?'

'Aye, I did know about the village, Mum, but where are you going with this? I have things to do.'

'I started work there just before you left school. Do you remember?'

'Of course I do! I had to take the job at the picture house not long after that, remember? If I had been able to train to be a nurse, I could have saved my wee boy!' Chrissy's nostrils were flaring as she waved her arms in the air.

'Ifs and maybes will drive you mad, Chrissy, they will get you nowhere except deeper into the depths of the despair you have been wallowing in, lass.'

'Wallowing? I can't believe I'm hearing this; I don't need to sit here and listen to this!' she said as she jumped to her feet.

'Aye, you do, and you will! Sit down.' Maggie nodded curtly towards the chair.

Chrissy sat down with a thud, angry tears prickling her eyes.

'James had been killed by the time I took on that job, and I had no idea where John and Billy were.'

'I know all this, Mum.' Chrissy held her head in her hands and exhaled loudly.

'We were a prime target for German raids. Imagine, with all that gelignite, cordite and guncotton inside, one hit and we would have been blown to smithereens, and half of Ayrshire too, no doubt. Fusiliers patrolled the perimeter barbed wire fences, looking out to sea for U-boats. We worked in air you could have cut with a knife; the chemical smells were overpowering at times. It was hard and dangerous work, but let me tell you this, Chrissy, when I was there, I felt so close to my boys! I felt that James was looking down on me with pride, knowing his mither was doing her bit. I was too late to help him, but I could help others just by being there and carrying on.'

Chrissy was silent; salt-laden droplets dripped from her cheeks.

'Listen, lass, I'm just trying to tell you, you are not being singled oot. What has happened to you isn't a punishment for something you have done or haven't done.'

'I've seen you gaze at wee Jack's photo with tears in your eyes,' she continued. 'You will never forget him, nor should you, but it's all right to remember the good times and not feel guilty about being alive. And I know what you are going through every day wondering where John is. War is a brute, a merciless raging swine of a thing, it doesn't care who or what it destroys, but we can't let it control us. I worked in that place day and night for what felt like an eternity. Think what it would have been like for me if I allowed myself to imagine the worst every time I opened the door and walked in. Aye, some of us turned as yellow as canaries, some of us lost friends, but we clung onto the fact that we were performing crucial war work. The boys at the front couldn't have won if we hadn't been doing our work. We had good times as well as bad. I will never forget the friends I met there.

The whole country is in this together, and I bet not one soul will come out of the other end unscathed and without a tale to tell. You are kind to everyone else, Chrissy, but it's time for you to be kind to yourself. Mrs Durnie would'nae have asked for your help if she didn't need it. She obviously trusts you. Don't let her down.'

Chrissy's sobs resonated like thunder coursing through her bones, shaking her to the core of her very being. She rose, walked to the couch and almost fell into her mother's open arms where she stayed until her sobs subsided.

'Thanks, Mum,' she whispered.

'For what, my pet lamb?'

'For being you.'

CHAPTER NINETEEN

Chrissy, 1940

Chrissy walked smartly along Irvine Road towards the doctor's house. She hadn't felt this alive for such a long time. She almost felt happy. She was still swamped by the thick black cloak of guilt that covered her from her head to her feet. But she just had to learn how to throw it off, hang it up in a closet and slam the door shut.

She must appear to be professional and dependable no matter what. She could not and would not betray the trust Mrs Durnie had in her. Rex trotted along by her side, looking up at her occasionally as if to say, *You will be fine, Mam, and I promise I won't chase the chickens.*

It had been agreed by both Mrs Durnie and Chrissie when they had set a start date that Rex could tag along if he behaved himself. They had a large, enclosed garden, and even an old kennel. It had seen better days but would suffice in a shower. Chrissy couldn't bear to leave him home alone all day, even though Bob would be in at lunch time.

It had been just under two weeks ago that Bob had come home, tired, weary and wearing his own black cloak of helplessness.

He longed to have his old Chrissy back, the Chrissy who could light up a room just by walking in to it. He pictured her humming to herself as she baked and cooked, creating dishes from their meagre rations that many housewives could only dream of. He told her she should write a cookery book; she just laughed but flushed with delight.

He wished and prayed every day that he could find a way to help her; to get her to open up, to let the bad feelings leave to make room for good ones. Instead of letting them fester inside, to talk and reminisce about the amazing years they had enjoyed with their precious son before he was taken from them way too soon.

They had received a telegram informing them that John was listed as missing in action. He had been named John to honour his uncle who still lay who knew where in France, and Bob hoped the name wasn't cursed. He knew this defied all logic, but he couldn't help thinking it.

Chrissy had accepted the news with an eerie calmness. In fact, she felt as if another piece of her frozen heart had been torn from her body and been shattered into tiny pieces that would never fit together again.

Tonight, Bob removed his boots, made a fuss of Rex who was delighted to see him as usual, wagging his tail so madly it almost went round in circles.

Chrissy was sitting at the kitchen table, sipping on a cup of cocoa, her favourite drink in the evening. Most nights it was a watery affair, but tonight, there had been enough of the milk ration left over allowing her to indulge in a creamy, milky chocolate drink.

He was expecting a bland greeting, the usual monotone, 'I've been keeping your dinner warm. I'll get it for you once you have washed your hands,' but instead Chrissy stood up, pushing the chair away with the backs of her knees and hesitantly walked towards him.

'Mrs Durnie was here today.'

'Mrs Durnie? What did she want?' Bob frowned, all sorts of scenarios swarming around in his head.

'We had a long talk.' Chrissy took in a deep breath and blew it out again slowly through pursed lips. 'She offered me a job, a good job. She says she has every confidence in me, that I am a quick learner. Imagine that, Bob, she asked me to help her!'

She pressed herself against his muscular body and looked up into his eyes.

'I'm terrified, Bob, absolutely terrified!'

Bob opened his mouth to speak, but she gently touched his lips with her left hand and pointed to her ring finger with the other.

'This gold band means you and I support each other, through sickness and health. You have been there for me, Bob, when many another man would have given up on me by now, but you have stood by me. You have been grieving, too, and I haven't been there to support you. Bob, I'm so sorry.'

The words tumbled out; they had been imprisoned for far too long. Now that they had escaped there was no stopping the flow.

'I'm terrified, but I want to do it. I want to take the job. I have a feeling inside me that I haven't felt for years now; it might be hope, who knows. I might always feel guilty about what happened to our wean, guilty about being alive when he is gone, but suddenly, it's as if someone has opened a door, swept all the stale and musty air out of my head, and blown fresh pure air in. I'm rambling now, I just don't know how to explain it!'

Bob took her in his arms and kissed her gently. She didn't pull away; she kissed him right back. They held each other tightly as if afraid to let go and find that the conversation hadn't really taken place. Chrissy was first to release her grip; she didn't want to, she had forgotten the warm secure feeling of being held in the arms of the man she loved.

'Chrissy, you know I will support you, no matter what you decide, don't you?'

Unsure of how to react, she simply said, 'Enough of this! Get washed – dinner will be on the table in five minutes.'

She tucked a chestnut curl behind her ear, smoothed her apron and headed for the oven.

After Bob had eaten and the dishes were done, instead of going straight to bed, they sat together on the couch. Bob's arm draped around her shoulders protectively. She nestled into his body, enjoying the feeling of his solid chest and his masculine smell. She tucked her feet up onto the couch, sending a silent prayer of thanks into the ether.

'Don't move, Mrs Ramsay.'

Bob got up and strode over to the sideboard. He fished around in the back left-hand corner and brought out a bottle of sherry. Chrissy had completely forgotten it was there. He poured out two small glasses from the nearly full bottle; it was only ever used in Christmas cakes and trifle, but rationing had put that particular gas at a peep. He returned and sat down beside her again.

'Here's tae us and here's to the future, Chrissy! We have a lot of damage to do yet, eh, hen?'

'That we do, Bob. Here's to us, to Katie and our boys. May John come back safely, and here's to Jack. I know you are here with me, son, I know that now. You are in my soul and that will never change, I promise you.'

They walked hand in hand upstairs to bed, both tired and weary. Bob thought his heart might erupt with joy.

CHAPTER TWENTY

Chrissy, September 1940

The old Chrissy re-emerged from the cave of darkness that had surrounded her for so long, slowly but ever so surely.

Her first day working for Vera Durnie had been a baptism of fire and she enjoyed every minute of it. When she was learning, her mind had to stay focused on the job at hand. It could not afford to stray into the past.

Charles Durnie's nephew had recently arrived from London. Vera and Charles were sitting at the breakfast table listening to the news one September morning as usual, when a disturbing broadcast chilled them to the bone:

This is the BBC. Good morning. We begin today's programme with a special report.

Last night, the capital endured its most sustained aerial assault since the outbreak of war. Beginning shortly after tea-time, enemy aircraft launched a heavy bombardment across East London, the docks, and surrounding boroughs. The raid continued into the early hours. Fires are still being fought in Rotherhithe, Poplar, and the Isle of Dogs.

Casualties have been reported, and emergency services are working with great courage and speed. We commend the fire brigades, ambulance crews, and wardens who remained at their posts throughout the night. Their bravery is matched only by the resolve of Londoners who, despite the destruction, emerged from shelters with dignity and determination.

The Prime Minister has issued a statement: "London can take it and will take it. The enemy shall not break our spirit."

They looked at one another and decided there and then that Martin must live with them for the duration of the war. The subject had been raised by Martin's parents once or twice, but they thought that he would be safe at boarding school. This latest assault on London changed everything.

Vera introduced Chrissy to Martin. He was a bright boy, his blond hair, cut into a pudding bowl shape so common now, shone, as did his shoes.

He politely shook Chrissy's hand, but he couldn't take his eyes of the scruffy looking dog sitting patiently by her feet. His blue eyes shone as he inspected every inch of Rex.

'Can I stroke him?' he asked and looked up at his aunt.

'You better ask Mrs Ramsay, Martin.'

Martin shifted his gaze to Chrissy, his eyes silently pleading.

Chrissy felt her heart miss a beat when she looked at him. *He must be about the same age as Jack*, she thought as she took in his grey short trousers, knee-high grey socks, grey short-sleeved shirt and sleeveless patterned pullover.

'Of course you can. He loves having his tummy tickled. Just ask him to roll over!'

Martin blinked his eyes; they were almost popping out of his head.

'You mean if I ask him to roll over, he will?'

He was incredulous.

'Not only that, but he also sits when you tell him to, and he will give you a paw. He can sit up and beg too, although that's usually when you have a treat for him. He loves raw carrots, and he barks when you ask him to speak.'

Martin's eyes widened and he shuffled from one foot to another, unable to contain his excitement.

'Mother and father wouldn't let me have a dog. Mummy said she was allergic to their hair, but I don't think she really wanted a dog.'

Vera glanced at the boy; he had hardly said two words since he arrived, and now here he was talking animatedly with someone who was a complete stranger to him

'Why don't you and Rex go into the back garden and you can ask him to do his tricks for you?' Vera was mindful that there was important work to do. She really did need help to keep things running smoothly.

'I'll call you when *Children's Hour* starts.' She already knew he loved to settle in with a glass of milk and listen to his favourite programme.

Chrissy looked into her shopping basket, rummaged around a bit and brought out a bright red rubber ball.

'This is his favourite. He loves to play fetch – you just throw the ball, and he will bring it straight back to you.'

'Really?' the boy gasped, anxious to set off with his new friend who was already gazing at the ball, waiting for it to be launched into the air.

The two women smiled knowingly at each other.

'I know it's early days. He's been very homesick and he misses his friends terribly. I hear him crying at night; he pretends to be asleep when I go into his room. I think having Rex as a companion is just what he needs now. Thank you for bringing him. Now, a quick cup of tea and then down to business.'

Once inside, Chrissy marvelled at the size, shape and décor of the house she had only entered twice before: once when she had a nasty chest infection and once to collect medicine for Jack. She hadn't seen further than the entrance hall where she had admired the stained-glass window at the top of the stairs, but here she was in the kitchen, a cavernous looking place with a high ceiling and cream-coloured range. There was also a small free-standing gas cooker with a plate warming rack above it.

She admired the large pine table in the middle of the floor. She glanced through to what she presumed to be the scullery. There were a huge pantry and a large wooden pulley hanging from the ceiling. It had several items of clothing hanging from it including men's pyjamas. Involuntarily her cheeks flushed; she had just seen the doctor's pyjamas! It almost caused her to panic, but she scolded herself. *Chrissy, he is a man, just like any other man, and his pyjamas are just like everyone else's. Pull yourself together!*

'Mrs Bell used to come in a couple of times a week to help with baking, cleaning and a bit of washing, but she is now in the WRVS.'

Chrissy followed Vera out of the kitchen, across the hallway and through a door which led to the doctor's surgery. Once inside it was just as she remembered it, especially the pungent aroma of surgical spirit, medicines, ointments and carbolic cleanliness. The fire grate was set with kindling. A lace curtain wafted backwards and forwards in the warm autumnal breeze coming through the open window.

'Dr Durnie is on duty at Kilmarnock Infirmary this morning, so it is an ideal time to show you around.'

Vera pointed out what was in each cupboard and drawer except for the desk drawers, explaining to Chrissy almost apologetically: 'Dr Durnie knows where to find everything in the desk drawers. I'm not sure how he can, they always look so disorganised to me, but there you have it.'

'We must make sure that we are always stocked with essentials, Chrissy. I will show you where everything is kept shortly. We place orders for supplies regularly, but more often than not we don't get everything we need, when we need it, so just like everyone else we make do and mend.'

Vera smiled. 'Don't look so worried – all of this will soon be second nature to you, I promise!'

Chrissy nodded and smiled nervously, and pushed yet another imaginary lock of hair behind her ear.

'I would also like you to clean this room. Mrs Bell never came in here. I have taken care of it until now. There are some delicate instruments and other medical equipment, but I will show you how to clean them properly another day. The microscope gets dusty, but the doctor prefers to see to it himself. It was his father's, you see.'

Vera walked towards a door that Chrissy had failed to notice. It was tucked beside a large mahogany bookcase. She turned the burnished brass doorknob and opened it. Inside was a clinical looking room lined with shelves and cabinets full of boxes, packages and bottles of every shape and size.

One cabinet held a supply of freshly laundered white coats. A large stainless-steel, box-shaped cabinet with a gauge in front of it caught Chrissy's eye, and Vera noted her growing look of concern.

'It's not as scary as it looks; it's an autoclave, used to sterilise instruments. That smaller one over there is to sterilise cotton wool, swabs and the like.'

Chrissy started to perspire; her neck felt stiff with building tension, the palms of her hands were wet to touch. *What I am doing here? I can't do this.*

As if reading her mind, Vera put her hand on Chrissy's shoulder.

'You will not be expected to do anything alone until you have been trained and feel confident enough to do it. Do you know anything about the Civil Nursing Reserve, Chrissy?'

'I may have heard a little about it here and there, but no, not really,' she admitted.

'The CNR teaches women just like you how to perform basic first aid, home nursing and hospital work. I have taken the liberty of writing to Miss Dunlop to inform her that you may apply for a place and what I foresee your duties at the surgery will be. Working here until the course starts will give you a head start.'

Chrissy was speechless; her eyebrows rose as her mouth gaped open.

Once again, Vera smiled reassuringly. 'It's a lot to take in. I understand you will have concerns, questions, even doubts, but I wouldn't be proposing it unless I was sure you were capable, and I know that you are more than capable. Now, let's take your measurements, I need them for your uniform. I have a leaflet here for you, it explains what to expect in more detail, take it home and discuss it with Mr Ramsay.'

*

Her head was thumping; it had been filled to bursting with so much information she felt mentally exhausted. The day had passed so quickly and had felt almost surreal. She couldn't quite believe it was happening! After all her childhood dreams of becoming a nurse, this was an opportunity she could never have imagined as a married woman with grown children.

Chrissy flopped into an armchair to read the leaflet Vera had given her.

AYR COUNTY COUNCIL

CIVIL NURSING RESERVE

WOMEN OF AYRSHIRE

YOUR COUNTRY NEEDS YOU

In this hour of national trial, the call to service echoes not only on the battlefield but in our hospitals, rest centres, and homes. The Ministry of Health, in cooperation with Ayr County Council, urgently seeks capable, compassionate women to join the Civil Nursing Reserve.

Whether you are trained in nursing or simply possess a steady hand and a kind heart, you are needed.

WHAT YOU WILL LEARN

All volunteers will receive instruction in basic nursing duties.

Hygiene, feeding, bed making and wound care

First aid and casualty handling during air raids

Infection control and hospital protocols

Emotional support for evacuees, the elderly and the wounded

Procedures for blackout emergencies and mass casualty events

Training will be held at designated centres in Ayr, Cumnock, and Girvan. Transport assistance may be arranged for rural volunteers.

WHO MAY APPLY

Women aged 18 to 60, of sound health and good character

No prior nursing experience required, just a willingness to serve

Preference given to those available for evening or weekend shifts

Uniforms and protective garments will be issued. Tea and light refreshment provided during training sessions.

Apply in person at your local council office, or write to:

Miss Margaret L. Dunlop

CNR Coordinator

Ayr County Council Offices

Wellington Square, Ayr

Chrissy was trembling with anticipation. The conversation with Vera had been the spark, but reading the leaflet had fanned the growing embers, and she hoped that Bob would not try to extinguish the blaze that now raged deep in her belly.

Chrissy wasn't sure how to tell Bob about the plans Vera had proposed. She was excited at the prospect, but at the same time she doubted her ability to cope with a demanding new role. Lord knows, she had enough to do around here! What about her volunteer work?

It crossed her mind not to mention it at all, but when Bob came in, something deep inside made her stand tall, take a deep breath and proclaim:

'Sit down, Bob, I have something to tell you.'

Once she'd told Bob about the plans Vera had for her, she asked defiantly: 'What do you think of that, then?'

He took her hands, stepped backwards and looked at her from head to foot.

'My wife the nurse, eh? Oh, Chrissy I am so proud of you, not just about this but about, well you know, everything. You are brave, kind and capable, Chrissy. I ken ye think about John every day. I also ken that we say no news is good news. We are both trying so hard to believe that and pray that it's true, that one day he will walk through that door, or we will at least get a letter.'

Bob then eased the moment by winking and saying, 'And wait until he sees his mum in her uniform!'

They chuckled at his last statement.

'Seriously, Bob, I am a version of every story I have told myself. In my head I've been a teacher, standing in front of a classroom full of children, writing on the blackboard, teaching them to read and write, to count, to tie up their shoelaces. I've also been a secretary, working in an office, typing letters, answering the telephone, organising everyone and everything.'

Bob smiled. 'Nothing new there, then, apart fae the phone of course, hen.'

She shushed him with a stern look.

'And ever since I went to the Dick Institute all those years ago, I have imagined being a nurse. I've longed to know how to help people, to ease their pain, to do things for them that they couldn't do themselves, to make someone feel better just by being a reassuring presence, giving them hope.'

This time Bob didn't smile or speak; he stepped towards her, took her in his arms and kissed her forehead.

'Again, nothing new there, Chrissy, you do that here for us every day.'

'You know what I mean.'

He nodded. 'Of course I do.'

'Training to be a nurse was my dream, Bob. My teacher told me I could do it, but Mum and Dad needed me at home. Then I met you, I became a wife, a mother and I love those roles, you and the weans are my whole life, but I must make a space for this. It's something just for me ... do you understand?'

He nodded again, not sure what to say.

'I feel so guilty; if Jack hadn't died, the minister would never have spoken to Mrs Durnie and I wouldn't be getting this chance. I feel as if I'm responsible for losing him all over again.'

'Sit here.' Bob patted the couch. 'Chrissy, Jack dying was tragic, but it was due to an illness. You did nothing to cause it, and he couldn't be cured. I miss him and think of him every day just like you, but he's gone and nothing we can do will change that. You said Mrs Durnie remembered you when you went to visit Billy ... she thought you were a natural. She would have remembered that fact even if Jack was still alive and well. I know you need to do this for yourself, but you can do it for Jack too.'

Chrissy leaned into him. 'I love you, Bob Ramsay ... underneath all that dirt and coo dung you're made of marshmallow, aren't you?'

'Coo dung coated marshmallow! You have loads of good ideas and recipes, but I don't think that will catch on somehow.'

Chrissy slapped him playfully on his dungaree-covered thigh.

'You will train to be a nurse, you will be good at it, and you are going to make your whole family proud, ma girl. Wait until oor Katie hears about this!'

'I hope she gets a day off soon. Mind you, this boy she is seeing is taking up more space on the pages of her letters than anything else. These days, no one else gets a mention.'

'I hope we can meet him some time soon. I expect he's kept busy, though.' Bob looked pensive.

Katie had explained in a previous letter that Alan had been deemed medically unfit for active service. He now drove a bus on the Ardrossan to Kilmarnock route, and helped the local firefighters on a part time basis.

'Aye and what about Katie writing about the awful shock he had the other night? He can hardly see at night, what with the blackout and only tiny slits for the headlights, but still he managed to see a dead body on the road between Springside and Crosshouse! Can you imagine, Bob?'

They sipped on their steaming cups of watery cocoa and listened to the wireless. Among their favourites were *It's That Man Again*, *Bandwagon*, and *Monday Night at Seven*, but tonight they were listening to Vera Lynn singing and reading out messages to and from servicemen. It was an emotive show; Chrissy usually had her handkerchief at the ready, and her thoughts always turned to John. Where was he? If only she knew if he was dead or alive. Should she be mourning the loss of another son? Should she allow the agony of losing a child to seep into her bones like water into a sponge? *No!* She refused to give up hope. John would come home. *He's safe and being cared for.* She must believe that. He IS alive. She must not give up hope .... without it, what was there?

'She should have a day off coming up soon. We can save our rations, and you can bake her one of your special pies.'

Chrissy smiled and allowed a tear to trickle down her cheek as Vera Lynn sang *We'll Meet Again*.

CHAPTER TWENTY-ONE

March, 1941

Chrissy loved every minute of the nursing course. A quick learner, she was top of her class, and this alone made her happier than she could ever have imagined.

Helping Dr and Mrs Durnie in the surgery had prepared her a little for what would be expected of her. Items that had once been completely unknown to her were now familiar, less scary, and she was extremely proud of her achievements as was her husband.

Chrissy and Bob had spent the last couple of hours in the air raid shelter with the other villagers. The atmosphere had been cold, damp and oozing with anxiety and tension.

When all-clear sounded, they quickly made their way home.

'Come on, Rex, get a wiggle on, I can't wait to hold a nice hot cup of tea in my hands. They're frozen, and you should thank your lucky stars that nobody minded you being in there tonight.'

Rex lolloped along the pavement, stopping to sniff at every gate and thoroughly enjoying this nocturnal outing.

'I tell you what, I'll stay here and let him enjoy his walk, while you go back and get the kettle on,' said Bob.

'Thanks, Bob don't be too long though. *It's That Man Again* will be on the wireless soon. I'd like us to be settled in before it starts.'

Chrissy had just poured the tea when Bob appeared through the back door.

'Perfect timing, Mr Ramsay. Oh no, there's someone at the front door. Who can this be? I hope it's not Mum, she should be well settled in for the night by now.'

Bob made his way to the front door.

'Mrs Durnie! Why? I mean, come in.'

'I'm sorry to call at this hour, but could I speak to Mrs Ramsay for a moment please?'

By this time Chrissy was by the door. 'Come in, Mrs Durnie.' Chrissy frowned when she saw the other woman's expression.

'You will have heard the bombs nearby.' It was a statement rather than a question.

'Yes, we have only just come back from the shelter.'

'A block of flats in Culzean Crescent in Kilmarnock has been hit, other buildings too. People are speculating whether the Luftwaffe have been targeting Ardeer or Prestwick. Maybe they were returning from another raid, but no matter, the rescue teams are working as we speak, searching for casualties in the rubble. Chrissy, you are indeed not obliged, but I would be grateful for your assistance. Dr Durnie is in the car now, heading for the Infirmary. I offered to go too; he is just outside. Could you come and help? We may not be on the front line, but we can provide back-up, fetch and carry, make tea, anything to help the regular staff who will be working flat out.'

Chrissy walked to the closet in the hall, grabbed her coat and hat, and headed for the door. Bob fetched her bag and hugged her.

No words were required; this is what she had been trained for after all. If she could be there to help someone the way the staff had helped her when Jack had died, to make them feel less scared and alone, she was determined to do it.

*

'Listen to this, Chrissy.' Bob flicked and rustled the newspaper to remove a large crease and began to read: '"Last night, the town of Clydebank endured a sustained and ferocious aerial bombardment by enemy forces. The attack commenced shortly after 9 o'clock and continued into the early hours. Fires still burn across the shipyards and tenement rows. Emergency services are working tirelessly to contain the damage and assist the wounded.

'We regret to report significant loss of life and widespread destruction.

Many families have been displaced. Temporary shelters have been established at Kilbowie Church Hall, Dalmuir School, and the Singer Recreation Grounds. Citizens are urged to offer blankets, food, and assistance where possible.

'Despite the devastation, the spirit of Clydebank remains unbroken. Firemen, nurses, and volunteers have shown extraordinary courage. We commend the workers of John Brown's Yard, who returned to their posts at dawn, determined to carry on.

'Let it be known that Clydebank stands. Scotland stands. We shall not be cowed by terror from the skies."'

'The poor souls! We got off lightly by comparison, not that I thought that last night. It was awful, Bob, I'm just so glad I was able to help, even if it was in a small way.'

'What is it all about, eh? So many lives lost or changed forever. I will never understand it for as long as I live.'

CHAPTER TWENTY-TWO

Vera, 1944

Vera was overcome by tiredness; she had never succumbed to it before, but recently the tiredness had been unworldly. This afternoon she had given in and gone up to her bedroom to lie down for a short while.

Charles was at the Dreghorn surgery attending to patients there for the afternoon. Chrissy had the afternoon off and had invited Martin to spend some time with Bob on the farm. She and Vera thought the change of scenery and activities might help to take Martin's mind off the reports from London. The wireless had been reporting that the air raids were getting worse, not like the Blitz of 1940, but unyielding and destructive just the same. On top of that, Martin hadn't received a letter from his parents for well over a month now. Charles had tried to telephone his brother both at home and at his workplace but with no luck.

Charles told Martin not to worry, explaining that the telephone lines had probably been damaged, but Martin could tell that his uncle was worried by the way he did not meet his gaze.

Vera was becoming increasingly worried about her symptoms. She knew the "change of life" could be horrid; her own mother had experienced an early menopause, and although she hadn't gone into detail, Vera knew with some certainty that it had been more than an unpleasant experience. Vera thought that she was made of stronger stuff and had been through much worse having had three miscarriages. Charles had been preoccupied when she first broached the subject; he shrugged his shoulders and told her not to worry.

'You are too young, Vera. You really have been overdoing things lately. I thought having Chrissy to help you would make a difference, but you have continued to take on more and more war work. You must learn how to say no to people.'

Vera sighed; she knew most of this was true but expected him to be more concerned.

She tried not to, but she couldn't resist scouring through some of the textbooks housed in the sizeable bookcase in the surgery. Reading them had done nothing to allay her fears; the opposite, in fact. Her symptoms could be indicative of cancer. This had taken her by surprise, and yet, somewhere in the back of her mind she knew what she was experiencing was more than just "the change".

Then, there was that conversation with Mrs Todd in the Co-op. Most people in the village viewed Mrs Todd as a bit of an eccentric: she was always coming out with weird statements and stories, which were usually taken with a pinch of salt.

Mrs Todd had been on her way out of the shop and noticed Vera was standing in the queue. At first, she walked past after saying good morning to her, then she turned back, put her hand on Vera's shoulder and whispered, 'It's different this time.' Vera had dismissed this as more nonsense, so why was she thinking about that proclamation over and over again? What did the old woman mean? Were the Germans going to win this war? It just did not make any sense.

As she lay on her bed, the bed she shared with her beloved Charles, her thoughts drifted to the night they had their first proper conversation.

*

It had been two-thirty in the morning. The dimly lit ward was unusually quiet except for the sound of snoring, the odd cough and other bodily noises. Vera was struggling to keep her eyes open; there had been new admissions today, some of the men were shell-shocked and at the very start of the road to recovery. Morphine had been administered as much as was allowed, and, for now, the men were asleep albeit fitfully.

She had updated her nursing notes in her meticulous handwriting. Nobody ever complained that they couldn't read her handwriting, unlike that of some of the doctors, Charles Durnie being one of the worst offenders. Vera would softly run the tip of her finger over the words he had written and sigh.

Would he ever notice her? She thought she was being obvious, but she was obviously more discreet than she imagined or he wasn't in the least bit interested in her.

Who can blame him? she had thought. *I was born on London Road, brought up on London Road, and now here I am, back on London Road having never left Ayrshire even for my training.*

He looked so rugged! He must have seen lots of places far and near, seen lots of girls too! She sighed and glanced towards a patient who was coughing and expectorating into an enamelled spittoon.

Satisfied that he had settled, she opened the book on the desk and started to read about dressing amputees' stumps and the risks of infection.

She became aware of footsteps approaching and sighed; Sister on her rounds. What would she find to complain about this time? She turned her head and gasped loudly. Dr Durnie was right there, looking at her. She jumped to her feet immediately.

'Sit down, Nurse Brownlee. Sorry if I frightened you. I don't need anything, I just needed to see a friendly face.'

Vera hoped that he wouldn't be able to see her hot blushing cheeks.

'Do you mind if I take a seat?' he whispered.

'Not at all, I was just going to make a cup of tea to keep myself awake. I am useless on night duty, it just doesn't come naturally to me. I truly don't know how you do it...'

She stopped mid-sentence, thinking she may be being overfamiliar, but she was also incredulous and overjoyed that he had remembered her name.

'To tell the truth, neither do I, it just sort of happens. I think to myself, would I rather be in one of these beds, or be here, being me, and that sobering thought keeps me going through thick and thin.'

In that instant, Vera knew that the infatuation she had for this untidy but ruggedly handsome man was love, real love. She found it hard to resist reaching over and touching his hand. She stood up again and said rather too quickly, 'Tea, that's right, I'm going for tea,' and she scuttled off.

When she returned with tea and a plate of home-made biscuits, donated by a grateful mother, Charles looked as if he was asleep. His eyes were closed and his head was lolling to one side. Vera placed the tray down as quietly as she could, but his eyes opened immediately. Were they brown? Were they green? It was hard to tell in this light.

Soon they were chatting in animated whispers.

'Where are you from?' Charles asked a still flustered Vera.

'Honestly, if you were to look out of one of the first-floor windows, you could see my parents' house.'

'Really?' He let out a soft whistle. 'Which one?'

'It's across the road. It's a red sandstone building; it has a stable block to the left of the entrance and black wooden gates.'

'That narrows it down,' he chuckled, 'but I think I know the one you mean. Do your parents still live there?'

'Yes, just the two of them.'

'Where are you from?' she enquired.

'Glasgow born and bred although nothing as grand as your home. I have two brothers and two sisters. They are all doing their bit one way or another. Mother is so relieved that I wasn't sent to the front. My older brother works in London, but I have no idea what he does to be honest. He doesn't talk much about it. My younger brother is a vet and is somewhere in France.'

Another bout of frantic coughing caused Vera to jump to her feet, and she walked towards her patient with Charles at her heels.

'When is your next day off?' he asked shyly.

'A week on Monday.'

'If I can arrange it, would you like to meet me somewhere? Lauder's Tea Room is meant to be excellent, in spite of rationing, that is.'

Vera thought she might faint! She was elated.

'Yes, that would be lovely, Dr Durnie, I'd love to.'

'I'll speak to you tomorrow and we can decide where and when to meet.

Oh and by the way, it's Charles.'

Just then the coughing patient gasped for air. Vera wiped his lips with a piece of gauze and offered him some water. She noticed the spittoon was full. She fetched a fresh receptacle, covered the full one with a cloth and took it to the kitchen. She tipped the contents into the pot by the sink. Tomorrow, someone would have the task of boiling the lot before it could be safely disposed of. Vera ordinarily baulked at the undertaking, but tonight, with Charles's words flooding her thoughts, she did not bat an eyelid.

*

Vera wiped away a rogue tear; those days had seemed so difficult to navigate, but this ... how would she deal with this?

She made up her mind that she would not mention her symptoms to Charles again, or anyone else for that matter. She would take a step back and carry on as best as she could. After all, there was nothing else for it.

She would have a word with Chrissy, though; she trusted her. Chrissy would step up, she knew she would ... she had to.

CHAPTER TWENTY-THREE

Chrissy, 1944

'Bob, Mum will be here soon. We're heading to Lauder's, have you remembered? It's my afternoon off ... Bob?'

When there was no answer, she called out again, 'We need paraffin, matches, candles. Are you listening tae me?'

'Of course I am, my turtle dove! Oh she that must be obeyed, are you planning a bonfire? You'll be telt tae put it oot by the ARP.' He choked slightly as he laughed at his own joke.

As per usual, the cows had been milked just after five that morning. Bob only had time for a quick slice or two of bread and a slither of butter, but more often than not it was dripping. The national loaf the people of Britain were being encouraged to eat for health purposes had quickly become known as "Hitler's secret weapon". It was dry, grey and unappetising, and almost everybody hated it.

The pantry was pitifully bare these days. Thank God for their veg patch and farm connections. Chrissy even came home with an egg or two courtesy of Mrs Durnie's chickens.

Bob was tucking into his lunch with gusto: a huge pile of potatoes, topped with a knob of margarine, salt and pepper, a slice of ham, Chrissy's homemade pickle, a mountain of carrots and a glass of milk.

'Don't forget the black paint! There are chinks of light showing through the blackout boards. We don't want a fine.'

Just as he spoke, Maggie came into the kitchen. As usual, she had a tin of goodies with her; she only used her margarine and butter rations for baking and she was frugal with her sugar rations. Having lived through rationing before, she didn't see it as much of a hardship, just something she had to deal with as well as she could.

Bob's eyes lit up.

'What have you brought for us the day, Ma Barnes?'

He grinned broadly.

'Oaty biscuits and jam tarts this week. Mind and keep some for Katie. I got a letter from her this morning. She says she has a day off on Friday and she'll be on the early bus.'

'You know more than us, Ma! Did you know she was coming, Chrissy?'

'No, I did not, we haven't had a letter for about a week now. Maybe ours will arrive in the second post. Now, Bob, as God is my witness, I will swing for you if you eat too many of those biscuits and tarts! I mean it!'

Bob nodded and gave her the thumbs up, winked and headed for the tin.

'Right, lass, Lauder's the ironmongers is a must, Lauder's the baker's tearoom is another must. I hope they have French fancies! Is there anywhere else you would like to go?'

'Before we get the bus, I need to put one of these on the church notice board and one in the shop. It won't take long.' Chrissy held up two notices.

CROSSHOUSE WOMEN'S RURAL

Official reminder of the registered jam-making session using the Ministry Sugar Allocation

At the doctor's house – use back entrance.

Thursday 28th September, 2pm

The Ministry has granted us an additional 14lbs of preserving sugar following Mrs Durnie's persuasive letter.

Mrs Fulton will demonstrate the Dixie Hand Sealer and proper canning technique.

Mrs Marshall will oversee all labelling, all record-keeping and Ministry compliance. She will log fruit weights, sugar usage, jar counts and distribution notes.

Please bring washed (unchipped) jars, aprons, wooden spoons and saucers for set testing.

Also bring any surplus fruit from gardens or hedgerows.

Reminder

This is a Ministry-approved preservation session. All jam produced will be returned for official distribution under government guidelines. Sugar has been allocated by the Ministry of Food and must be used strictly for registered jam-making. No personal use permitted. Any surplus jars must be declared and labelled accordingly.

Mrs Jean McMurray, President of the Crosshouse Scottish Women's Rural Institute.

'Mrs McMurray asked Mrs Durnie if she could put these up, but she is so tired, I offered to do it. It will be like all hell let loose that day. I've never seen such competition over a bit of jam.'

'I wouldn't mind a wee look in Lewis's and...' she hesitated, 'I don't suppose you'd come with me to the Dick Institute; I want to look for some library books.'

'I think I could make that. I'm no decrepit yet. Everybody gets breathless when they get to my age; as they say, auld age disnae come itself. Now let's go. You pick the order we do them in.'

They were walking along Bank Street just as the Laigh Kirk bell chimed eleven. Maggie glanced towards the Cross and scrutinised the groups of people who were chatting animatedly, catching up with gossip, mostly hatches, matches and dispatches, finding out if MacFisheries had any fish and if the greengrocer had any fruit. Maggie squinted to see if she recognised anyone, and to her surprise and delight she saw someone she had worked with at Ardeer.

'Chrissy, while you go into Lauder's, I'll go over and see Minnie. She and I worked together. I would love to have a catch up.'

'Go ahead, Mum. We agreed we would get the paraffin last – they won't thank us for stinking out the tea shop, will they?'

'True, lassie, never mind, it was just a thought.'

'Tell you what, Mum, I will go to the Dick Institute on my own. I know you weren't keen on walking up that hill or going in there and I understand. I'll meet you back at the Cross in say an hour?'

'Perfect, you're on, cheerio, hen.'

Maggie puffed towards her old friend as Chrissy walked in the direction of Duke Street.

Walking towards the impressive building that housed a library, a museum and an art gallery, Chrissy marvelled at the sheer size and elegance of it. It never ceased to amaze her. She stared at the four great pillars, the dome and the statue, and the lions and crest above the front entrance before going in.

As soon as she pushed open the door and stepped inside, she took a deep breath to drink in the aroma of old books, old wood and floor polish that exuded from the building. Heading straight for the library, Chrissy looked for the medical section, by-passing her usual autobiography and history sections.

Since she had been working with Vera and Dr Durnie, she had been amazed by the amount of information she had to absorb, but the more she learned, the more she wanted to find out. Being a married woman meant that she couldn't train to be a fully-fledged nurse, but nothing and no one would stop her from teaching herself.

Chrissy chose a reference-only book, carried it to a reading room and sat down at long wooden desk to read, absorb and learn. She already had two books in her bag that would be going home with her. She planned to take notes from the colossal book in front of her and had remembered to bring her notebook and pencil. The room was silent apart from the sound of pages turning and the odd sniff and cough here and there. Chrissy could sit reading for hours on end but was mindful that she had to meet her mother in just over half an hour now. The book was open at the cardiology section. Chrissy had been concerned about her mother's general health for some time now, particularly her dizzy spells, fatigue, breathlessness and chest pains. She knew that her mother tried to keep them under wraps, but sometimes she failed miserably.

As it turned out, the skin yellowing her mother had experienced although undesirable was harmless, but Chrissy was convinced that there was a link between her mother's condition and her war work. None of her symptoms had been evident before she went to work in the munitions factory. Now, one of Katie's friends worked in Ardeer and had already developed some of Maggie's symptoms albeit milder, but she was a young girl. What would she be like by the time she was Maggie's age?

Chrissy read everything she could lay her hands on about working in close proximity to explosives. She was aware that improvements had been made since her mother's time during the Great War: better training in handling explosives like TNT, gelignite and cordite, how to minimise friction, static and contamination, better protective clothing and efforts to reduce exposure to the chemicals. She found out that the symptoms of chemical exposure mimicked cardiovascular strain. What if there was some other treatment her mother could receive that would help to make her feel better?

Chrissy glanced at her watch and saw that she was already late. She hurriedly gathered up her notebook, pencil and library books, returned the reference book with thanks, and rushed for the door.

Maggie was nowhere to be seen when Chrissy arrived at the cross. A group of people had congregated outside the newsagent. Women in headscarves some shaking their heads and some were nodding. The men, some smoking, others pointing authoritatively this way and that, all grim-faced. Chrissy suddenly felt cold. *Something has happened, something bad.*

She walked over to the gathering and asked what was going on.

'A wee wummin just fell. One minute she was standing there, the next wallop, she was flat on her face!'

'Did you see what she was wearing? Did she trip?'

A man approached her. 'She didn't fall, she collapsed. Someone ran to the phone box and called for an ambulance. She will have been taken to Kilmarnock Infirmary I expect.'

Meanwhile, a woman described exactly what Maggie had been wearing.

CHAPTER TWENTY-FOUR

Vera, 1944

Vera and Charles were sitting at the kitchen table surrounded by row upon row of jam jars, each filled to the brim with various autumn fruit jams and jellies, mostly gooseberry thanks to Mrs Martin having a gooseberry bush "the size of Troon" in her garden. There were stacks of cans, too. The canning demonstration had been received well, and everyone was keen to give it a go. The atmosphere was still warm and heady after numerous pans of boiling sugar and fruit had been bubbling and spluttering all afternoon. Vera had always encouraged the village women to not only come and pick the fruit in the garden, but to make use of the generously sized kitchen when it was appropriate, but now it was an official and hence serious business that required strict controls.

The tangy air had been thick with good humoured but spirited banter during the proceedings, much to Vera's amusement although she did have to remind them that what they were doing was about community spirit and not culinary warfare.

She had been glad of the distraction knowing that she and Charles were going to have a serious chat with Martin that evening. It had been an unusually hot day, perfect for fruit picking, but not so much for jam making. She felt exhausted and nauseated, and longed to go to bed but refused to let Charles talk to Martin by himself.

Vera sat beside Martin while Charles sat opposite.

Martin's cheeks were speckled with tiny freckles that had not been there when he had arrived from London. He now spent most of his time outdoors. He had made firm friends at school, and although they teased him about his accent at times, it was always good humoured. Also, they loved being able to visit him at his aunt and uncle's home where they were allowed to pick apples from the trees and were often gifted small paper bags with a smattering of precious sugar in them to dip stalks of rhubarb in. When the women were baking or making jam, often little tit-bits would find their way in the boys' direction, much to their delight, and today had been no exception. Martin looked suitably sated and tired. He had had a marvellous time when he came home from school, fetching and carrying baskets and boxes of fruit and being thoroughly spoilt by the throng of women in his aunt's kitchen.

Now, sitting opposite his aunt and uncle, he sensed something was wrong. He shuffled uncomfortably in his seat and fiddled with his earlobe.

'Martin, I have something to tell you. You must try to be brave, but it will be hard.'

Martin tensed; he could feel his Aunt Vera's hand press down onto his bony shoulder.

'You know we have been trying to contact your parents, don't you, Martin?'

The boy nodded.

'We have had it confirmed that they ...' Charles stopped; he had broken bad news more times than he could remember, but surely this had to be the hardest thing he had ever had to do.

'Your parents were on a ship. I still don't know where they were going or why, but the thing is, the ship was torpedoed, no survivors have been found ... so far, that is.'

Martin blinked and moved away from Vera's hand.

'Why were they on a ship, Uncle Charles? I don't understand!'

'I don't know, Martin, it may have been to do with your father's work, you know he worked for the government, but even I don't know exactly what he did or where he went. It was special work, to help the war effort, important work. You should be very proud.'

Martin blinked again. 'Why was Mother with him?'

'I'm so sorry, Martin. I'm afraid I just don't know.'

Martin stood up and threw his chair back so hard that it crashed to the floor.

'Then you are no use at all then, are you? Even if you did know, I bet you wouldn't tell me, would you? Grown-ups love secrets!'

Vera was about to scold him for the outburst, but a glance from Charles told her to leave it be.

Martin ran out of the back door into the garden and made his way to the den he had been building with his friends; they even had a straw bed in it for Rex. They imagined they were like *The Children of Cherry Tree Farm*; Martin had read the book by Enid Blyton many times and felt it could have been written especially for him.

'Leave him for now, Vera,' Charles coaxed as she made to follow the boy. Daylight had moved aside to make way for dusk, but it wasn't dark enough to stop them seeing where he was, and Rex was by his side.

'He will need time to think. He will have lots of questions; I only wish I had the answers.' He frowned. The probability was that his brother was dead, but right now that was somehow unthinkable.

'Why don't you go to bed, Vera? You haven't stopped all day. You look all in.'

For once she didn't argue; she simply said, 'Yes, I think I will.'

Charles sat alone at the table consumed by thoughts of Martin, his brother and sister-in-law, and now his Vera. Vera was his life; he had loved her since he first met her in the Dick Institute. It had just taken his head a little while to catch up with his heart. He knew he had been neglecting her recently – she mentioned a few symptoms she had been suffering some time ago, but he had brushed her off, choosing to believe that if he ignored them, they would go away. What was that saying about the shoemakers' bairns?

He vowed that once Martin was safely in bed, that he would have a proper chat with his wife and get to the bottom of things. He rose slowly and made his way out into the garden.

*

Charles climbed into bed, mentally and physically exhausted. The chat with Martin had been much more difficult than he could have imagined. He had made him some supper and took him up to bed. He'd kissed his forehead and said goodnight, but Martin remained tight-lipped.

'We can talk more in the morning, Martin.'

'No, I don't want to talk about it anymore, not now, not tomorrow, not ever!'

*

He did not say goodnight; he turned his back on his uncle and stayed that way until he was sure he had gone. He got out of bed and padded towards the window. His lamp was switched off so he pulled the curtains apart to look out at the garden. He wanted to cry, but he couldn't – tears refused to come. What he truly felt like doing was screaming at the top of his voice until everyone in the village could hear him. He wanted to run until he dropped with exhaustion, but none of those options were realistic right now. He froze when he heard his bedroom door open and then softly close again. When he turned around, he saw Rex sitting in the shadows, his eyes glinting in the moonlight.

'Rex, come on boy. Who let you in here?'

Martin didn't care how he had got there; he scooped the little dog up into his arms, closed the curtains and then plopped him on top of his bed. They snuggled in together and Rex managed to fall asleep and give a little snore even although his head was soaked with tears.

*

'Are you asleep Vera?' Charles whispered.

'No, still awake. How is Martin?' She pursed her lips together in concern.

'Asleep now, I hope. He is angry, he hasn't shed a tear. This is going to be challenging; he is already shutting himself off. I've broken the no dogs in the bedroom rule, I'm afraid. I just thought that under the circumstances…'

'I've just been sick again, Charles,' Vera murmured. She felt so exhausted.

'What do you mean *again?*'

'Well, that's the third time today, and I haven't eaten anything. I have no appetite.'

'Vera, why didn't you say? When did you last eat?'

'Yesterday at lunchtime. I had a scone and jam with a cup of tea. I really enjoyed it. First thing I have enjoyed in ages, to be honest.'

Charles sat up and switched on the light. He looked at Vera, properly for the first time in a while. He took in her pale features, her sunken eyes. She had lost weight too.

'Right, tomorrow I am going to call a chap I went to medical school with. He specialises in gastroenterology. I will ask him to see you, and we will get this sorted out, Vera, I promise you!'

'Be careful of making promises you can't keep, Charles.'

Her reply rocked him to his core. Vera was the most positive person he knew. She rarely complained or made a fuss. All at once, Charles felt very frightened.

CHAPTER TWENTY-FIVE

Chrissy, 1944

Chrissy walked into Kilmarnock Infirmary and was instantly hit by the smell of strong disinfectant. The smell of the place brought back so many memories: the night of the bombing, doing everything she could to help, but mostly of Jack, her sweet boy who had died here so prematurely. Her boy who had such spirit. Who loved going out to play, who loved his dog, who shone with happiness at the simplest of things. Without the intense grief for her beloved boy, Chrissy still doubted that she would have been asked to help Vera. She would not have found out her natural aptitude for first aid and nursing. Suddenly the infirmary no longer made her feel afraid, apprehensive. She was familiar with the green and cream walls, the black and white floors, the large airy Nightingale wards. She recognised the bustle for what it was. It wasn't frightening or sinister; it was positive, it was professional people doing what they had been trained to do.

Her mother was in ward two, the female medical ward. Chrissy opted for the stairs; the lift was in constant use, transporting patients between departments and wards.

It was not visiting time; Chrissy approached the ward doors cautiously and pushed the left one open just a crack and peeped in. She saw a nurse standing by a medicine trolley chatting to a colleague. Taking a deep breath, she strode in purposely and waited until they had finished their conversation.

'You are much too early for visiting,' said the younger of the two.

'Thank you, Nurse, I will deal with this.'

The older nurse smiled. She recognised Chrissy, but couldn't remember where from.

'Can I help you?'

'Yes, thank you, my mother, Maggie, that is Margaret Barnes, was brought to this ward about an hour ago. She collapsed…' Chrissy faltered.

'Ah yes, and you are?'

'I am her daughter, Chrissy Ramsay.'

'Your mother is indeed here, Mrs Ramsay; she is still in the process of being admitted. Why don't you take a seat outside and I will find out if we can allow you to come in and see her for a moment. Don't worry, she is quite comfortable.'

Chrissy had enough experience of medical speak to know that "comfortable" wasn't necessarily a good thing.

She followed the nurse through the heavy swing doors, their brass handles gleaming under the stark electric lights, into the corridor. Her heels clicked and resonated with the hard floor. She sat on one of the chairs that were placed together in a regimental row.

'It shouldn't be too long.'

The nurse in her smart starched cap and pristine uniform turned quickly, making her rubber heels squeak, and disappeared into the ward again.

After what had seemed like an age, the same nurse returned. She smiled and said, 'You can come in now, Mrs Ramsay, just for five minutes. Visiting is restricted to one hour in the afternoon, only two visitors to a bed and strictly no children.'

Chrissy walked into the ward, noticing the tables in the middle of the floor, the bay window that housed two beds, and the parallel rows of green metal beds sporting crisp white sheets and pillowcases, and pale green blankets.

Maggie was on the first bed on the left, right outside the duty room.

She looked pale, but cheerful enough.

'How did I get here, Chrissy? One minute I am running towards my old pal, the next I am lying here.'

'You collapsed on the street, Mum. Someone called an ambulance for you.'

'An ambulance? I've had all ma tablets this morning before you start.'

'You shouldn't leave the house without them, Mum. You know that.'

'Don't start, hen, I'm fine. In fact, Minnie was saying she feels the same as me most of the time, tired and dizzy, she can hardly catch her breath at times too, it must be an age thing, just like I telt ye.'

'If it was just an age thing as you put it, the hospital would be full to brimming with old biddies like you.'

Maggie beckoned Chrissy to come closer and whispered, 'Look around ye, hen, what do you see, eh?'

Chrissy smiled and hugged her mother.

'Oh Mammy, what will I do with you? I will bring your night things later, there's hardly any soap left, but maybe they will have some here. Is there anything else you'd like?'

'Just my book, but don't forget ma comb and toothbrush.'

'I'm sorry, but I must ask you to leave now,' said the nurse.

Chrissy kissed her mother's cheek and made for the door.

'Before I go, could I have a word with the nurse in charge, please?' Chrissy was shaking but determined to have her say.

'Certainly, Mrs Ramsay, I will ask Sister if she is free, please take a seat.'

'It's fine, I'll stand if you don't mind.' *If I sit down, my legs will give way and I won't be able to get back up,* she thought.

'This way please, Mrs Ramsay.' Chrissy prayed that her mother wouldn't notice this change of events.

'Good afternoon, Mrs Ramsay, I am Sister Nelson. Please take a seat. How may I help you?'

'My mother worked in Ardeer Munitions Factory during the last war. I have read that some of the chemicals used to make the explosives can cause all sorts of medical problems. Will you mention her previous occupation to the doctor who is looking after her, please? It may not make much difference, but I think it's better that he knows about it.'

'We have had several patients who worked there, Mrs Ramsay. The doctors have acknowledged that some of the older workers may have struggled with the long hours, heavy lifting and lack of rest, all of which can cause breathlessness and chest tightness and palpitations.'

'I appreciate that, Sister, but I truly believe that my mother is experiencing problems with her heart. I think she might benefit from some tests if only to rule out the possibility.'

Sister looked quite taken aback and had been about to dismiss this lay person, but something about Chrissy's manner and earnest face stopped her.

'I will mention our conversation to the consultant when he comes in to do his rounds. Try not to worry, we will take good care of your mother.'

'Thank you, Sister,' Chrissy gasped with relief.

She knew that without her albeit basic training and newly found confidence that she would never have dared to have such a conversation.

Walking down the stairs she unexpectedly felt a warm muzzy feeling. It started at her toes and moved slowly towards her head. It was a comforting but surreal feeling. Then, suddenly she felt Jack's presence. She closed her eyes for a moment and felt sure she would see him when she opened them again, but all that she could see was the long-chequered empty corridor.

CHAPTER TWENTY-SIX

Vera, 1944

'What is taking so bloody long?'

Vera raised her eyebrows; it was unusual for Charles to swear, especially in public.

'Darling, he is a doctor just like you. He gives his time to people who need it just like you do. Our time will come ... calm down.'

Vera felt more like herself these days. Some colour had come back into her cheeks. Charles had made an effort to make sure she was at least trying to eat. She did feel stronger but wondered if it was because all her attention had been on Martin lately, with less time to feel sorry for herself.

Martin had returned to the introvert he had been when he had first arrived. He spoke when spoken to, he kept himself to himself except when Rex was on the scene. The scruffy little dog seemed to have a way of communicating with Martin in a way that neither Vera nor Charles could explain.

When Martin was playing with Rex, he looked completely different. Vera knew he spoke to the dog; she had heard him in the den. Martin loved nothing more than taking a sandwich, a drink and a treat for Rex into the den and confiding in his canine friend. Was it because he knew that Rex could never disclose what he had been told? Vera thought that might be part of it. Another part was that Rex had never ever abandoned Martin in his hour of need. He had no expectations; he offered unconditional love and made Martin feel like he was the most important person in his life. Who else could claim to come close to that?

Chrissy had mentioned to Martin that Jack had shared his thoughts and dreams with Rex which had immediately piqued his interest. However, Jack had not depended upon Rex in the way that Martin seemed to. Chrissy wanted the boy to know that it was a good thing, a natural thing, in the hope that Martin would then find a way to open his heart to his aunt and uncle.

'Dr and Mrs Durnie, please come in.'

The voice cut through Vera's thoughts like a hot knife through butter.

She had been dreading this consultation; it was safer to think about Martin and ways to support him. She hated the focus and attention being pointed in her direction. She did not want to know what might be uncovered. What was that saying, "ignorance is bliss"? Oh, how true that was!

The men shook hands in a familiar and friendly way. Each knowing and understanding what was at stake, but refusing to acknowledge it.

After a chat, Dr Mitchell asked to see Vera alone.

He talked to her, questioned her and then examined her.

When they were back in the office, Dr Mitchell addressed both of them.

'This isn't really my area of expertise. I want to refer you to a colleague of mine. He is a gynaecologist, Mrs Durnie.'

Vera's brow furrowed, and she looked at Charles with an *I told you so* look.

'I have suspected for a while now that I am experiencing some sort of premature menopause. Is that what you think too?'

'Vera ... may I call you Vera? This is out with my level of expertise. I really cannot comment at this moment in time. I am happy to see you again if my colleague wishes me to, but I think he will be able to help you more than I can.'

Vera and Charles looked at each other, worry imprinted in every nook and cranny of their faces.

'Thank you and may I just ask for reassurance that you and Charles ...' she looked directly at her husband, '... will not discuss this behind my back? We find out what is wrong with me together or not at all.'

Vera wasn't sure where that statement had come from, but she meant it.

Charles looked startled. He nodded, stood up and shook his colleague's hand.

When they were outside, Charles stopped and looked at her.

'Vera, I love you. I love you more than life itself. I will do, or not do whatever you wish, my darling girl. I'm sorry I haven't been there for you – you tried to tell me, and I brushed you off!'

'That's enough, Charles Durnie, I don't want to hear another word!'

They walked towards the car, too frightened to speak.

CHAPTER TWENTY-SEVEN

Chrissy, 1944

'Right, Mum, no buts about it, you are moving into Jack's room. I am going to look after you.'

Maggie laughed out loud.

'You mean you want a chief shortbread maker and general dogsbody on tap!'

Chrissy looked at her mother's face and grinned.

'Oh no, you've worked it out! Well, you better stick to your side of the bargain.'

The two women looked at each other, their expressions saying so much more than words ever could. Bob gave a thumbs up.

'I am expecting a lot of baking, Ma, your butter ration cannae go to waste. Shortbread, cake, biscuits, pies, anything but nettle soup.'

'There is nothing wrong with nettle soup! It kept us going through thick and thin during the last war, lad, and don't you forget it!'

'Chrissy, don't forget that Katie is coming for a visit this weekend.' He tried but failed to conceal his glee. 'Her letter arrived today. Oor wee Katie will be here at the weekend.'

Bob hugged Chrissy and winked at his mother-in-law. He did not add that he was thinking, 'I just wish we could find out something about John.'

'Chrissy, have you enough sugar for this?'

Maggie pointed to the mason cash baking bowl on the work top.

'I've told you a thousand times, Mum, yes, we do. I've been saving sugar to match your quota of butter, get baking.'

Maggie chortled. She felt better than she had in ages. She also felt safe here with her daughter and son-in-law. She loved having her own space, but the company of her family made her feel secure.

She carried on baking, her favourite thing to do. Chrissy came into the kitchen to help her wash up. The aromas wafting around the house were delicious. So comforting and reminiscent of days gone by.

'My, Katie is going to have her socks blown aff wi this spread!'

Bob beamed, soaking up the sights and sounds of his wife and mother-in-law cooking up a storm in the tiny kitchen.

'Some of us have coos tae milk in the morning. I'm aff tae hit the hay. Goodnight, ladies, I will try not to wake you in the morning.'

He blew a kiss to each woman and headed for the stairs.

'Are ye coming, Rex? Come on wi yer dad.'

Rex looked towards Bob and then back at the kitchen. He decided that he fancied his chances where the food was and stayed firmly put.

'Traitor! You're the only other man in here, but good luck to ye.' Bob laughed as he climbed the stairs.

Chrissy knew that the little dog now had another love in his life: Martin. Rex stuck to the boy like glue when she took him over to the Durnie's. She knew in her heart of hearts that the boy needed Rex as much as she did, more if she was being truthful. She also noted that the dog seemed to sense his importance, and he did not take it lightly. He had stuck by Chrissy's side when Jack had died. He'd backed off when he knew she was living her life again, and now it was Martin's turn. Rex knew where he was needed by some sort of sixth sense and he fulfilled his duty with undying faithfulness.

*

'Here she comes!'

Bob had been watching for the bus to pass the house. It stopped and he saw the unmistakeable figure of his beloved daughter walk along the pavement in the direction of the house.

He looked again; she wasn't alone. By her side walked a tall young man wearing a bus driver's uniform. They were walking hand in hand and Katie was carrying a basket in the other.

At last, they reached the house. Chrissy and Maggie were standing in the hall. Bob had gone out to greet them.

Katie shrieked as she ran into the hall and into her mother's arms. She then ran to her grandmother and gave her a huge hug. Suddenly she remembered her companion and rushed over to take his hand.

'Mum, Dad, Gran ... this is Alan.'

Alan smiled nervously at the assembled family members.

'Hello, pleased to meet you.'

Chrissy thought the boy might pass out with nerves.

She walked over to him and gave him a hug, then Maggie did the same.

'Welcome, Alan, come away in and we will have a cup of tea.'

Before long all five of them were blethering, comparing stories about families, who might know who, and finally about how Katie and Alan met.

'Mum, you won't believe this, but ...'

She looked at Alan, and he flushed with embarrassment.

'Alan says he saw me standing at the bus stop and that as soon he saw me, he knew he was going to marry me. Imagine that?'

Katies eyes were glistening with happy tears and Alan's cheeks flushed to a deep shade of red.

'What are you trying to say, Katie?' Bob asked, already knowing the answer.

'What I am saying, Dad, is that Alan and I are engaged to be married!' She dramatically thrust her left hand under her father's nose.

A whoop of joy rose from each and every one of them.

'This is a celebration if ever there was one! This calls for a toast!'

'Bob, it's only two o'clock in the afternoon!' Chrissy was shocked.

'There's a war on. We need to grasp at what pleasure we can and hang on to it. We need to celebrate and party while we can. Chrissy, get on your knees and grab that bottle of sherry from the back of the sideboard, or what's left of it.'

*

'So, when is the big day?' Maggie asked.

'I don't know yet, Gran, you know how it is. John is missing, Uncle Billy is working down south. I know he is doing important work and that it is difficult for him to get away, but I would love it if he could be here.'

'There is no rush, is there?' Chrissy asked tentatively.

Katie laughed. 'No rush whatsoever, Mum!' Katie gave her mother a knowing look that made her blush.

'My brothers are in active service, my mum is a widow and still grieving for my dad,' said Alan. 'That said, she always will be. Katie and I are just thinking everything through, you know, wondering what would be best for everyone under all the different circumstances.'

'Alan, son, don't think too long, and remember you can't please everyone. These are difficult times. You two need to grasp what happiness you can, when you can. If you wait until all the pieces of this crazy jigsaw fall into place, you might never get married. That's my tuppence worth.'

Maggie and Chrissy nodded in agreement.

Chrissy had been shaken at the mention of John; she had accepted that what will be will be; after all, she had absolutely no control over the situation and she was determined to take things one day at a time, but for now she would plough her energy into her work, just as Bob was doing.

'Does everyone have a glass? Wait for it, Ma Barnes, wait for it!'

'Bob, away ye go, I don't even like the stuff,' Maggie said and pretended to scowl.

'To Katie and Alan, may they have a long and happy life together, and let's hope this war is over soon, and we can have a huge celebration when everyone is together again. Alan and Katie!'

'To Alan and Katie!'

CHAPTER TWENTY-EIGHT

Vera, 1944

'Well, here we are again, another day, another hospital! This is getting to be a habit.' Vera smiled at her husband, but it didn't reach her eyes.

'Do I really need to be admitted? What about Martin? I know he is getting better every day, thanks mostly to Rex, but he isn't out of the woods yet. I should be there for him! I will just lie here and worry about him.'

'And I worry about you. I can take care of Martin. Chrissy has agreed to help out, too, and she has agreed to let Martin look after Rex for a few days, day and night. I've even said the dog can continue to sleep in his room if he wants to. Anyway, it won't be for long, just until they can carry out some tests. You need a rest, lie back, relax and let everyone run after you for a change.'

Vera smiled and tried to swallow the rock hard lump of emotion caught in her throat. Her head was filled to capacity with "what if" questions. They had been through them all before and she knew that there was no point in going over them again. *What will be will,* be she thought, *and we will need to deal with it no matter what.*

The ward Vera was admitted to house an eclectic mixture of patients, some older but mostly younger than she was.

It was very strange to be in a hospital bed; to be on the receiving end of things and she hated it. *I don't want to be in it; I'd rather be making it!*

When the screens around the bed opened, she rested her head on the stack of pillows behind her and scrutinised her fellow "inmates".

Directly opposite was a young girl. *She looks about sixteen,* Vera thought. Her face was almost the same colour as the white pillowcase under her head. There was an unmistakable bump beneath her blanket.

How could they put me in a ward like this, she thought, *with expectant mothers?* She knew that the war had brought changes in protocol, but all the same it seemed to be thoughtless. At best, cruel. Surely, they had read her medical history?

The girl caught Vera looking at her and stuck her tongue out.

Vera was shocked. *Why, the young madam!*

The girl sat up and seemed to thrust her pregnant belly towards Vera, and grinned with some kind of self-satisfaction, almost as if shocking Vera was a victory of sorts.

'Mrs Durnie?'

A white-coated doctor approached her bed. He asked the sister to pull the screens around for privacy. *Privacy, huh,* thought Vera. She had witnessed so many scenarios where some doctors and nurses forgot that the flimsy curtains were not soundproof.

'I must apologise, we really wanted to give you a single room, but I'm afraid its mayhem in here right now. I hope you understand; we will move you as soon as we can. My consultant has explained that he was a colleague of your husbands and that you are a nurse. We usually try to look out for our own, the only perk of the job some might say, but these are difficult times. I hope you understand?'

The doctor sounded confident enough, but his eyes were almost pleading with her not to create a scene.

'No need to apologise, I do understand.' Vera reassured him, and his shoulders visibly dropped.

'We will do our best to look after you and get to the bottom of why you have been feeling so wretched.'

Wretched! Vera wondered just how old this young doctor was. She felt so old, but she knew that she had no other option than to lie there and agree with him. "Wretched" actually came close to describing how she had been feeling. Tired, scared, unrelentless vomiting and weight loss she could ill afford.

Now, here she was lying opposite a rude young girl who seemed to have all that Vera had yearned for all her married life and yet did not even begin to understand how fortunate she was. It was so unfair.

The screen was opened and Vera was once again in full view of the other patients. Some openly stared, others feigned disinterest whilst sneaking a peek at her now and then.

She looked to her left and saw a woman about the same age as her. Her hair was unkempt and she had a look of hopelessness about her.

On her right was a cheerful looking woman. She was knitting, and she smiled when she saw Vera looking at her.

'Socks for my son,' she mouthed.

Vera smiled at her and continued to look around the ward.

In the bay window she saw a woman who was vaguely familiar. Her hair was salt and pepper grey, and she looked older than any of the other patients. When she caught Vera looking at her, she immediately looked away and pulled her bedclothes high around her neck.

Oh Charles, I miss you. I don't want to be here! Please come and take me home. Whatever is wrong with me, we can handle together!

Vera hated that she wanted to cry. She wanted to cry so much, for Charles, for Martin, for Chrissy. She knew that Chrissy still grieved the loss of her boy. Being here was a stark reminder, not that she needed one, that she could not give Charles a child. He never gave her cause to feel that way, so she had to admit that she was angry with herself for failing to have a baby. A baby that would have been so loved, so cherished, who may have followed in his father's footsteps and become a doctor, or her mother's footsteps and become a nurse. Then she corrected herself; there were lots of female doctors these days. Yes, her daughter would have become a doctor.

She looked at the girl opposite and couldn't help feeling just a little contempt.

There had been an air raid warning in the night, but they hadn't been evacuated to the shelters. Vera was thankful for that. She was as close to the other women in the ward as she wanted to be. The thought of being holed up in a shelter made her shudder. *I don't want questions. I don't want answers. I just want to be left alone.*

Vera was allowed to get up and go to the bathroom on her own. The bathroom consisted of three sinks, one actual bath and three toilet cubicles.

Standing at the sink, she washed her face, applied some Ponds cold cream and a spritz of Yardley Violets. Charles was visiting today, and she wanted to look and smell her best.

The woman at the sink on her right kept her head down, avoiding any kind of contact but Vera was now certain that she recognised her.

'Sister Reid, is that you?' She couldn't believe she had just asked it out loud.

The woman gripped onto the sink with both hands; she seemed to be unsteady on her feet. She drew up her shoulders, picked up her toilet bag and turned towards the bathroom door without acknowledging Vera's presence.

'It *is* you, isn't it?'

The woman could not ignore the question any longer.

'I used to be,' she answered flatly.

'Sister Reid, it's me, Vera Brownlee. Durnie now. We worked together at the Dick Institute during the last war.'

Mima Reid turned to look at Vera.

'Nurse Brownlee,' she said deliberately. 'This is an unexpected meeting.' Her words were guarded, to say the least. 'Ah yes, I think I remember you. Ward one, wasn't it?'

'Yes, that's correct, ward one.'

They looked at each other, and in an instant Vera recognised the apprehension she was feeling was mirrored in Mima's eyes. Both women were silently relaying the same message to each other: *Please don't ask me why I am here.*

*

Mima was suffering from a pelvic organ prolapse. The symptoms had been gradually getting worse over the years, forcing her to seek help.

Giving birth to her son had been difficult and not without complications. For one thing, he weighed almost eleven pounds, and as she had a slight frame, she ended up having a forceps delivery.

Obviously, she had been honest when she was asked if she had ever been pregnant and given birth. There was no record of it, after all. Mima thought she would die of shame when she admitted to having an illegitimate child. She wanted to justify the situation, but the doctor merely raised his hand.

'No need for any explanations, Miss Reid. You aren't the first, and you certainly won't be the last. The main thing is we get this sorted for you.'

And that had been that. Mima felt grateful that she did not need to elaborate.

Mima had not chosen to give her baby away. She had had no other option, and she tasted the bitter unjustness of it every day. She had carried on with her life as a single woman. She'd undertaken her nursing training and dedicated her life to looking after others. There wasn't a day that went by that she didn't think of her son. Yes, he belonged to another family now, and she knew they could give him the life that she could not. She would have been disowned by her parents. How could she have worked and looked after him at the same time? He would have been called names at school; the list of cons was endless, and she replayed them in her head over and over again. Even if she had fabricated a cover story and had been believed, she was certain that she had made the right decision back in 1901. She had to believe it in order to survive, but he was still her flesh and blood, her son, and she loved him with all her heart.

CHAPTER TWENTY-NINE

Chrissy, 1944

'My, that was just the perfect day! Katie looked like a picture in my old wedding dress, didn't she, Mum?'

Chrissy glanced at her mother, noticing that Maggie looked exhausted but happy. Now that she was receiving treatment for her heart complaint she had been like a new woman, but being on her feet for almost the whole day had taken its toll.

'She did, aye, hen, she really did. It's amazing what a nip and tuck here and there can do to a frock. It was a lovely service; the minister did us proud. When he spoke about keeping faith, hope and the future, I really did believe him. I feel, for the first time, that this bloody war might be coming to an end and that Katie and Alan have a lot to look forward to; we all do. If only we knew about John! Where *is* the lad?'

Maggie's voice cracked a little. She would never forget his namesake, her own boy John, whose body was lying somewhere overseas, only God knew where, but his spirit would forever be in her heart. Maggie knew she would be reunited with him one day, just as she knew she would see James and her Jim again, not in this world of course, but she just knew it.

'Right,' said Bob, 'now that the newlyweds are on their way to Largs for a couple of days, I think we should put our feet up and crack open that bottle of brandy that Dr Durnie handed in.'

'How is that young lad Martin doing now? Is he talking much these days? You haven't mentioned him for a while now.' Maggie asked as she took a sip of her brandy and grimaced. 'Chrissy, hen, do me a favour and get me a cup o' tea. I don't ken how anybody can drink this stuff.'

'Coming right up, your ladyship, just you sit there, and I'll wait on you hand and foot.'

Chrissy laughed and made her way to the kitchen which seemed empty without Rex waiting patiently for a scrap or two, or scratching at the back door to go out and chase next door's cat.

'I don't suppose there is any of that cake left, is there?'

'You know there is, Ma,' said Bob. 'Coming right up.'

While she waited for the kettle to whistle, Chrissy ambled back into the living room and sat on the arm of her mother's chair.

'Martin is much better these days; he has been a bit quieter since Mrs Durnie has been in hospital, but he and Rex are inseparable. It's like me and my shadow. I miss having Rex around the house, but it's as if he knows his place is with Martin. It reminds me of when Jack was sick – Rex hardly ever left his side. He just seems to know that he can make folk feel better just by being there. He is a special wee dog, indeed, he is, and I still get so see him every day, don't I?'

*

Chrissy had felt a similar emotion of late. She knew the doctor was missing his wife, but she also knew that she was helping in more ways than one. There was her nursing work, of course, and keeping the surgery stocked and running smoothly, but she and Martin had developed a special bond that hadn't gone unnoticed by either Vera or Charles.

Martin liked to sit at the big kitchen table and watch Chrissy as she busied herself cooking and baking. She had taken this on, even before Mrs Durnie had been admitted to hospital, on the days that Vera was just so exhausted that she had had to have a lie down.

'What was your son Jack like?' Martin had asked.

At first Chrissy had been taken aback by the question, and would have preferred not to answer, but as time passed, she actually welcomed the chance to talk about her boy. Martin lapped up the stories she told him and the questions came thick and fast. *What did Jack like to do? What were his favourite games and books? Who were his friends?*

Martin had been delighted to find out that he already knew some of Jack's friends, but none of the boys had ever mentioned Jack; he was sure if he asked them, they would talk about him.

The pair were comfortable and relaxed in each other's company. Chrissy wanted to tell Martin that he could talk to her about anything, but she didn't want to overstep the mark. It wasn't her place to get him to open up about his parents, but she felt that he would when the time was right. She also suspected that if Rex could talk, he would have a tale or two to tell!

*

'Kettle's boiling!'

'Really, Mum, I hadn't noticed!' Chrissy laughed. She hadn't felt this happy for a long time.

Katie's mother-in-law, Alan's mother, was a lovely lady; they had promised to see each other again soon. The sun had shone on her beautiful daughter and son-in-law. Although it had been a small wedding, the church had oozed with love, happiness and hopefulness.

'Have you warmed the pot?'

'As if I would dare not to, Ma, and yes, I've given a spoonful to the pot since it's a special occasion!'

She turned to look at the table and noticed that the sugar bowl was empty. Tutting, she walked over to the wall-mounted cabinet to fetch the half empty blue paper bag of sugar sitting there. She closed the cabinet door and looked out of the window. Her heart skipped a beat, and she felt faint. Chrissy grasped the table and sank into a chair.

A GPO telegram boy was walking up the path towards the house.

CHAPTER THIRTY

Chrissy 1944

'Bob!'

The urgency in her voice made Bob jump. In a second, he was on his feet and in the kitchen.

'What's happened – have you burned yersel'?'

'Look!'

Chrissy pointed at the window. Bob dutifully looked but couldn't see anything. She rose and walked over to look for herself; she knew she hadn't imagined it.

There was a loud knock on the front door. Bob answered it and walked back into the living room carrying a telegram like it was an unexploded bomb.

Maggie immediately entered mother mode.

'Come on, son, open it, it has to be done,' Maggie spoke with much more authority than she felt.

Bob slowly opened the envelope carrying an official insignia and sat down to read it out.

Telegram from: Air Ministry London to:

Mr and Mrs Ramsay, Irvine Road, Crosshouse

Regret to inform you that your son, Temporary Flight Sergeant John Ramsay, is reported missing in action as of May 1941. Subsequent information received indicates he is now a prisoner of war in enemy hands. Further details will follow when available. He is being treated in accordance with the Geneva convention.

Deepest sympathy from the Air Ministry

For a moment, all three sat and looked at each other. Maggie was first to speak.

'Thank God, the boy is safe!' she sobbed uncontrollably.

The telegram unearthed emotions she had tried so hard to suppress, but she knew they were still there, indelibly etched in her heart just waiting for a chance to escape and be heard again.

Chrissy remained quiet and strangely calm.

'I always felt in ma gut that he was still alive, but I couldn't let myself believe it. He's alive, Bob, he's alive!'

She rose and walked over to her husband. Bob couldn't hold back his tears as they hugged each other so tightly that it was almost impossible to breathe.

When they parted, Chrissy went to sit beside her mother. She squeezed her hand tightly; no words were adequate or required. Chrissy knew what her mother must be feeling.

'I think you need a brandy, Ma.'

Bob smiled warmly at Maggie and got the reaction he was expecting.

'Away wi ye, keep your brandy, I'll stick to ma tea, thanks.' Maggie wiped away the tears that were still trickling down her face and pooling in the wrinkles around her mouth.

'Temporary Flight Sergeant! My, he's done well – he went in as an aircraftman, and now he's been promoted, Chrissy.'

'Well, I hope he didnae do anything stupid to get it. I wonder where he is! Will we be able to write to him?'

'I expect so if they know where he is. I wonder why he hasn't written to us?'

'The telegram says further details to follow – maybe that will shed some light on it.'

'Aye,' said Maggie.

'The main thing is that the lad is alive, and hopefully well. I'll ask the minister to mention him on Sunday. We are blessed, truly blessed.'

Both Chrissy and Bob researched reasons for missing in action reports.

Chrissy found out that capturing forces often didn't inform the presence of POWs to international bodies like the Red Cross. They both knew that with the chaos of war, especially if men had been captured in a remote area, news about them may not reach home.

They had been informed, without any trace of emotion, that until a soldier's fate had been confirmed, they remained officially missing in action.

Now that it had been confirmed that John was alive and a prisoner of war, Chrissy would leave no stone unturned until she found out where he was.

With Dr Durnie's help, she found out who to contact for more information. She wrote a letter to the War Office, The Ministry of Defence, the International Committee of the Red Cross, and local military units, hoping for more information, but so far none had been forthcoming.

'My boy is alive! John is alive. Thank you, God, I can cope with anything now!'

CHAPTER THIRTY-ONE

Vera, 1944

Mima was back in bed after her surgery. The operation had been successful, but she had lost a lot more blood than expected. A nurse took her temperature and pulse, and checked her respirations. After satisfying herself that the intravenous fluids were running smoothly and in a timely fashion, she swiftly made her way down the ward to answer a call bell.

Suddenly there was a commotion and several staff members moved quickly towards a side room.

Everything was quiet and Vera was just closing her eyes when she heard Mima call out, quietly at first, and then with more urgency. She was writhing in pain and thrashing her arms around, making the cannula in her arm leak blood.

Vera looked up and down the ward, but there was no one to be seen. She got up, pulled her dressing gown around her shoulders, shoved her feet into her slippers and crept towards Mima's bed.

She placed her hand on Mima's arm and whispered, 'Can I do anything to help, Sister Reid? It's me, Vera. You are back in bed now.'

Mima stared at Vera; her face was flushed, her eyes bulged, and she looked terrified. Vera truly felt sorry for this poor woman who never had any visitors. There were no flowers by her bedside, no bottle of barley water, not even a card, nothing to say that there was anyone in the world who cared about her.

'It's all my own fault,' Mima murmured.

'Nothing is your fault. You have had your operation, but maybe you are due some pain killers. I will try to find out.'

Mima's free hand grasped at Vera's. Her grip was unyielding.

'It *is* my fault ... my son ... I must see my son ... he is just a baby ... I must see him ... I need to look after him ... what if he hates me?'

'You are running a temperature. I will get help as soon as I can. You don't have a son. Please don't worry!'

Vera tried to leave, but Mima gripped her hand tighter.

'I am not hallucinating, I do have a son, I do!'

Rivers of tears held back by shame began to course down Mima's face.

'Please don't tell anyone. Oh, I am so cold!'

Mima was getting more distressed by the minute.

A nurse with an unmistakeable disapproving look on her face appeared at the bedside.

'I can handle this, Mrs Durnie, please go back to bed.'

'I was just trying to help. I know this lady – we worked together during the last war. She is very hot to touch!'

'I am aware of that. I have just taken her temperature, everything is in hand, now please go and rest.'

Vera went back to bed, seething at having been dismissed in such a way. As she lay there, she wondered if what Mima had been saying about a baby boy, a son, was real or a fragment of febrile delusions mixed with a drug-induced stupor.

Should she mention it if she happened to be talking to her again? Vera began to view her ex-colleague in a whole different light. Gone was the starchy, judgemental sister who ruled with a rod of iron, and in her place was a frightened lonely woman who may have a secret past that neither Vera nor any of the other nurses at the Dick Institute could never have imagined.

CHAPTER THIRTY-TWO

Chrissy, 1944

Chrissy and Bob sat opposite each other at the kitchen table.

'Read it again, Bob.'

'I'll try, but I don't know how to say half of the words.' He frowned, took his cap off, and ran his hand over the top of his head.

'To the parents of John Ramsay ...'

'Ocht, I don't mean that bit, Bob, skip that bit!'

'Well, you read it then, smarty pants, it's going to be the same as the last time we read, though.'

Chrissy grabbed the letter from his outstretched hand and read out loud.

'We hope this message finds you with strength and courage during this difficult time. We are writing to provide you with updated contact details and support resources.'

'Aboot time if you ask me,' quipped Bob.

Chrissy flashed him a look that said shut up and continued again.

'Regarding your son ...'

'Temporary Flight Sergeant John Ramsay,' Bob chirped.

'We don't need that bit either!'

'Behave yersels, you two, you're acting like a pair o' school weans!' Maggie called over her shoulder from the kitchen sink with more than a hint of frustration.

'Please know that he is being monitored closely and we are committed to ensuring his safety, wellbeing and eventual return home. We understand the emotional toll this situation brings, and we want to assure you that you are

not alone. Our team is available to answer your questions, provide updates as they become available, and connect you with counselling and support services.

Please do not hesitate to reach out at any time. Your strength and resilience are deeply admired, and we are here to walk alongside you every step of the way.

'And then it says he is in Stalag Luft 1, Barth, Northern Germany.' Chrissy said the last part of the sentence slowly and precisely. She placed the letter on the table, and they looked at each other. Maggie placed two steaming cups of tea and an obligatory piece of shortbread in front of each of them.

'Bob, we can write to him! We can send him a parcel! The letter did say we could do that, didn't it?'

'Aye it did and I'm no readin' it again, Chrissy! You just want to laugh at ma German accent!'

'Is that what it was, Bob, I thought you just had a bad cauld!'

Maggie chortled at her own joke and then promptly choked on her biscuit.

'Serves ye right, Ma Barnes,' Bob laughed.

'I'll get ma knittin' needles oot, and I'll make some bramble jelly,' Maggie said. She relished the thought of being useful and busy. 'Do you think wee Martin would like to help me pick some brambles? We can take Rex with us; there should be plenty doon the Whin Road.'

'He'd love that, Mum, he's doing so much better these days. He's joined the boys brigade, and often has pals at the big house. They've been learning about first aid. I can see him following in his uncle's footsteps at this rate. Oh and by the way, Ma, he calls brambles blackberries.'

'Once he's tasted one of my bramble and crab apple pies, he'll never call them that again,' Maggie said haughtily.

'Right, knitting needles, wool here we come!'

And at that she almost skipped out of the kitchen.

CHAPTER THIRTY-THREE

Vera, 1945

Vera tip-toed over to the cot and cooed at the baby snugly wrapped in a lovingly handknitted shawl. Golden wisps of hair glistened like strands of gossamer on top of her head. She had developed a bald patch where her little head had rubbed against the muslin square underneath it. She snuffled softly as she lay there, oblivious of the happiness her birth had caused.

Vera knew that she could quite happily sit and gaze at this tiny human for twenty-four hours a day. She marvelled in everything about her, constantly counting her tiny fingers and toes. She never tired of offering her a finger and the thrill she felt when her daughter gripped it tightly.

'Snooze well, little Alice. I must go and get ready for your aunty coming to visit.'

Vera reluctantly tore herself away from the baby. She still couldn't believe how she had reached such a momentous chapter in her life She could never have imagined this moment in her wildest dreams; she would not have dared to.

Vera recalled the day she was told that she was not menopausal, but that in fact she was pregnant. She truly thought it was some sort of malicious joke, but only for a moment. When Charles had squeezed her hand tightly and then gazed into her eyes, she knew it was not a joke or a dream – it was actually happening!

'But how, I mean why? Oh, I don't know what I mean! I feel giddy!'

All at once, Charles was on his feet and placed a protective arm around her shoulders.

'It *is* rare, to be honest, Vera,' said the consultant. 'You have been suffering from hyperemesis gravidarum – that's why you have been vomiting morning noon and night. The tests eliminated any gastrointestinal causes. I have to say, given your profession, the doctors assumed that if you were pregnant, you would have known about it!'

Vera and Charles looked at each other, slightly embarrassed.

'We have been so busy!' said Charles. 'My nephew is living with us and has been going through a traumatic time. We hardly get the time to talk to each other!'

Charles stopped when he saw his colleague's raised eyebrow.

'If I may say so, Charles, all evidence to the contrary!'

Vera flushed bright red, but she didn't care; she was pregnant, and this man had just confirmed it. And not just a little bit pregnant but a six whole months' worth of pregnant!

'We will monitor you carefully. We have a plan in mind which we will discuss, but you must rest. No more working. The district midwife will be a regular feature in your life from now on. If she detects or suspects the slightest abnormality, you will be admitted to hospital for complete bedrest, and I know that is the last thing you want. You will be aware that you are classed an elderly primigravida, which is cause to take extra precautions, and given your history of miscarriages we must not take any, and I mean *any* unnecessary risks. Do you understand?'

'We do, and you can trust me, I will take the greatest care of her.'

Before leaving the hospital, Vera had something she wanted to do.

She had asked Charles to bring some flowers from the garden, and a bottle of her homemade elderflower cordial.

While her husband had a catch up with his colleague, she went to visit Mima Reid who was still recovering from her operation.

She sat down on a chair beside Mima's bed and told her what was happening, and about her news.

They had chatted openly during their time together on the ward and had got to know each other.

'Vera, I know you thought I was unjust, that I treated you unfairly.'

'Please no, not at all!' Vera became flustered, unsure of what to say.

'But, you see, I trusted you. I knew I could depend on you, Vera. I could trust you to look after the ward and the patients in the same way as I did myself. Some of the others ...' she paused, '... they were good girls, but not all of them had the instinct you had. In fact, you reminded me of myself when I was newly qualified.'

Mima told Vera about her baby. She confirmed that she hadn't been hallucinating, well, maybe a little, and that she hoped she could trust Vera with her secret.

'I have wanted to tell someone for ages. The secret has been like a lead weight I have carried with me for so long. My sister was the only living soul other than my son's adoptive parents who knew anything about him and his history, and now Lizzy is in a world of her own, albeit quite happy in that world for now. She has no idea who I am, and I have no idea how much time she has left to live. I'm glad I had that outburst, and I'm glad that you are now my friend.'

Vera's eyes filled with tears.

'I'm sorry, Mima, I suppose I'm a bit hormonal.'

'Please stay in touch; here is my address.' She handed Vera a slip of paper. 'I know you won't be able to visit again, but hopefully I will be discharged soon. Would it be acceptable if I came to visit you and the ...?'

She nodded towards Vera's abdomen.

'Little one?'

Mima held her breath. It had taken all the courage she possessed to ask the question.

'Of course, Mima! In fact, I insist upon it!'

Mima felt a lightness of heart she had not felt in years, decades even. Vera kissed her cheek, and they said goodbye. They were still Vera and Mima, but now they were so much more, and each woman was thankful for it.

CHAPTER THIRTY-FOUR

Chrissy, 1945

Life continued at quite a pace. Bob was as busy as ever on the farm. During the summer months, Chrissy almost forgot what he looked like. Maggie appeared to be knitting for the whole of the British Army, Navy and Airforce, and Chrissy found herself taking over many of Vera's duties as well as continuing with her own. She didn't mind one bit, and, in fact, once the baby had arrived the whole atmosphere at the surgery and the house had changed.

Martin was completely smitten with his baby cousin. He loved to hold her and rock her to sleep. He watched over her like a mama bear over her cubs and loved to help Vera with bathing and even nappy changing.

Rex too seemed to recognise that this tiny new addition to the family was precious, and he guarded her pram and cot with a steely doggy determination.

Martin had become closer to Maggie. He loved nothing better than to sit with her, helping her to wind wool and listen to tales of the great war. He loved to hear her talk about her three sons, James, Billy and John. The stories he had heard about Billy and his work in Aldershot had convinced him that he would be a plastic surgeon one day, even though Uncle Charles had brought him down to earth with the realities of medical training and doing his time as a junior doctor.

But he especially loved the stories about Chrissy, her love of books, how she'd loved going to the pictures when she was small, and then becoming an usherette. He had even borrowed *Anne of Green Gables* from the library, hoping that none of his friends would spot him doing it. Much to his surprise, he had really enjoyed it and decided that Chrissy reminded him of Anne Shirley. He knew from what his aunt and uncle had mentioned that Chrissy was a quick learner, intelligent and resilient, but he had seen for himself how forgiving and kind-hearted she was. Yes, Chrissy and Anne were similar, no doubt about that, and he liked and admired everything she did and stood for.

Maggie in turn adored being with Martin; she often wondered if he and Jack would have been firm friends, like brothers even. She felt nothing but joy and a sense of peacefulness when she was with Martin, but she could not put it into words.

The news in papers and in cinemas was an amalgam of grim realities and growing optimism; several developments offered hope and a sense of progress. Allied forces were gaining ground in Europe. The Battle of the Bulge saw Germany suffering devastating losses.

There seemed to be light at the end of the tunnel, but that would not and never could diminish the hardships, heartache and loss suffered by the armed forces and civilians both in Britain and the rest of Europe.

*

Maggie sat alone at the kitchen table. She had been to bed but had been unable to sleep.

She loved living here with her daughter and son-in-law, but she missed sitting alone with her thoughts. Of course, she could think when she went to bed, but inevitably she would fall asleep.

'What is it all about?'

She spoke out loud, albeit in a whisper, to no one in particular.

'I just don't understand it. Why can't people, countries, religions just get on, respecting each other? Why do we end up going to war?'

She thought back to 1918, and armistice. There were celebrations, street parties, and of course she had been relieved, but she couldn't be happy. The price she had paid was way too heavy.

'Two of my boys are dead. I don't even know where one of them is. He is lying in a field somewhere in France. My bright wee boy who was so full of life is reduced to nothing but skin and bones, buried in mud never to see the light of day again. Please, God, let me know that his soul is free, flying high above those fields so far away. Let me know that he is happy and that he is reunited with his brother and his dad. And Billy, maimed and scarred for life, but so positive and doing so much for others.' She sighed.

'Ah, Billy, lad, I'm so proud of what you have achieved. The difference you are making to so many lives is heart-warming, son, to say the least, and you've met a lassie, and if she makes you happy, I know she will make the rest of us happy too. Chrissie, ma wee lassie, you have done so much to help others too. I am one heart-broken mither, but a very proud one too.'

She heard a creak on the stairs, and saw Chrissy appear in the doorway.

'I thought I could hear voices, Ma – is everything alright?'

Maggie placed her now empty cup of cocoa in the table.

'Aye, hen, it is. I never imagined I could feel like this again. I feel contented, aye, that's the word, contented wi ma lot in life. Do I wish it had been different? Of course, but as it is we are all doing well each in our own way.'

'We are that, Ma. Now, come on, I'll fill the hot water bottle for you and bring it up.'

'Thank you, lass, thank you for everything.'

CHAPTER THIRTY-FIVE

Vera, 1945

'And how is my little goddaughter today?'

Mima clucked like a mother hen as she peered into the navy-blue pram.

'Well, apart from keeping me awake half the night, she is doing just fine. She took to breast-feeding like a duck to water, but I just don't seem to get any rest. She had a bit of colic...'

Vera stopped and apologised

'I am so sorry, Mima, I mustn't complain, I love her more than life itself, but I am so tired.'

Vera could have kicked herself; what would Mima have given to have experienced sleepless nights and painful breasts! That was such an insensitive thing to say.

'Of course you are, Vera. You had a difficult pregnancy, and you are an ...'

'An older mother!' Vera finished.

'Well, yes, it does make a difference, you know.'

'It's not just that; I've had to give Chrissy some time off. Her daughter is expecting, early days yet, but she slipped at work and broke her ankle. Chrissy was worried of course; she has been a godsend to us and has never complained or refused to help in any way she could. I had to give her time off to help Katie in her hour of need.'

Martin skipped into the kitchen. 'Hello, Aunt Mima, how are you?'

'I am fine and dandy, young man. Speaking of which, come here.'

Martin did as he was bid; he loved Mima almost as much as he loved Maggie, and the feelings were reciprocated ten-fold.

'I have not one, but two *Dandy* comics here for you and ...' She held out a paper bag filled with humbugs.

Martin threw his arms around Mima and planted a kiss on her forehead.

'You are the best auntie ever!' Then, realising what he had just said, he corrected himself. 'After Auntie Vera, that is.'

The women laughed, causing Alice to stir in her pram.

'Shush,' Vera whispered.

'Why don't you go and see if Tom is at home? You could read your comics together and share your sweets?'

'Good idea, Auntie. Can Rex come too?'

Vera looked at his pleading eyes, but would not be drawn.

'What have I said? Tom's family have rabbits in the back garden, and you know how Rex loves to bark at them; it upsets everyone in earshot. He can stay here with me.'

She glanced over at the little dog who was lying in front of the range snoring softly. As he had grown older, he had developed a likening for warmth at all costs.

'I'll be back in time for dinner,' Martin whispered as he headed for the back door.

'I know you will ... I know you saw Chrissy leave a pie before she left to catch her bus.'

Chrissy made the best pies; you would never think they had been made with rations.

Vera made a pot of tea, set out cups and saucers, and sat down opposite her friend.

'I've brought us something too,' said Mima.

She opened her bag and produced some home-baked gingerbread.

'Oh, I can't resist your gingerbread! I have a slither of butter in the pantry – I'll go and fetch it.'

While they were enjoying their afternoon tea, Mima noticed that Vera was on edge.

'What's the matter, Vera, is something wrong?'

'I need to ask you something, but I don't know how to broach the subject.'

It was Mima's turn to look concerned.

'Fire away.'

'I know you have a lot on your plate visiting your sister. It's such a long trip to Ailsa.'

'Vera, spit it out!' Mima coaxed.

'Right, here goes … it's a big ask.'

Mima nodded but said nothing.

'I mentioned that Chrissy is taking some time off, and, well, I wondered … I wondered if you would consider moving in here for a couple of weeks to help Charles in the surgery …'

'I'd be delighted!'

'You will?'

Vera was surprised and delighted. The request had been much easier than she had imagined.

'I mean there would be some red tape to sort out, but I can't think of anyone else I would trust to live in, help Charles and be here for me and Martin.'

'I visit Lizzy once a month, Vera – she doesn't even know who I am. The volunteer work I am doing … well, what can I say? I know I am capable of so much more. Yes, I am considered unfit to work in hospitals anymore because of my nervous exhaustion, but I know I can do more, *safely* do more,' she added.

'You know you wouldn't be employed as a registered nurse; you would undertake the duties that Chrissy carries out.'

'I am well aware of that; it will suit me down to the ground.'

'And it will be temporary, just until Chrissy comes back.'

'Yes, I understand that too. Once a nurse, always a nurse! My background can only be an advantage, surely. I will love being here, being with you, Martin, Alice and Charles, of course. Thank you, Vera! I don't know how or why our paths crossed again, but I am so glad they did.'

CHAPTER THIRTY-SIX

Chrissy, 1944

'Bob, are you listening to me?'

Chrissy was feeling anxious and exasperated. Since she had been told that not only was Katie expecting a baby, but that she had been in an accident at work, she had been beside herself with worry.

Now that she knew that the accident had caused nothing more than a broken ankle, she had relaxed a little, but she wanted to see Katie as soon as possible.

A newspaper had recently reported that a young mother had died after falling downstairs during an air raid. Because of the black-out, she had lost her footing and broken her neck. The story haunted her; how would Katie cope with one leg in plaster?

'Why don't you go and see her?' said Maggie.

'Mrs Durnie has baby Alice to look after now. I can't leave her in the lurch, Mum, it wouldn't be fair.'

'Chrissy, your daughter needs you. All's fair in love and war after all. Mrs Durnie will understand, and it will only be for a week or two. It will do you good – you have been looking stressed out lately. I'm not handless, I can make sure Bob has a decent meal on the table when he gets home. Rex is with Martin. Think of yourself and your family for once. Go!'

*

'BOB!'

'Good grief wummin, what is it noo?'

'Listen to me, Bob, Rex is with the Durnies but send what scraps you can their way for him. Ma will see to breakfast, dinners etcetera, Martin will probably visit from time to time so mind your Ps and Qs!'

Bob grimaced.

'Thanks for the faith you have in me, Chrissy, I'm sure we will manage just fine, or is that what you are afraid of?'

He grinned the schoolboy cheeky grin that always managed to melt her heart, even after all these years. She slapped him playfully on his shoulder.

'You will miss me, Bob Ramsay, just see if you don't!'

Bob hugged her and whispered, 'More than you will ever know …'

'That's it, am no' goin'!'

'Don't be daft, Mrs, Katie needs you much more than anyone else right now! Get that bag packed – you have a bus to catch!'

'I just need to hand a pie in for Mrs Durnie …'

'Enough, Chrissy, you can hand it in on your way to the bus stop. They will cope just fine.'

Bob leaned in to kiss her neck.

'I love you, Chrissy Ramsay, don't ever change.'

Dressed in her Sunday best, Chrissy made her way to the bus stop. Maggie walked along with her, carefully carrying the pie.

'I'll stand here wi yer case while you drop it off, but don't be long – the bus is due in ten minutes.'

'Right-o, Mum. I have a wee treat for Rex too, I hope he's in and not out with Martin.'

'Honestly, Chrissy, you talk about that dog as if he was human.'

'He is one of the family, Mum, don't ever forget it!'

'Get on wi' ye, or you definitely will miss that bus.'

Chrissy knocked on the back door and called out, 'Vera, are you there?'

She was surprised to see Mima, wearing an apron and with the kettle in her hand.

'Miss Reid, I … I was looking for Mrs Durnie.'

'How many times do I have to tell you it's Mima!'

Chrissy smiled. 'Right you are, Mima.'

'Vera has gone for a walk to the shops, she needs some things from the drapery, and it's our day to collect Hitler's secret weapon.' She laughed.

'Ah, the blessed national loaf! Still, it fills a hole.'

'I need to run, my bus will be here any minute. Here is the pie I promised for Mrs Durnie. It's the doctor's favourite.'

'The poor man, he never gets a minute's peace, between the surgery and the hospital, plus he loves helping Vera to look after Alice whenever he can. He looks so tired, though.'

'He does that... Mima, I really need to run now.'

'Quickly before you go ... Vera said to tell you that she is fine, that she will have me trained up in no time, Martin is happy and so is Rex, so go and enjoy being with Katie, oh and one last thing ...'

Chrissy looked round as she opened the door.

'What's that?' She frowned.

'Vera said ... and I quote ... please don't ever let Martin know where you get the rabbits for the pie.'

*

Vera had been waiting in the queue for some time. Every few minutes she would ask the woman behind to keep her place while she went out to look into her daughter's pram to make sure, she was still asleep and safe.

'Good morning, Mrs Durnie, how can I help you?'

'Did you manage to find me some safety pins, Mrs Ferguson?'

'I did so. Mrs Smith from Annadale Crescent found some old ones in a drawer and she handed them in for you.'

Mrs Ferguson rummaged in a drawer and fished out a crumpled brown paper bag.

'I am so grateful, thank you, Mrs Ferguson, I must thank Mrs Smith too. I don't suppose you have any white thread, do you?'

'Sorry no, that I don't, and I have no idea when we will be getting any in. I will ask my mother if you like, she has a big old sewing box – she might have some spare.'

'I don't want to cause any trouble.'

'No trouble at all. I'll get oor Charlie to hand it in if she has some.'

'Thank you. Now, last but not least, do you have any muslin?' Vera raised her eyebrows and tilted her head to one side and crossed her fingers.

'I kept a yard for you ... don't let on, though.' Mrs Ferguson laughed and touched her nose with her index finger.

'Mum's the word, eh?'

Mrs Ferguson wrapped the cloth in some brown paper.

'No string, I'm afraid, it ran oot yesterday.'

'Not to worry, it will be fine like that. How much do I owe you?'

'That will be one shilling and sixpence, please.'

Vera handed over the money and hurried outside to check on Alice who was still fast asleep. She noticed a silver sixpence lying at the top of the mattress, placed there by a well-wisher to bring good luck. She smiled.

She popped the paper package into the pram bag and started to walk towards the Co-op. She saw Mrs Todd approaching in the distance. She had just crossed the road and was walking straight towards her.

'Oh no, I don't have the energy for this today. I haven't seen her since Alice was born, and she will want to ask twenty questions!'

*

'Mrs Durnie, how nice to see you! I've been a stranger to the village lately.' she pointed to her leg. 'Ulcers again.'

'Oh dear, that's not good, Mrs Todd, maybe you should see the doctor?'

'Naw, it'll be fine, my sister put some honey on it, and she found some old bandages.'

Vera raised her eyebrows.

'Dinnae worry yourself, she biled them first.'

'Of course, I didn't think for a minute that she wouldn't have boiled them first,' she lied.

'So, I was right then!'

It was a statement, not a question.

'Aboot, the wean. What have you called her?'

'Alice,' Vera was still puzzled.

'That's a braw name. It suits her. I love her wee pink bonnet.'

'Thank you. Mrs Ramsay knitted it. She has mittens to match,' Vera said proudly.

'That last time I saw ye, I told you that this time would be different, didn't I?'

Vera stared at the woman, not sure how to answer. She recalled the short conversation.

'I think so, yes, you did, but I admit I wasn't sure what you meant by it.'

Vera was not unconvinced that the old lady, although harmless, was a bit of a fruit cake.

'I meant aboot the wean.' She pointed to Alice. 'I kent that you would produce a fine healthy baby, and just look at her, she is the picture of health.' Mrs Todd beamed at Vera with self-satisfaction and smiled at her with a gap-toothed grin. The old woman leaned into the pram and placed a sixpence next to the other one.

'Really, there is no need, Mrs Todd, you must ...'

'It's tradition, silvering the wean. A wee bit of silver for luck, not that she'll need it, lass – she will go places. But you tell your man tae look after himself.'

'Thank you, Mrs Todd, remember to come and see the nurse if that leg doesn't get any better.'

As Vera made her way home, she couldn't stop thinking about the strange conversation she had just had. She mulled it over, trying to remember when the first strange conversation had taken place – was it the day she had nearly run Chrissy over with her bicycle? It couldn't have been, could it?

No one knew I was expecting at that time ... not even me!

CHAPTER THIRTY-SEVEN

Vera, 1944

Vera watched as Alice suckled from her breast, tiny droplets of milk escaping from her rosebud mouth. There could be no feeling quite like it in the world, she thought as she gazed at the infant, so small and so dependent on her for everything, so vulnerable and trusting.

'I will always be here for you, Alice. I will keep you safe. Mummy and Daddy love you very much.'

Alice stopped sucking for a moment, as if concentrating on her mother's words. She seemed to smile, and Vera knew that most mothers would say it was just wind, but she was certain that her daughter had just smiled at her. Her heart was so full of love and tenderness for this little girl that she wasn't sure how she could carry the weight of it.

Alice suddenly stopped feeding, her tiny semi-open mouth allowing milk to dribble down her chin and onto the muslin cloth. Her huge eyes blinked once, then twice, and then succumbed to slumber. Vera wiped Alice's chin gently, restored her dress and then tenderly placed her in her pram.

Mima knocked and brought in a cup of tea.

'Get it while it's hot and put your feet up for a wee while. I'm going back to help Dr Durnie with the afternoon surgery.'

'Thank you on both counts! I will.'

Mima made her way to the surgery. It hadn't taken her long to find her feet, much to Chrissy's annoyance. Chrissy knew that it was uncharitable of her to think so, but she had hoped that Mima would find it more difficult. A few days before her departure, Mrs Durnie had asked her to show Mima what happened on a typical day, where everything was kept, her order book, etc. She had done it willingly, but she couldn't help feeling that she would not be missed and hoped that she would still have a job to come back to.

Mima knocked, then, hearing nothing, she opened the door. Charles was sitting at his desk, feet propped up on a wooden chair. His right elbow was resting on the desk, his splayed-out fingers buried in his hair supporting his head. He was fast asleep. She had been thinking for a few days now that he looked pale, and he seemed to be extremely tired. Of course, she realised that new parents suffered from disturbed sleep, but her instinct told her this was more than that. He had been a bit short-tempered with her, only once, but she had also witnessed it with an albeit trying patient. This was almost unheard of for Charles. Even when she cast her mind back to him working as a junior doctor at the Dick Institute, all she could remember was a caring and capable young man, and she felt sad to see him so exhausted.

She hadn't mentioned any of this to Vera, of course; it wouldn't do to worry her, but even young Martin had expressed his concerns.

'Aunt Mima, when Uncle Charles was reading me a story the other night, he fell asleep in the middle of it, right-on top of my bed!'

'I expect he is very tired, Martin, he is a very busy man, and there are a lot of sick people he needs to look after. Now, don't you worry, I will do all I can to help him.'

Mima hoped she had sounded convincing.

Now she noticed Charles's sandwiches lying untouched on the desk; beside them was a cup of tea with barely a mouthful taken out of it.

Mima instinctively knew that this was much more serious than tiredness due to overwork.

'Dr Durnie,' she whispered, and then again louder than before.

Charles stirred and immediately sat bold upright; his hand moved automatically to his abdomen.

'Mima, I'm so sorry, I must have dosed off.'

'Pardon me for asking, Doctor, but do you have abdominal pain?'

'A little ... probably hunger pains,' he said and pointed at the uneaten food.

Mima immediately entered "ward sister mode". She wasn't having this, not for one minute longer.

'Dr Durnie, I would like to suggest that you did not eat lunch because of your abdominal pain, am I correct?'

'That might be the case. I have been working around the clock as you know, and when I am at home, I want to spend as much time helping Vera with Alice and Martin. I'm just tired, really. I'll go and splash my face with cold water and get ready for afternoon surgery.'

Charles stood up and immediately fell back down heavily into the chair. Mima was at his side in an instant, immediately taking charge.

'Lie down over there, on your couch. I am going to check your pulse and your blood pressure.'

Charles was feeling so weak that he did not argue. Mima pulled his arm around her shoulders and helped him over to the couch. She undid his tie and opened his jacket.

The thready rapid pulse and low blood pressure told her all she needed to know.

'Stay right there, Doctor, and don't move a muscle. I'm going to call for an ambulance.'

Charles was about to argue, but he was suddenly wracked with excruciating abdominal pain. Mima swiftly walked back over to the desk, picked up the telephone and dialled 999. She competently and clearly conveyed her findings, explained she had been a ward sister on a surgical ward and finished by saying: 'If I'm not mistaken, we have the beginning of a perforated ulcer! Please send an ambulance immediately!'

*

By the time the call ended, Charles had begun to vomit. Mima ran to the trolley and picked up a stainless-steel kidney dish and held it under his chin, speaking to him reassuringly as she did so.

The dish was quickly filled with dark and grainy fluid which she recognised instantly as old blood. She had seen enough of it in her time to know what was happening. She only hoped the ambulance wouldn't take too long.

'The ambulance is on its way, Charles, just stay calm. Is there anything you want me to do?'

'Fetch Vera,' he moaned, semi-consciously.

Mima saw Martin playing with Rex in the front garden. she opened the window and called to him.

'Martin, go and fetch Aunt Vera, there's a good boy. Tell her I need to speak to her for a minute. Tell her you will stay and keep an eye on Alice. Take Rex with you, quickly now.' She tried to sound calm.

Martin, sensing some urgency, did as he was asked without question.

A few minutes later, Vera walked into the surgery, not sure what she would find. Martin had sounded anxious when he relayed his message. She took in the scene before her: she looked at her husband's pale face, the kidney dish, and then at Mima.

'Charles! Oh no!' Her hands flew to cover her mouth to prevent a scream.

'Now, Vera, don't worry, the ambulance is on its way. It will be fine if you stay calm,' Mima said.

Vera tried for her husband's sake, but she couldn't prevent tears from forming.

'Oh Charles, I should have noticed, I should have known!' He weakly shook his head.

'Vera, pull yourself together, this is not helping anyone! Now, go and get some more gauze and another dish, this one is nearly full!'

The sharpness of Mima's tone stunned Vera into action.

Soon, they could hear the ambulance bell ringing just as Charles vomited a copious amount of fresh, bright red blood.

CHAPTER THIRTY-EIGHT

Chrissy, 1944

Chrissy sat in her daughter's living room and couldn't believe what she was reading.

Katie was having 40 winks on the couch; this was the time of day she became weary and drained of energy. Chrissy making lunch for her had become the usual pre- nap routine, and how she had missed her mum's vegetable soup with chunks of potato in it and a sprinkling of parsley on top! It was her ultimate comfort food and would always remind her of home. Alan had been enjoying Chrissy's cooking, too. When he and Katie had both been working shifts, he often came home to an empty cold, dark, quiet house, just as Katie did, but these days a small fire was always burning; although it was early spring, there was a nip in the air, and summer seemed to be a long way off yet. The small house was filled to the brim with aromas of cooking and, if they were lucky, baking too.

While Katie slept, Chrissy would go foraging for wild garlic and nettles to use in her soups. She often found some wild sorrel and a few wild strawberries too. She also collected elderflowers to make cordial and gathered rose hips to hand into the local chemist to make syrup.

On top of that, she volunteered at a local children's nursery, on a temporary basis, as often as she could. She was missing her job in the surgery, but no one could accuse her of slacking.

Another bonus of this visit was that she was getting to see more of Alan's mother, Mary, and discovered that they had lots in common.

Chrissy continued to read and before she could stop herself, she gasped out loud, making Katie wake up with a start.

'What is it, Mum, is it a letter from John?' Katie yawned, rubbed her eyes and tried to focus on her mum's face.

Since they had received news from the War Office, letters had begun to-ing and fro-ing between them and John. It made such a difference to Chrissy and Bob to hear that their son was doing well and was being well cared for. He had also received the care packages they sent. It was progress indeed and Chrissy lapped it up like the cat that got the cream. Katie prayed that this was not bad news about her brother.

'Sorry, hen, I didn't mean to wake you. No, it's a letter from Mrs Durnie. You will never guess what has happened!' Chrissy was frowning and looked ashen.

'Stay there, Mum. I'll put the kettle on – you look like you are about to faint!'

'If you can manage, I'll come through when the kettle boils and finish off.'

Katie hobbled to the kitchenette on her crutches. She had filling up the kettle and putting it on to boil down to a fine art now, but Chrissy wouldn't let her fill the teapot or carry any cups of tea while she was still non-weight bearing.

Katie gingerly made her way back and sat down opposite her mother.

'Tell me, then, Mum, what has happened?'

'It's Dr Durnie. He's in hospital ... just made it in time from what I can gather. He's been looking peaky for a long time now. Well, *I* thought so. I just thought he was just overdoing it. It sounds as if Mima saved his life!'

Chrissy looked over the top of her reading glasses at Katie, who was sitting open-mouthed.

'Vera says if Mima hadn't been there, he may not have made it to hospital at all.' Chrissy took off her glasses and swung them between her fingers.

'But surely if Mima hadn't been there, you would have been, and you would have done whatever she did, if you see what I mean?'

'No, Katie, I'm not sure that I would. If the doctor had told me he was all right, I wouldn't have dared to argue. You just don't do that. Well, *I* wouldn't do that. You just don't think about doctors being sick and admitted to hospital, do you?' Chrissy frowned and bit her lip.

'Vera says that Mima went into ward sister mode and completely took charge of everything calmly and efficiently. She even took his blood pressure and pulse; I couldn't have done that. It says here …' Chrissy pointed to the letter written in Vera's meticulous handwriting, '… that she called the ambulance even though he'd told her not to and that she looked after Alice and Martin while Vera went with the doctor. I would have panicked, I know I would, Katie. If you hadn't broken your ankle and if I hadn't come down to look after you, and if I had still been there doing my job, he may have died!'

'That's an awful lot of ifs and buts, Mum! You don't know what you would have done. As it is, you weren't there, and the story has a happy ending so why are you so worried about it?'

Chrissy heard the kettle whistle and went into the kitchenette to make the tea. She almost wished that she could lay her hands on some brandy; her hands were shaking and she clutched onto a chair to stop herself from swaying.

'I wouldn't have done what Mima did. I'd have left him and probably found him on the floor.'

The thought of it made her shudder. She handed a cup of hot sweet tea to Katie; she had even taken some sugar for herself.

'What if they don't want me back, Katie? What if they decide that Mima is much more useful? After all, she is a fully trained nurse with years of experience.'

'Aye, Mum, but she's not employed as one; she had a nervous breakdown or something. What if she has another one of those, eh? You need to have more confidence in yourself.'

Katie put her arm around her mother's slender shoulders and hugged her.

'I'm sure your job is safe and will be waiting for you when you get back. I will be allowed to bear weight soon, and there will be no stopping me once that happens! You'll see, everything will be just fine.'

CHAPTER THIRTY-NINE

Vera, 1944

'Alice is fine, Charles, just her first tooth is coming through, I'm certain of it. I have her teething ring ready. I think she is too young for bread crusts. I've also managed to get some teething syrup. She loves it when I rub her gums with my pinkie.'

Charles laughed, then winced as the sudden movement pulled on his stitches.

He did not like being on the receiving end of medical treatment and nursing care one bit. He was an agreeable enough patient but he longed to be back at home, to lie beside his wife at night, to talk about the day's happenings, to ask her opinion of this and that, and to hold her in his arms, just the two of them in their own little cocoon, hidden away from the rest of the world. He relished skin-on-skin contact, even if they were both too tired to make love. The intimacy they shared just by lying together was indescribable.

He gently placed his hand on hers, and they looked deeply into each other's eyes.

'Charles, I have been so scared! To think I almost lost you is unbearable!'

'Vera, you and I have a lot of damage to do yet, and now we have Alice as an accomplice, the world is our oyster!'

'I don't want the world, or oysters for that matter. I just want you and our daughter.'

'Madam, your wish is my command.' He smirked, and immediately she felt the familiar fluttering in her stomach that she had felt the very first time he had smiled at her.

'Have you been reading the papers?' His eyes shone and he couldn't keep still.

'Not really. It's been pretty hectic between one thing and another. Why, what's happened?'

'Reach into my locker and bring out the newspaper – it should be near the front. It's early days yet, but progress is being made. Do you remember the Berveridge Report back in 1942?'

Vera nodded. 'I think so.'

'Just listen to this.' Charles started to read aloud: *'A Bold Prescription for Britain's Future – Government White Paper Proposes National Health Service for All.'*

He paused for dramatic effect and to take in Vera's reaction.

'In a move hailed by some as "the most ambitious social reform since the Poor Law", the Government this week unveiled its long-awaited White Paper outlining plans for a comprehensive National Health Service. Published under the auspices of the Ministry of Health, the document sets forth a vision of medical care, free at the point of use, available to every man, woman, and child in the United Kingdom.

The proposal, which builds upon the principles laid out in the Beveridge Report of 1942, seeks to unify Britain's patchwork of hospitals, clinics, and local health authorities into a single, coordinated system. Under the scheme, responsibility would rest with the Minister of Health, while local councils would be tasked with administering services in their districts. The health of the nation is not a matter for charity, but for justice.'

Charles paused. 'It's really going to happen, Vera! Can you imagine it? I know there will be divided opinions; some of the older chaps think it's too idealistic and see it as a threat to their livelihoods, but I see a fair system. Patients won't need to worry that they can't afford treatment, people will be treated earlier so we should see fewer serious illnesses, and doctors like me will have easier access to specialists and a steady income from the government.'

'Calm down, Charles, your blood pressure will go through the roof at this rate,' she grinned. 'I agree with you one hundred percent. Not just on the matter for charity but for justice. Powerful words, indeed, but I suppose I can understand why some doctors might have concerns. I expect you will be throwing yourself into this when you get home? Have they said when you can come home, by the way?'

'Not yet, but it shouldn't be too long now. I mean look at me, I'm the picture of health, rosy cheeks the lot!'

'Only because of the iron tablets and the liver you've been having.' It was Vera's turn to smirk; she knew that Charles hated liver and that, according to him, the ward sister was more intimidating than Mima. He had mentioned that she even stood over him until he ate it.

'I will not come home at all if you insist on giving me liver to eat! I'm not joking, I mean it!'

'Luckily for me, Mima is still staying with us. I will delegate your menu to her and I know she won't let me down!'

'You're joking! I love her, but I will not allow her to force feed me with liver!'

They laughed in unison, happy to be together, but longing to be alone.

'How is Chrissy? Any news?'

'Yes, her daughter is now almost self-sufficient, so she's planning to come back this weekend. Judging by her letters, Bob has had quite enough of quality time with his mother-in-law and can't wait for his wife to return. Poor Bob, he works so hard. Do you know he still sends scraps for Rex every week? Martin and Rex are inseparable; it worries me sometimes as Rex isn't getting any younger.'

'None of us are, darling, but let's cross that bridge when we come to it. It's time I was home, looking after you and baby Alice. I forgot to mention, a locum has been arranged to look after my patients for now, until I get back on my feet.'

'That's wonderful news, Charles! You mean for the first time in our lives we will be able to spend time together, guilt-free?'

'Sounds like it. Maybe we should get away somewhere, just the four of us. My old friend Gordie has a cottage on Arran. He says we can use it whenever we like. He's based down south for now. What do you think?'

Vera's face lit up, and she smiled from ear to ear.

'What do I *think* ...?' She flung her arms open wide and hugged him gently. 'I could dance, but sister might disapprove! Charles Durnie, you are the sweetest, and most handsome man I know! I think a few days on an island will be the best medicine of all for you. I can't wait!'

*

'Chrissy, I am so pleased to see you. Come in, sit down, and tell me all about Katie!'

'Thank you, Vera, it's so good to be back.'

Vera was ecstatic; Charles was coming home, Mima had been admirably holding the fort and now her beloved Chrissy was back where she belonged.

'Can I ask you something, Vera?'

'Of course, you can, what is it?'

'I know you have Mima to help you. I also know that she saved Dr Durnie's life. She is so much more qualified than me, and I want to say that ...'

'Chrissy, I have missed you, more than I care to admit. Yes, Mima has been working here and has been invaluable, but, Chrissy, you are also invaluable. Things just haven't been the same without you. Hopefully the war is coming to an end, but people will always get sick, sad but true. We need you, Chrissy. There are big changes in the pipeline for medical services, and you will be needed more than ever.'

Tears pooled in Chrissy's eyes before tumbling down her cheeks.

'I was so frightened that you wouldn't want me anymore. I mean what do I have to offer compared to Mima?' she sobbed.

'Stop right there, Chrissy! You are and will always be welcome here, and, more to the point, you are a valuable member of our team. We have known each other for many years now. Remember when Billy was a patient of mine? I showed you around the hospital and I could tell even then that you are a natural nurse. You instinctively knew what to say to the patients, and that is a gift, a gift you still possess. And some of those boys were pretty broken, but you were able to look them in the eyes and not focus on their injuries. We need you, Chrissy, the patients love you, they have been asking about you on a daily basis. Martin adores you, Chrissy! You are not just an employee, you are part of our family.'

Chrissy was overcome with emotion – all that worrying about not being good enough, about being superfluous to requirements vanished in an instant.

'I have just one question, well, two actually. Where is Alice and can I see her? And where is my boy, Rex?'

'Mima has taken Alice out for a walk. They will be back soon, and, just between you and me, I think there may be a touch of romance in the air!'

She touched her nose conspiratorially.

'We had a visit the other week, a physiotherapist from Kilmarnock Infirmary, Donald Lochlon. I'd say he is about the same age as Mima; they just seemed to hit it off. I wouldn't be surprised if they start to see each other socially.'

'Really? I hope so, she certainly deserves some happiness in her life. She has spent her whole adult life looking after others.'

'So have you, Chrissy.'

'Aye, but until recently it was only family ... I don't mean *only* but...'

'I know what you mean. Anyway, Rex is next door lying on the rug pretending to help Martin with his homework.'

'How is Martin? Does he talk about his parents at all?'

'Occasionally, but I think Rex knows much more than he lets on. He has been an absolute blessing! I hate to think how Martin would be without him.'

'He is a special wee dog, no doubt about that. Can I go through to see them?'

'Of course you can, you know the way. I'll make some tea.'

'Hello, boys!'

Rex ran to her side and jumped up with excitement. His tail was wagging so hard that a newspaper sitting on a table by the fireplace flapped in the breeze. He licked Chrissy's hands and let out doggy squeals of delight.

Martin also jumped up off the floor.

'Chrissy! I'm so happy to see you, you've been away for ages! I don't like people going away!' He said and then hugged her. 'Why, if I had a tail like Rex, I'd wag it too!' he laughed.

'Well, this is the best welcome home ever! I thought you might have forgotten who I am.'

Rex cocked his head to the side as if to say, *That's the daftest thing I ever heard.*

'Chrissy, I could never forget you! I'm glad you got my letters and I loved receiving yours in the post.'

'Let me get my breath back.' She sat down on the sofa. 'Pass me my bag, please, Martin, there just might be something in there that will interest you and Rex.'

Chrissy loved this room: two wing-backed blue armchairs sat either side of the large fireplace and a standard lamp stood to attention behind each chair, modelling matching floral, fringed lampshades.

A small wooden table sat beside each chair. Vera's reading glasses lay on one and there was an ashtray on the other. The velvet curtains in the bay window were also blue, but a much darker, richer shade than the chairs.

Soft, squishy floral cushions were dotted here and there, and cream-coloured antimacassars lay over the back of the chairs and sofa. Two additional windows were situated opposite each other allowing light to flood in, giving the whole room a bright, airy feel. The mirror above the fireplace reflected the large painting that was hanging on the back wall. There were several other oil paintings on the walls, and the wireless set had a table of its own next to the fireplace. The mantlepiece displayed a chiming clock, photograph frames and two gleaming brass candlesticks. The whole room exuded classic comfort.

Rex was already sniffing her bag, one paw up, one paw down so fast it looked like he was dancing. His brown eyes stared at the bag as if he was hoping to see right through it to the contents.

'I have a wee treat for you, Martin, but only if Aunt Vera says you can have it now. Promise you will keep it until after *Children's Hour* if she says no?'

'I promise!' he replied earnestly.

Chrissy pulled out a copy of *The Beano*, a brown paper package with string tied around it and a paper bag.

'Thank you, Chrissy, I love *The Beano*! Can I open the parcel now?'

'Of course you can, just be careful with it.'

Martin untied the knot in the string and carefully unravelled it, wrapping it around his fingers just like his aunt Vera did before she popped it into her "everything" drawer in the kitchen.

Inside the brown paper that he folded and set aside was a thick layer of newspaper. He tore it off to find a handmade wooden spitfire. His eyebrows shot up and his mouth gaped open. He held it aloft turning it this way and that.

'It's perfect, Chrissy! Wait until the boys at school see this!' He made the aircraft fly by running around the room, making growling aeroplane noises.

'The propeller moves, look Aunt Vera!' he squealed as she came into the room with a tea tray.

'Oh, my goodness, so it does! It's wonderful, you're very fortunate to receive a gift like this!'

*

'Katie's man, Alan, made it. I think it made the nights pass quicker when he was stuck in listening to two blethering women!' She laughed.

'Chrissy, will you give me your son-in-law's address, please? I want to write and thank him.'

'Of course I will. Now, how about this one?'

She passed the paper bag into his now outstretched hand.

Whimpering with self-pity, Rex was reaching out a paw to anyone who would take it. He sat and begged, trying hard to be noticed.

'Yours is coming, boy, have patience.' Chrissy waved her index finger at him after which he lay down and groaned the loudest doggy groan, making everyone laugh.

Martin opened the paper bag to reveal a bar of chocolate. He almost dropped it in surprise. He was speechless.

'My goodness, Chrissy, where did that come from?' Vera cried out in surprise.

'Alan had some GIs on his bus. They even gave him a pair of stockings for Katie. she can't wait to get her plaster cast off so that she can wear them. They asked Alan for directions to where they were staying and once they reached Ardrossan, because it was his last run of the night, he took them right to the doorstep. They were very grateful and thanked him with some gifts. I even brought home a tin of fruit for Mum and Bob, plus a tin of spam.'

'Well, one good turn deserves another. Mima made a batch of jam tarts this afternoon. I'll give you some to take home with you.'

Thank you, Vera!'

'Now, young Rex, I think this is what you have been waiting for!'

Chrissy reached into her bag once more and brought out a bone that had seen better days.

'Katie was making some bone broth; I saved the bone knowing that this young man would love it.'

Rex was now focusing all his energy on the bone; he sat completely still and fixed it with a stare.

'It's for outside, mind.' Chrissy stood up and walked towards the back door with Rex glued to her heels.

'Here you go.' She popped it between his tiny teeth and playfully pushed him outside. He did not take much persuasion, and bounced down the steps like a rabbit and then trotted down the garden with his new prized possession held firmly in his mouth.

CHAPTER FORTY

Vera, 1944

'Martin, can you help me, please? Uncle Charles is coming home today; I want everything to be just right.'

'It will be, Aunt Vera. Aunt Mima left me a list before she went shopping, and Chrissy will be here soon. What do you want me to do? I can look after Alice for you.'

Vera smiled; she loved how Martin looked after Alice. He talked to her, he even read her stories. She was much too young to understand, but she seemed to lap them up and react appropriately with a gurgle here and a wave of the hand there.

Chrissy had been delighted when he began to read *Anne of Green Gables* to her, and, if truth be told, she loved to stand behind the door and listen. She was almost word perfect – she had read that book so many times, it was etched into her being, and knowing that a brand-new generation was being introduced to it filled her with joy, even though baby Alice would not remember a word.

Mima came in the back door, her basket looking pitifully empty.

Vera could immediately tell by her face that the shopping trip had not been successful.

'The Co-op butcher had some skirt of beef, and I did buy liver.' They grimaced in unison.

'Will you tell Charles, or shall I?'

'The store had no soap, no tins of corned beef, but I did buy a tin of peaches and some dried egg. Still no cotton thread in the drapery, I'm afraid. And last but not least, there were no cigarettes!'

'Quite the homecoming! Sorry, dear, you have no cigarettes, but just to make up for it have some liver ... he may well tell me to put it in my pipe and smoke it!'

'Did you manage to make the pie, Chrissy?'

'I did, and no, before you ask, Martin still has no clue where the rabbits come from.'

Vera sighed. 'He's not a stupid boy. He is probably just humouring us, bless him.'

'Probably but let's not worry about that now.'

'Charles will want to look at his surgery. He'll want to sit at his desk if I know him, just to convince himself that nothing has changed without his approval.'

*

'It's spick and span, Vera,' said Mima. 'I've put a small vase of flowers from the garden on his desk. The fire is ready to light if he wants it; we are short of coal, or I would have gone ahead and started it. All the instruments are spotless, and we are as stocked up as supplies will allow. How long will the locum be staying?'

'Just a few days to handover; he is needed elsewhere. It's not ideal, but better than nothing. Needless to say our trip to Arran has been cancelled, plus, there have been a few developments with a number of his patients. He will need to familiarise himself with all the changes.'

'Thank you, Chrissy, and thank you too, Mima. I know you were planning to go home so I truly appreciate you staying on to help out.'

'Not a problem, Vera, so long as you don't mind Donald popping in later this week?'

'Not at all, he may be able to give Charles some exercises to strengthen his muscles. He's going to be weak for a while yet.' Vera smiled

'I'm sure he would be more than happy to help in any way he can. He is such a lovely man; he's been on his own for several years now since his wife died. We enjoy each other's company. He is so easy to talk to, I feel like I've known him all my life. I've even told him about Lizzy.'

'I am so pleased for you, Mima. How is Lizzy? You haven't mentioned her for a while.'

'Not good, not good at all; she is skin and bone, she has a chest infection, they are querying pneumonia, and she is confined to bed. Truth be told, I don't think it will be too long before she passes away. Is it wicked for me to think it will be a blessing? She has had a hellish life. I wouldn't wish what she has gone through on my worst enemy.'

'It's not wicked, it is understandable that you might feel that way. Remember some of those boys we looked after in the Dick Institute, the pain they were in? The day and night terrors, the quivering, staggering, crying in the night. Physical scars can be seen and invite sympathy most of the time, but mental scars can mean that people are misunderstood. They can be ostracised if people don't understand. Many don't know how to react. We saw it with our own eyes when families came to visit. But you have done your best, Mima.'

Mima smiled and glanced over towards Chrissy.

'I'll stay for as long as you need me, Chrissy, no longer.'

'That might be a longer than you think, thank you Mima.' Chrissy understood what Mima was saying and was deeply grateful.

A loud whimpering noise coming from the room next door stopped the conversation. Rex appeared at the door and ran out again as if beckoning the assembled women to follow him.

Vera was first to arrive in the front room; Martin was on his knees in front of the fire, tying newspaper knots for kindling. He was holding one sheet between his two trembling hands.

Kneeling down beside him, Vera put her arm around his shoulder; she noticed that he was white as a sheet.

*

'Look, Aunt Vera!' Pools of unshed tears lay dormant in his eyes, just waiting for the order to escape.

He held out his trembling hand and gave her the sheet of newspaper. At first Vera thought it was the headline about the V1 bombs being used against Londoners, but beneath that she read:

'"Extraordinary Discovery: Shipwreck Survivors Found Alive in America

Twenty-one survivors from a passenger ship, the SS Star of Cardastria, long believed lost with all souls aboard, have been discovered in the United States. The vessel, which vanished after a reported U-boat attack in 1941, was presumed to have sunk with no survivors. However, reports have revealed that a small group managed to escape and were rescued by a merchant vessel..."'

'Wasn't that the name of Mum and Dad's ship?'

Vera helped him to his feet and led him over to the sofa.

'Yes, it was, Martin! Uncle Charles knows about this report. While he has been in hospital, he has written to several people who may know if your mum and dad were amongst the survivors. We didn't want to say anything until we found out more. Uncle Charles is still waiting for some replies to his letters, and a friend of his has made a few telephone calls. It's all a bit muddled right now – mail is taking a long time to cross the Atlantic and there have been so many developments recently that have added to the chaos of it all.'

Mima came in with a glass of rosehip syrup and handed it to Martin who gulped it down, causing him to choke and splutter. He blew his nose before asking huskily, 'When will we find out?' Fat wet tears, defying orders, trickled slowly down his pale cheeks.

'I really don't know, Martin, but Uncle Charles has left no stone unturned. If they did survive, we will find them, you must believe that.'

'I do believe that. I ...' He hesitated. 'I talk to Rex about it all. He really listens. He turns his little head to one side and I know he's really listening to what I am saying. He puts a paw on my hand as if to say, *It will be alright, Martin.* I know it sounds silly, but I believe him too.'

'Not silly at all!' Vera pulled the boy into her arms and hugged him tightly while she stroked his soft hair.

'Martin, you are such a brave boy! I want you to know that Uncle Charles and I are so proud of you. Chrissy and Mima love you too. You are so precious to us! You are Alice's big brother – remember that no matter what happens. You are and always will be, and yes, it will all work out in the end. I know it will.'

CHAPTER FORTY-ONE

Chrissy, 1944

Her home was just as she remembered it. Chrissy wasn't sure what she had been expecting, but finding everything in order and in its place was a comfort and a relief. She knew she had her mother to thank for most of it. Bob was a good, kind and hardworking man, but housekeeping was not in his repertoire.

Being back at home filled her with a warm fuzzy feeling somehow, and she could not explain it. She knew deep in her heart that Jack was close by. This brought her so much comfort it made her cry, but with happy tears, something she could not have envisioned even a few short months ago.

They had received a letter from John. He was safe and well, at least that is what he said. She knew that mail was censored, but she chose to believe that what he said was true.

She had written to him telling him that he was going to be an uncle, that she was training to be an auxiliary nurse, that his dad was doing well, and that Maggie was as strong and stubborn as an ox as usual. She tried to keep the news as upbeat as possible. She mentioned Rex and how he was helping Martin, and told him that Dr Durnie was recovering well. Knowing that the letter would be vetted made her curb her enthusiasm for telling him all the village news. 'You just never know,' she had said to |Bob, 'I can't afford to let anything slip. Who knows who will read his letters before he gets them?'

Just knowing he was alive was enough; her boy was alive and for that she was truly thankful.

Chrissy thought that her mother had lost weight; she was also very pale. The sparkle in her eye was lacklustre, and there had been no comical quips about her return.

Chrissy could tell that her mother was anxious to appear as normal as possible, but she refused to be drawn into the picture that was being painted for her.

'How have you been, Mum?'

'Oh, you know me, hen, I'm fine. I've got a lot of damage to do yet,' she quipped.

'Mum, tell me the truth – how are you really? I need to know.'

'I'm fine, Chrissy, really fine.'

'Right-o, Mum, the *really* has convinced me otherwise.'

'My heart has been playing up a bit. I've been a bit more breathless, but that's nothing new, is it?'

'No, but there is something else you aren't telling me, I know it!'

'Let's just say ...'

'Let's just say nothing, Mum, tell me the truth!'

'I saw a specialist while you were away. He says I have heart failure. My heart can't pump blood fast enough or something, and that's why I am out of breath and tired all the time, and that's why my ankles are so swollen.'

'Why didn't you write and tell me?'

'Chrissy, my pet lamb, you have had more than enough on your plate with work and Katie. They take priority over an old biddy like me.'

'Is that what you think? It's not true! You are and always will be a priority for me.'

'Chrissy, listen to me, I shouldn't be. You have Bob, Katie and John to think about – *they* are the future, especially that wee baba who is waiting to be born. I have had my day. I've known heartache, of course I have, but I have known joy, and I have known love, true love. Your dad and I were almost like one person. The minute I saw him I knew he was the one for me. How lucky am I? We spent so many happy years together, very happy years. I want you to know that and remember it. We didn't have a lot when it comes to material things, but we had the world and more when it came to feelings and love. I'm not scared to die, Chrissy.'

'Stop it, Mum, I don't want to hear it!'

*

'You are going to, hen; I want you to hear it. I am not scared to die, I have so many folks waiting for me: John, Jack and your dad. Why would I be scared of that, eh?'

'Oh, Mum, what will I do without you? I just can't imagine my life without you in it!'

'Chrissy, my pet lamb, you can, and you will, but for now, I'm going nowhere. Understand? Nowhere! Now, could I trouble you for a Horlicks before I turn in?'

*

'I've made you a cocoa, Bob, I've got Horlicks but I'm happy to swap.' Chrissy held both cups to her nose and sniffed and looked at the contents. 'They are both wishy-washy but at least they are hot.'

'I don't mind, you choose.'

'I had a chat with Mum earlier. Did you know she had been to see a specialist?'

'Yes, I did, guilty as charged, but I agreed with her, there was no need to worry you about it when you were looking after Katie.'

'I'd rather have known. I should have been with her for the appointment. We had a frank talk, I even told her I loved her, and she said she loved me.'

'My, that was a frank chat! It's not often we talk like that in this hoose! How do you feel?'

'I feel that I need to accept what has been laid out for me. As they say, *What's for ye, will not go by ye.* I firmly believe that is true, I really do. When Jack died, I couldn't accept it; I thought we were being punished, for what I just don't know, but I realise that we are dealt cards in life and we need to play them to the best of our ability, no matter what they are, no matter how difficult. We deal with what we are dealt.'

'I think you are right, Chrissy love, we do.'

'When will this bloody war end, Bob? When will our boy come home?

When will things get back to normal?'

'Oh hen, what is normal? Can you even remember? We need to carve out a new normal when this war ends. We can't look back, Chrissy, we need to look forward, because if we don't, we will go mad. I believe there are many things to look forward to, and you need to believe that too.'

'Our parents believed that there was a lot to look forward to. The war to end all wars, they were told, and yet here we are ... twenty-one years the peace lasted.'

'I ken. I think about that tae, but we need to believe that we are fighting for something better than what old Adolf has in store for us. What else is there, Chrissy?'

CHAPTER FORTY-TWO

Vera, 1944

'Martin, are you asleep?'

'No, Aunt Vera, I'm still awake.'

'May I come in?'

'Yes, Rex is here, beside my bed, don't tread on him.'

'I won't. Come on, Rex.' She patted on the bedclothes to invite the little dog up onto the bed.

Rex hopped up without hesitation making Vera smile; she had suspected that he slept on the bed, curled into Martin. After what the boy had come through, was still going through, how could she deny him his best friend's cuddles at bedtime?

'Aunt Vera, can I ask you something?'

'Of course, Martin, anything.'

'Am I bad for thinking that I would rather be here with you, Uncle Charles, Chrissy, Mima and Rex? I want Mum and Dad to be alive, of course I do, but I hardly saw them, they were both so busy. I felt lonely, even at boarding school. I just didn't fit in. I have friends here, I love this house, I love you and Uncle Charles, but I especially love Rex. He is my best friend in the whole world.'

'Darling, Martin, no, you are not bad. You have had so much to deal with for a little boy, it would be a lot even for an adult. You have been so brave, and we are very proud of you. There have been so many changes in your world, but you mustn't doubt that your parents love you very much. They sent you here to us to keep you safe. London was almost razed to the ground, the bombing was incessant, night after night. The people there have been very brave too. Your parents sent you here because they love you so much.'

'I know that, Aunt Vera, but I love it here. I love the garden, the chickens, my friends and this boy here.' He clutched the little dog so hard that he groaned like a teddy bear.

'If they have survived, will that mean I need to go back to London?'

'I think so, Martin, if that is where your parents will be living. Surely you want to be with them?'

'I thought I did, but I feel so happy here. I would like to stay here with you. I love Alice, she is so cute, and I think she likes me too.'

'She loves you too, Martin, she is little, but you have been like a big brother to her, and she really does love you. As I told you, you will always be her big brother no matter what happens.'

'What if Mum and Dad come back and I want to stay here, what happens then?'

'It's late, young man. We will cross that bridge if and when we need to. Rex is trying so hard to sleep, so we need to stop chattering now. We can talk again in the morning. Now, cuddle in and keep each other warm.'

'We will, Aunt Vera. I love you.'

'And I love you, Martin. Things will work out for the best in the end, I'm sure of it. Good night, sweet boy.'

As Vera closed Martin's bedroom door, she could not stop the tears welling in her eyes. She truly loved the boy; he was like the son she had never had. What had been an almost empty house was now a home full of love. Alice and Martin adored each other. Chrissy was almost part of the fixtures and fittings now; it was as if she had always been there, and Mima, although she would be venturing to pastures new, she would always be a welcome visitor, and Donald, too, no doubt.

The house had become a home, and there was not one member of it that Vera could imagine living without.

*

'That's it, you are going to see Dr Durnie!'

'Chrissy, the poor man is barely out of hospital himself! I'm not going to bother him with my troubles.'

'They are not troubles, Mum! You could hardly breathe when you got upstairs. It's his job, and he would hate to think that you weren't being honest with him.'

'Chrissy, listen to me, I will not go to see the doctor, but what I would like to do is get on a bus and go to visit my granddaughter before she gives birth and mayhem begins.'

'Really? That's what you want to do? I will try to arrange a day off, but now that Mima has gone it's a bit more difficult. But it's not unsurmountable.'

'Woo, get my daughter and her big fancy words!'

'Mum, stop this! Let me see what I can arrange.'

'Why do you need to come with me? Can't I go to visit my only granddaughter on my own?'

'On your own?' Chrissy was incredulous.

'Yes, Chrissy, my pet lamb, on my own.'

'Are you sure you are up to it, I mean...?'

'Chrissy, I get on a bus at the bottom of the street, I get off at the bottom of Katie's street, where either she or Alan will meet me. How hard can it be?'

'Fine, I will write to her and make arrangements.'

'Too late, that's already been done. I'm catching the bus tomorrow; do you have anything you want me to take to her?'

Open-mouthed, Chrissy stared at her mother. she wasn't sure how to react, but then suddenly she laughed.

'You win, Mum, you always do. You have always known what is best for me ... for us. I will look in the pantry and see what I can send. Don't stay too long, though, Bob will miss his cooked lunches.'

*

'Grannie, let me help you with your bag.'

'You will do no such thing. I can manage – you need to look after that great-grandchild of mine, lassie.'

'Whatever you say, Grannie. Come on, it's not far. It's pretty basic, you know. I hope you aren't expecting too much?'

'Katie, compared with what your grandpa and me started off with I'm sure it will be a wee palace, and so long as it's filled with love, who cares?'

'It certainly *is* full of love. Alan is really looking forward to your visit. I've told him lots about you.'

'Uh oh, I'm not sure if I like the sound of that.'

'Don't worry, it's mostly about your baking and cooking ... he can't wait!'

'No pressure then, hen!' Maggie laughed out loud.

'You will love getting to know his mum better. She has been so good to us.'

'Lead on, McDuff, I can't wait!'

'We are almost there. There it is, this wee one at the end of the terrace. We even have a wee garden at the front and a slightly bigger one at the back. Alan has been growing leeks, potatoes and carrots. They're a bit on the small side, but he is so proud of them. What do you think of the curtains, Grannie? I made them myself – can you believe that?'

Maggie looked at the gleaming windows crisscrossed with tape as per ARP regulations, but she could just see the dainty floral fabric hanging on either side.

'My, they're braw, lassie! Perfect for those windows.'

'They used to be an old dress belonging to Alan's grannie.'

'Wait a minute, I get it now! While I'm here, you'll be rummaging through my things and turning them into cushions or lampshades, I expect!'

'Oh Grannie, you are daft! Of course I won't!' Katie was chuckling as she opened the green wooden gate leading to the narrow path and the matching green-painted front door.

They were both panting now.

'I can smell the sea; hopefully we will manage a walk or two along the shore, it will be just the thing to blow away my country cobwebs and fill ma lungs with briny fresh air. Mind you, ah ken Ardeer isnae far away. I hope they behave themselves in there.'

Katie opened the door with a loud, 'Tarrah! Let's get in and get you a seat. Put your bag there for now.' Katie pointed to a space beside an armchair.

'Can I have a wee glass of water, hen, just to help me get my breath back?' Maggie flopped into the chair with a grunt.

'Coming right up.' Katie walked into the small scullery. She still had a slight limp, emphasised by her growing girth.

'Here you go.' She handed the glass to her gran and then she too flopped into the chair opposite.

'I'll be glad when he or she decides to show their face. Alan needs to tie my shoelaces for me, and as for swollen ankles ... I don't need to tell you about that, though, as you've done this four times. I reckon once will be enough for me, I'm so tired all the time.'

'Ah, but Katie, look at what you get at the end, a little baba, a little bundle of joy that will capture heart as soon as you lock eyes. Your heart will swell a lot more than your ankles – it will swell with pure, unconditional love that will last your whole lifetime.'

'Sorry, Grannie, I can cry at the drop of a hat these days.' Tears welled in Katie's eyes and she dabbed at them with her hankie.

'Do you still think of James and John?'

'Only every day, lass. I wonder what they would be doing now if they had survived. Would John be married, would I have lots more grandchildren, where would they be living? War is so cruel, so very cruel; look at your uncle Billy, he was one of the lucky ones in more ways than most. Aye, he lost an arm, a leg and an eye, but he has carved out a life for himself. He still works at the hospital, yet he could so easily have gone under, so to speak, but he climbed out of the dark hole he was in, and he makes me proud every single day. His wife is a lovely girl. I hope she makes it up here sometime, maybe when the war is over and she's not so busy. She has been working with a chap called Archie McIndoe. Apparently, he is another brilliant plastic surgeon. Their patients are mostly RAF boys who have been badly burned after their planes have been hit. She will be home again soon, though. Billy has had to get used to fending for himself for a few weeks, bless him. Now, I need to spend a penny, so point me in the right direction.'

'It's out the back, Grannie, no fancy indoor toilet here, and, I hate to tell you, there's no Izal left but there are plenty of newspaper squares.'

'I've had outdoor privies for more years than I've had an indoor one. More hygienic if you ask me. When I was a wean, we had nothing more than a hole in the ground with a wooden seat over it, wooden walls and a bit of a ceiling. When it was full up, ma dad would dig another hole, and we would move the walls etc, lock, stock and barrel. Later on, we used a bucket under the seat, and you lifted a handle that released a measure of earth into it when you had done your business. That had to be emptied, of course.'

Katie wrinkled up her nose. 'I don't feel so bad now; at least we have a flushing toilet, Grannie.' She grinned.

'It's just over there. I'll put the kettle on ready for when you get back. I don't suppose you brought any goodies, did you? My sweet tooth has almost given up hope of ever being fed again!'

'What a question! Open ma bag and right on top you will find ma special tin. We had a bit of a whip round. I baked, your mum did too, and Mrs Durnie gave us a jar of jam and two eggs! As if I would come empty-handed! War or no war, I will always find a way to bake.'

*

'Sorry it's a tiny room, Grannie. Mum made herself comfortable in it, though. It's warm, so you should be quite comfy.'

'Katie, stop fussing, I'll be fine. I'll get unpacked, come down and let you read a letter from your uncle Billy. His stepson and his wife have just had a baby son. Billy is just like the cat that got the cream… and Katie …' she called out as her granddaughter was leaving the room, '… I so proud of you too, lass. You have made this into a cosy wee palace! Well done, hen.'

'We have had lots of help, a chair here, a table there, some dishes and cutlery, but thanks, Grannie, that means a lot!' She beamed from ear to ear. 'I'll need to get dinner on soon. Alan is hoping to finish on time tonight to entertain his guest of honour.'

'I'll be down in just a minute to give you a hand.'

She is so happy, so hopeful. I pray that this will be the last war she will ever witness and that she will be spared what her mum and I have gone through, Maggie thought as she unpacked.

CHAPTER FORTY-THREE

Vera, 1944

'It is so good to be home, my darling girl. I have missed you so very much. I can't believe I will be sleeping in my own bed tonight beside my lovely wife.'

'Well, you will believe it when Alice starts howling with colic. It's been going on for a few nights now.'

'I'll soon sort that out. I might have just the thing, and anyway I will be happy to take my turn at pacing the floor at last. How is Martin? He should be home from school anytime now, shouldn't he?'

'Yes, and I know he is anxious to talk to you about his parents. I've explained that it is so difficult communications-wise right now, and he understands that, but I'm sure he thinks there is something I haven't told him.'

'I wish I did have some news; the truth is that we may not hear anything until the war is over. I suspect that my brother's reason for travelling on that ship may have more to do with it, but I will probably never find out, you know, with the Official Secrets Act. I always suspected he was more than a run of the mill civil servant.'

'I'm sure if you sit down and explain it all to him in simple terminology, he will understand. He is a clever boy, and has even mentioned that he would like to be a doctor. He has a kind and empathetic heart. I think he would make a good doctor, just like his uncle Charles.'

Vera kissed her husband's cheek.

'If he does go down that road, things will be very different for him. With luck, we will have a comprehensive, free health service funded by taxation, of course. Imagine ...access to treatment won't depend on whether a person can pay or not. It will be my dream come true, Vera, medical and surgical treatments available to everyone, rich or poor!'

His eyes were sparkling and he had the widest grin on his face.

'Can you imagine it, Vera, well actually, I don't think we need to imagine, I think it *will* happen! What a momentous thing to witness in our lifetime.'

'I hope you are right, Charles; it would be life-changing for most people if it does happen.'

'Look at this headline.'

Vera stood behind him, reading over his shoulder.

"Plans for a comprehensive, free, and universal health service for all citizens from birth to death – will it make your job harder or easier?"

'It will make it different. I know a lot of my colleagues still have deep concerns. There is a lot to be discussed and mulled over, but I truly believe as a doctor who genuinely wants to help people that it simply *must* happen.'

Rex, who had been lying at Charles's feet, sprung up and started to wag his tail furiously. Jumping from one paw to another in his unique doggy dance, he stared at the door.

'I think your nephew has come home from school judging by this young man's reaction!'

The door swung open and Martin breezed in.

'Uncle Charles, I've missed you! Why wouldn't they let me come to visit you?'

'Hey, I don't make the rules, and the nurses and ward sisters, well, what can I say about them? They rule those wards with a rod of iron – tyrants, they are!'

'Enough of that, thank you, or I'll tell Mima, and then where will you be?'

'Probably being force-fed with liver. Please don't tell her, I take it all back! Nurses are angels with lamps, or something like that.'

'Right, young man, before you go out to play in your den with Rex, homework. You will need to work hard if you want to be a doctor, you know. Go and sit at the kitchen table. I'll bring you a glass of milk and an apple.'

*

'Right-o. Has Rex dug up that smelly bone again? He digs it up and then buries it again in a different place. I keep telling him I don't want it, but he seems to think that it is the most precious thing in the world and that he needs to hide it from everyone!'

'As long as he doesn't bring it in here, I don't care. The last thing Alice needs is a bone landing on her while she is kicking on the rug.'

'She loves Rex too, Aunt Vera, her eyes follow him wherever he goes, and she kicks really hard and squeals when she watches him. I'm so glad that Mrs Ramsay doesn't mind sharing him.'

Martin got up and walked towards the door.

'Can I have a chat with you later, Uncle Charles?'

'Of course you can! Let's get homework, dinner and *Children's Hour* over first. I will tuck you in tonight and we can have a chat then ... deal?'

'Deal!' And he skipped out into the hall and through to the kitchen.

'I love that boy, Charles. He is so sweet and kind, and he loves Alice. I suppose never having a sibling of his own he feels protective of her, just like a big brother. He even reads to her! That said, when it comes to nappy changing time, he beats a hasty retreat!'

'I can't say I blame him for that,' Charles grimaced. 'Now, I am going through to my surgery to catch up with some paperwork. I'll be flying solo again soon; I want to be ready!'

'Speaking of which, do you think Chrissy is ready to deal with some of the more minor injuries on her own? She is very sensible, but not overly cautious. She knows when to ask for advice or assistance.'

'You have a better understanding of what she is capable of than I do, so if you think she is ready, then I do too. What does Chrissy say about it?'

'I think what worries her most is how the patients will take it. This is a small village, they all know her, and they may not take kindly to her seeing them on her own.'

'Let's cross that bridge when we come to it. Given that being seen by her is considerably less expensive than seeing me for minor ailments, they may welcome her with open arms. Only time will tell.'

CHAPTER FORTY-FOUR

Chrissy, 1944

'Dr Durnie's surgery, how can I help you?'

'Is that Mrs Durnie?'

'Speaking. Who's calling?'

'I'm Mrs Ramsay's son-in-law, Alan. May I speak to you for a moment?'

'Yes, of course, is anything the matter?'

'Well, yes and no, I don't have much change, so I will need to make this quick. Katie, my wife, has gone into labour three weeks early. Her grannie, Mrs Barnes, has become more and more breathless. I think all the excitement got to her. Can you let Chrissy know, please?'

'I will do, right away, but try not to worry...'

The line went dead.

Vera ran to the kitchen; Chrissy was nowhere to be seen.

'Mima, have you seen Chrissy recently?'

'She's in the surgery, there's quite a queue out there. A few boys were fishing for eels and minnows when part of the bank gave way; a couple of them have deep cuts, and they will need stitches. Chrissy will be helping to reassure them or will be holding them down, one of the two. It has caused quite a backlog. Is something wrong?'

'Yes and no. Her grandchild has decided that it's time to make an appearance, and her mother isn't coping too well.'

'Oh dear, I'll go and relieve her. I'm sure she will want to be with Katie. Don't worry, Vera, I'm happy to help.'

Mima made her way through the door to the surgery while Vera went to the kitchen to gather a few things for Chrissy to take with her. She had a bag of clothes that Alice had outgrown already and there was a new batch of bramble jelly in the pantry. She picked up a jar and a jar of rhubarb and ginger as well, and added them to the bag just as Chrissy rushed into the room like a whirlwind, her cheeks flushed. She couldn't keep still.

'I wouldn't normally ask for time off, but when I heard Mum is breathless, I thought ... Oh, Alan must be so concerned and Katie won't be able to cope with labour, a new baby and a sick grannie ... I'm not sure what the plan will be, but I'm sure I will think of one on the way there. I'll run to the house now, leave a note for Bob and catch the next bus. I'm really sorry!'

'Go, go, go Chrissy, no need to apologise, take this bag with you! People were so kind to me when Alice was born. I received many hand-knitted clothes and other bits and pieces. I meant to give them to you a few weeks ago. I'm glad they're going to a good home.'

'You are too kind, Vera.' Without thinking, Chrissy hugged her and kissed her cheek. 'I can't tell you the difference you have made to my life.'

And she ran home to leave a note, then caught the bus to Ardrossan.

*

'Mum, I'm so glad you are here!' Katie was pacing around the living room in her nightdress and slippers. 'The midwife has been in, she says she will come back in an hour. The heartbeat is strong, and everything seems to be...'

Katie was stopped mid-sentence by another contraction.

'Whew, that was a bad one! Alan has told his mum, and she will come over as soon as she can. That was a stroke of genius when he thought to telephone Dr Durnie to get a message to you. The poor man has been like a headless chicken. Grannie has been great, but then she became very breathless. I've managed to convince her I'm fine, so she has gone for a lie down. Now she knows you're here, she will relax a bit, so will I for that matter. It's been six hours now, and still nothing, but the pains are coming quicker and the pain is much worse. I'm not sure how much more I can take. How long were you in labour with me?'

'You don't want to know that ...' Chrissy smiled sympathetically.

Katie groaned and held on to the back of the chair. This time she let out a yell and Chrissy had to remind her to breathe. Beads of sweat appeared on her brow; she was panting and tried to stand up again but couldn't.

'That was a bad one, Mum. I want to stand, but maybe it would be better if I sit. I just don't know what to do with myself. I hope the midwife comes soon. The nearest telephone box is about two hundred yards down the road, just in case we need to call her again ...out the door, first turn on the left.'

'I think you should sit down for a wee while, hen, before you fall down. You're as white as a sheet. I'll fetch you a glass of water.'

'What's all this noise aboot?' Maggie winked at Katie. 'You are going to be just fine, my pet lamb; it won't be long now.'

Chrissy flashed her mother a warning stare.

'It will take as long as it takes, Mum.'

Maggie frowned at her daughter, and shook her head, willing her to keep quiet; the girl needed encouragement, not misgivings at this moment in time.

Katie slowly lowered herself back into the chair then screamed in pain.

'I need to push, Mum, Gran, I need to push!' Her voice was weak and she was drenched in sweat. Chrissy could feel the panic rising. What should she do?'

Maggie was eerily quiet and calm. Chrissy had never seen her mother like this before.

'Chrissy, go and boil the kettle, fetch some old newspapers and as many towels as you can find. Katie, lass, have you got any string?'

Katie managed to answer once her contraction ended.

'In the kitchen, the drawer next to the sink beside the scissors.'

'Perfect, lass. Chrissy, bring the scissors and string too. Put the scissors in a cup of boiling water.'

'Grannie, what's happening? I can't stand it anymore! The pain! I'm so dizzy too!'

'You can and you will, Katie, but you must listen to what I am telling you and do as I say, do you hear?'

'Yeeeeeesssss! Oh, please help me!' The plea was heartfelt and the scream came from somewhere deep inside. Katie was terrified; being in labour was much worse than she could ever have imagined.

None of them heard Alan come into the room. Maggie took charge.

'Perfect timing, Alan son. Go and call for the midwife and the doctor, tell them to come right away.'

Before she had finished the sentence, Alan was halfway out the door.

'Sit right on the edge and hold your knees up with your arms, Katie, that's it. I can see baby's head, lovely dark hair, lass, now listen to me, when you feel the need to push with your next contraction, don't. It will be hard, but it is important. I can see that the cord is around the baba's neck. I need to slip it over to release it.'

Chrissy stood open-mouthed, her arms full of towels and newspapers.

'Quickly, Chrissy, put a pile of paper on the floor here, and put a towel on top. Keep a couple of towels to wrap the baba in. Bring the string and scissors and put them where I can reach them.'

Maggie expertly slipped the cord over the baby's head just before the next contraction came.

'Katie, remember what I said: just pant, pant, pant.' Maggie began panting to demonstrate what she needed her granddaughter to do while she controlled the speed of the head crowning.

'That's it, lass, the head is born.'

Katie gasped and nodded, unable to speak. She groaned loudly and pushed with all her might. The baby's little body slithered into Maggie's waiting arms along with a rush of deeply blood-stained fluid.

'Katie, you have a little lassie. She looks perfect!'

Maggie quickly wrapped the new-born in the towels after she skilfully tied the cord twice before cutting it between the two pieces of string. She handed the baby to an ashen-faced Chrissy just as Alan burst through the door. He couldn't believe what he was seeing.

'Alan, son, help Katie to support the weight of her legs. She's tired now, but there's still work to be done.'

Alan immediately did as he was told.

'Katie, you need to stay like that until the afterbirth comes, lass. With your next contraction, push again.'

Maggie noticed a steady trickle of blood. Katie hadn't torn, but this amount of bleeding was concerning her deeply.

After what seemed like an age, there was still no sign of the placenta.

'Alan, go to the door and see if there is any sign of the midwife.'

Alan, feeling faint, was glad of the excuse to leave and get some air. He quickly did as he was told once again.

Maggie knew she was out of her depth now. As a young girl, she had helped her father and grandfather with lambing; she had often seen them untangle cords from necks, and as a young woman she had often been called upon to help neighbours who were in labour. She was amazed that so many things had come back to her, but this bleeding and the non-appearance of the afterbirth was worrying her a lot.

'The midwife is here; she's just parking her bicycle.'

Maggie closed her eyes and thanked God. The door opened.

'Hello, Katie. I'm Sister Christie. Just give me a minute to take off my coat and I will be right with you'

Sister Christie got onto her knees and examined Katie who was still bleeding.

'You have a retained placenta, Katie. That means the afterbirth hasn't been delivered. I'm going to give you an injection to help expel but it in the meantime will someone call for the flying squad. Tell them we have a retained placenta with potential haemorrhaging, quickly, please.'

Once again, Alan was hot-footing it to the telephone box after searching for a handful of change.

Chrissy felt sick to her stomach as she cradled her baby granddaughter in her arms. She watched as the midwife tried to control the bleeding. Her baby girl, her Katie, was struggling to breathe. What should have been one of the happiest days of her life was turning into a nightmare. Her thoughts turned to her mother – the way she had handled the whole thing had been amazing, Chrissy had had no idea that her mother was capable of such a thing. How did she know what to do? How would she have coped if her mother hadn't been there? It didn't bear thinking about; she knew that she had frozen, she had felt incapable of doing anything useful. What if her mother hadn't been there? Guilt settled heavily on her shoulders, weighing her down with a mixture of gratitude and despair. She gazed at the tiny human in her arms, so helpless and so positively perfect and she knew she would do anything for her. She had never felt so humble in her life. Or so grateful.

A knock at the door brought her back to the here and now. The "flying squad", a group comprising of an obstetrician, an anaesthetist and a midwife, rushed into the already crowded room,

'Mother's pulse is weak and thready; there is no sign of separation. The fundus is soft and there is more bleeding than I would expect after giving 1ml of syntometrine intramuscularly ten minutes ago,' Nurse Christy informed the obstetrician.

After a short examination and administering some pain relief, the doctor spoke to Alan.

'We need to get Katie to hospital as soon as possible. Baby will come too as we will need to examine her properly.'

Katie called out, 'I want to see my baby, please let me see her.'

'All in good time, Katie, we must make sure she is warm and safe. You are very weak, but you can hold her once we have settled you in at the hospital.'

'Can I go with her?' Alan asked.

'I'm afraid not, we only have facilities for mother and baby. Call the hospital tomorrow. Now, we must hurry.'

Maggie, Alan and Chrissy sat in the living room sipping tea and staring into space. Alan's mother had arrived in the middle of the furore and had wisely decided to go back home to wait for news.

'I'll go to the phone box later and call the hospital to find out what is happening. I won't be able to sleep otherwise.'

'Good idea, son. The best thing you can do is to get a good night's sleep. You will be more use to your two girls tomorrow that way. Why don't you go to the pub for a quick pint? You look like you need something stronger than tea.'

'If you think so ... All right, I will.' His furrowed brow and grim expression mirrored what they were all feeling.

When he had gone, Chrissy stared at her mother.

'I don't know how you did what you did today, Mum, but thank you. I was useless, I didn't know what to do. I froze! I was so scared.'

'Chrissy, my pet lamb, remember I have a wee bit of experience, and that kind of thing is like riding a bike, you never forget how to do it. Plus I am her grandmother, but you are her mother and that is a bond like no other. Please, never forget that.'

CHAPTER FORTY-FIVE

1944

Chrissy put on her uniform and set off to work half an hour early. She had assumed that Vera, and Mima if she was still there, would have questions about Katie and her new granddaughter and she wasn't wrong.

As soon as she walked into the kitchen, she was greeted with whoops of delight.

'Oh Chrissy, we were so worried! Bob came and told us the news and kept us up to date. What a worrying time for you! And what about your mother? Isn't she the star of the show, after baby Meggie of course?'

'I know! I couldn't believe it myself. I felt helpless.' Chrissy frowned. 'I don't know how we would have coped without Mum. Alan, too, he was in the right place at the right time. It was *me* who let everyone down.' Her lip trembled and her eyes began to fill with tears.

'Come and sit down here, Chrissy. You didn't let anyone down, you had your part to play, and you did it.' Vera handed her a cup of tea. 'Have you had any breakfast? What about some toast?'

'No thanks, I've eaten, but that's kind of you.' She began to sob. 'Oh Vera, all my old doubts came back to me! Would Jack have survived if I had done more for him, if I had noticed warning signs, if I had called for Dr Durnie earlier ...?'

'Chrissy, stop that now!' Vera's voice was unusually stern. 'We have been over this time and time again. Jack became very sick and very quickly. Everyone involved in his care did everything they could have done. Likewise, you went to be with Katie as soon as you got the news that she had gone into labour early.'

'But that's just it! I went because I was annoyed with my mother! I didn't want her to go and visit, you see. When I found out she was breathless, I assumed she was going to be a nuisance. I told myself that she was the last thing Katie needed. How wrong was I? My mother saved the day. I couldn't believe how calm she was. I had no idea she knew so much about childbirth even if she did practise on sheep and lambs.' She allowed herself a small smile

''Have you spoken to her about it? Did she come home with you?'

'Yes, as soon as we knew Katie was recovering and that the baby was thriving, we left. Alan was making sure everything was ready for their return. They both thank you for the clothes. They were thrilled. Mum cooked up a storm before we left to make sure Alan doesn't starve, and we baked a few things too.'

'Uh oh, Alice is letting it be known that it's her breakfast time, too. I need to go and feed her. Will you be all right working with Dr Durnie this morning? Mima went home last night, but I can take over if it gets too much for you and you can look after Alice. I know a lot of people will want to congratulate you and it can get a bit overwhelming.'

'I will be fine, but thank you for the offer ... best to jump in at the deep end!'

'Good for you, Chrissy, but you know where I am if you need me.'

*

'Good morning, Dr Durnie,' Chrissy felt nervous.

'Congratulations, Chrissy, or should I say Grannie? It is good to have you back. Mima is very efficient, but if I'm being honest, she still scares me a little. She gives me "that" look sometimes when I'm doing something she disapproves of, and I'm right back in the Dick Institute under the beady eye of stern Sister Reid.' Charles laughed.

Chrissy relaxed a little. 'What do you need me to do first? I feel like I've been away for weeks, not days. My head has been all over the place.'

'I'm not surprised. From what I hear it was quite the dramatic entrance into the world your granddaughter made. I'm delighted that mother and baby are doing well now. I expect Katie will be very tired for a while after losing so much blood.'

'Yes, she is, but she is being well looked after. She hates the iron tablets, though, but like you, she prefers them to liver!' Chrissy grinned. 'Now, where do I start?'

'There are a few instruments waiting to be autoclaved, and the trolley in the surgery needs to be stocked up, if we have any stock that is. It was busy last night. The dressing clinic we set up is running well. It certainly frees up spaces in the normal surgeries. That was an excellent idea, Chrissy.'

'Thank you, but it was more of a joint effort really.'

'Well, thank you for helping to keep it running smoothly, I really appreciate it.'

Chrissy wondered why the doctor was being so nice to her; he was never rude, but he seemed to be more chatty than usual. Could he tell how she was feeling? Had Bob said something? Maybe he had just put two and two together. She was certain that the story about her mother delivering her own great-granddaughter would have spread around the village like wild fire. Suddenly she wished that she had taken up the offer from Vera, but she instinctively knew that it was better just to get on with it. Taking a deep breath, she set about her duties with her usual level of professionalism.

After a beetroot sandwich for lunch followed by a scone and jam, Chrissy felt ready to tackle the dressing clinic.

The surgery was lucky to have a small treatment room - come-storeroom. Chrissy would call a patient through, remove any old dressings and cover them with gauze. Once Dr Durnie came in to assess the wound and a treatment plan was decided upon, Chrissy was left to clean and dress the wound again. Today, however, Dr Durnie had suggested that she could see some of the patients by herself, do the regular ulcer dressings and more minor ailments.

'The treatment plan is written in the patient's notes.' Chrissy raised her eyebrows.

'I know, if you can read my writing, that is,' he smirked. 'You will see the patient, and record your findings and what treatment you gave. Are you happy to do that?'

'I ... I don't know,' she stammered. 'Are you ready to trust me with that sort of responsibility?'

'I wouldn't be suggesting it if I didn't.'

'Well, in that case, yes, I'm sure I can do it. I won't let you down.' She sounded more confident than she felt.

'I know that. No heroics, though. If there's something you aren't sure of, come and get me, and if I'm not available, fetch Vera. The patient won't mind waiting.'

The afternoon passed quickly. The first three patients were straightforward. She was about to call the fourth when Dr Durnie popped his head around the door.

'I have a very important phone call scheduled for three o'clock. I have taken a look at the notes, and the next patient is a regular, very straightforward. I shouldn't be any more than ten minutes, but you will be well on your way by then.'

Right, Chrissy, you can do this. She smoothed her apron and adjusted her cap before glancing at her reflection in the mirror. *You look the part. Now let's see if you can act the part.*

Chrissy walked to the waiting room and called for her next patient.

'Mrs Gibson, come through please.'

She held the door open and beckoned the woman through into the hallway. She heard the unmistakable sound of muffled laughter and instinctively she stiffened. She had a strong feeling that Mrs Gibson had been talking about her to another patient in the waiting room. This was not paranoia: Mrs Gibson had a habit of smiling sweetly at Dr Durnie and scowling at Chrissy behind his back, and she usually had some catty remark to make about nurses being heavy-handed followed by, 'I don't mean you, hen,' deliberately avoiding using either the title Mrs Ramsay or Nurse. Dr Durnie didn't seem to notice, but Chrissy certainly did.

'Put your foot onto the stool please, Mrs Gibson, and I will remove your dressing.'

'You'll need to help me, hen, ah canny dae it masel. Have you forgotten I have a very sair leg?'

Chrissy bristled with frustration thinking that Mrs Gibson had managed to lift her foot onto the stool the last time she visited, but answered, 'Of course I can help you, there you go.' She gently lifted the woman's leg by the ankle and placed it on the stool.

'Oi, be careful with ma leg! I'm no a piece o' meat, ye ken!'

'I'm sorry, Mrs Gibson; I'm being as gentle as I can.'

The old woman tutted loudly and made a point of crying out when her bandages were removed.

'Almost there. My goodness, that does look better than it did when I last saw it.' Chrissy gave her one of her best smiles.

'Aye, I heard you'd been off gallivanting and that your ma delivered the wean. Poor auld soul, pity you couldn't have done it yoursel'!'

The words landed like a knife to her heart and cut her deeply. She held back tears, and then realised that she was angry, *very* angry, with this woman who had gone out of her way to demean her since day one of her working here. She had also heard the odd whisper while she was queueing at the Co-op but had managed to rise above it. But this was a full-blown assault on her senses. However, she refused to give the older woman the satisfaction of seeing her cry.

She took a deep breath before saying, 'Now, then, I shall have this cleaned up in a jiffy and bandaged in no time.'

She turned to her trolley and poured some cleaning solution into a kidney dish.

'I don't think we need any sulphanilamide powder today. I will apply some antiseptic cream instead and then...'

Chrissy was stopped mid-sentence by a red-faced Mrs Gibson; her eyes were bulging out of her head and for one minute, Chrissy thought she was going to leap right out of her chair and hit her.

'What do you mean you don't *think*?' she cried. 'Who are you tae *think*, hen? I want to see the doctor now!'

'Dr Durnie is in the middle of an urgent telephone call; he is happy for me to see you on my own and ...'

*

'*He* might be happy, but *I'm* not! Get him in here right now! Yer nothin' but a jumped-up farmer's wife, and let me tell you this ...'

'Mrs Gibson, that is quite enough. I will not have a member of my trained staff being spoken to in that manner. You will apologise to Nurse Ramsay at once, then she will bandage your leg, and you will be free to go.'

Mrs Gibson was stunned into silence. Her mouth gaped open before she tutted loudly and crossed her arms tightly across her ample chest and said, 'I'm sorry, hen.'

'It is *Nurse* Ramsay to you!' Charles spoke curtly and quietly in a tone oozing with authority.

'I'm sorry, *Nurse* Ramsay.' She spat out the words like they were slices of bitter lemon.

'If you are not willing to treat my staff with respect then you will no longer be welcome at this surgery, and I suggest that you pass that message on to anyone else in the village who shares your opinion.'

'That's you, all done,' Chrissy said brightly.

Without speaking, the incensed woman rose from the chair and walked with a somewhat exaggerated limp towards the door. When she left, she slammed the door with a loud bang.

Chrissy was dumbfounded; she had never heard the doctor speak to anyone like that. He didn't even raise his voice once. She was delighted that he had stuck up for her like that; it had been unexpected but very welcome.

Vera appeared in the hall, coming through the door that joined the surgery to the rest of the house.

'What was that bang? It shook the house and woke Alice up.'

'Nothing we can't handle eh, Chrissy, what do you say?'

'I'd say nothing we can't handle, Dr Durnie.'

She couldn't remember ever feeling so valued in her life.

CHAPTER FORTY-SIX

Hogmanay, 1944

'I can believe I'm going to be allowed to stay up until midnight, Aunt Vera! Remind me what happens again.'

'Well, when the clock chimes midnight, we wish each other a happy new year, then we wait for a "first footer" – the first person to come to your door in the new year. They should ideally be tall and dark-haired, and they bring a piece of coal in to ensure the household will stay warm in the coming year, whisky to toast a "guid new year", and black bun, which is a rich fruit cake, but we won't be getting any of that this year, and maybe not the whisky either, come to think of it. Hopefully someone will be able to spare a small lump of coal. And then everyone sings *Auld Lang Syne.* It's an old tradition that brings communities, friends and family together.'

'Robert Burns wrote that, didn't he? I learned that in school. The teacher said that people are kept busy "redding the house" – what does that mean? Do we need to paint things red?'

Vera laughed. 'No, thank goodness, it just means cleaning the house from top to bottom, especially getting rid of ashes from the fire and any other rubbish to give us a clean start to the new year by getting rid of the old year.'

'I wish I had managed to stay up last year. I'm determined to do it this year!' Martin's eyes were shining at the thought of the evenings gathering. 'Remind me who's coming?'

'Here, take Alice for a minute while I fold these nappies.' She plonked the baby onto his lap. Alice immediately started to laugh and giggle when Martin jiggled his knees and pretended to be a horse.

'Chrissy and Mr Ramsay will be here, so will their daughter Katie, her husband Alan and their baby Meggie; Mrs Barnes will be here too if she is well enough.'

'I thought you said the baby was called Margaret Christine Isabella?'

'Yes, she is called after her two grandmothers and her great-grandmother, but she will be called Meggie for short.'

'Is Aunt Mima coming?'

'Yes, and her friend Donald.'

'I hope we all fit into the house. What do you reckon, Alice? I expect you will be asleep. You're still very little, but I'm a big boy now and I can stay up late. I'll tell you all about it when you're older, Alice.'

Alice stared intently at her cousin and gurgled, offering him a wide gummy grin with two white teeth peeping out like tiny glistening seashells. Martin was a natural with the baby girl, and they had developed a strong bond with each other, one that Vera could only have imagined, and more than she had hoped for. Their natural interaction with each other warmed her heart.

'Will we need to give them some food? How will we manage?'

'Don't you worry about that, we have been planning this evening for a long time now. Everyone has been saving rations when they could, and so they will bring food with them, and we will share what we have with everyone else too.'

'I can't wait! I'm so excited to see everyone here at the same time and to see what food they bring!'

Martin was growing fast, and his appetite was growing too. She hated hearing him say he was hungry, but he was no different to any of his friends in that respect.

'I wonder if Mum and Dad will be celebrating new year somewhere?' He was still convinced that they were still alive.

'I hope so, Martin, I really hope so. Maybe we will get some news in the new year.'

'And they will want me to go back and live with them?'

'Yes, they will.' She did not add if they are still alive. 'But maybe not until the end of the war. I've told you that things will work out, Martin, just wait and see, but please don't worry about it.'

'I feel really mixed up. I've been so happy here. I love it, I've got new friends, I have a baby cousin, I have my very own den, trees to climb, apples to pick and so many people coming and going ... I don't get the chance to miss Mum and Dad anymore, and I am never lonely.'

'When *were* you lonely?'

'At boarding school. I wasn't one of the popular boys – I often got left out of things, and then when I went home for holidays, Mum and Dad were so busy. Dad had to go into the city a lot, especially just before the war started. I'll miss school when I leave next year. What am I going to do?'

'Uncle Charles and I have been discussing it. We think it would be good for you to help Mr Ramsay on the farm. There are so many jobs to do. In the evenings Uncle Charles and I can help you to study the subjects you will need for medical school, if you still want to be a doctor, that is?'

'I do; I really do. Mrs Barnes has told me stories about her son Billy. He lost an arm, a leg and the sight in one eye, and has burns on his face, chest and hand. He was treated by a plastic surgeon and ended up working for him – it all sounds amazing! I might want to do that sort of work one day.'

'Work hard and I'm sure you will. Now, pass her to me.'

Vera held out her arms to take her daughter from him; Alice squirmed in protest.

'That enough playing horsy for now, young lady. Martin has his Hogmanay chores to do. Make sure your bedroom is neat and tidy, won't you?'

'I will, Aunt Vera. May I put the wireless on?'

'Of course you can.'

Soon strains of *Goodnight, Sweetheart* were easing through the atmosphere, soft ribbons of sound that made Vera want to dance.

'Come on, Alice, let's waltz.'

She twirled around with her baby girl in her arms, making her laugh and gurgle with joy, wishing that everyone in the world could be as happy as she was right now.

*

If it were able to, the dining table would have been groaning under the weight of all the food laid out on top of it.

Maggie had made two large bowls of pig's head brawn; it looked very tasty indeed, decorated with sprigs of parsley. Bob had been growing mushrooms in a bucket in the coal house, so she had also made a mushroom pie.

Maggie had delegated the shortbread making to Chrissy, much to her daughter's surprise. Chrissy also brought a Homity pie. Mima brought a bottle of homemade elderberry wine and an apple crumble, and Katie brought a bread-and-butter pudding and some corned beef hash rissoles.

Vera had been baking potato bread and had put out crystal dishes of jam and pickles, and bowls of mock cream. *Make do and pretend* was the popular saying, but Vera thought that if this was pretending, then they had nothing much to complain about; no one would guess that they were rationed. With this amount of food, everyone would be going home with bags of leftovers at the end of the night.

'My oh my, just look at this lot! I'll need to watch myself – I don't want set my ulcer off again!' Charles said. He had joined Vera in the dining room, leaving the guests to mingle in the sitting room.

'Don't you dare, Dr Durnie, there's far too much to do. I will need help with the washing-up for a start.'

Charles pulled her into his arms and kissed her so tenderly that she couldn't pull away even though she was worried that someone might come into the room at any moment.

'I love you, Mrs Durnie. Whatever did I do to deserve a wife like you?'

'I can't answer that, I'm afraid. You didn't even know I existed until I offered to make you a cup of tea on night duty!' She tried to look upset.

'Is that what you think? Why do you think we worked together so often?'

'What do you mean, Charles Durnie? Are you saying you changed the rotas to work with me? Sister Reid would never have allowed that!'

'She didn't know. God forbid I should alter her rotas. Let's just say I got on well with my superiors and colleagues and leave it there.'

'You did not! I don't believe you!' Her eyes were shining with unadulterated love for this man; she felt like she was eighteen again, a lovestruck teenager.

'You'll never know, but don't you dare mention this to Mima. She still frightens the life out of me!'

'Come on, we need to go and attend to our guests.'

'Before we go in, look at this.' He held up a bottle of whisky. 'It's been agreed that Alan will be the first footer. He has coal and shortbread, and now he will have this.'

'Where did you get it from? I can't believe it!'

'A gift from one grateful Colonel Pollock-Morrice over at Craig House, no less. He gave us a bottle of sherry, too, and a lovely bottle of port.'

'This is going to be a wonderful evening, Charles; we are so lucky. Let's go and invite everyone to come through.'

*

'Ladies and gentlemen, this way please. Supper is ready!'

Charles held his arm aloft, inviting everyone to join him. There were gasps of surprise and delight when they entered the room.

'You wouldn't think we were rationed, would you?' Chrissy gasped.

'Help yourselves, it's a free-for-all, stretch or starve as they say. The napkins are over there, and I borrowed a tea urn from the Women's Rural. Cups and saucers are on the sideboard, there is a small amount of sugar in the bowl, and … Mr Ramsay brought a quarter pound of fresh butter straight from the farm.'

With gasps of delight all round and much clinking of cups, the assembled gathering started to tuck in, chattering and laughing. Rex sat by Martin, hoping for some crumbs to fall onto the floor either accidentally or, more than likely, quite deliberately.

Suddenly, Vera Lynn's distinctive voice filled the room with the song, *When the Lights go on Again*. Everyone became silent, then one after the other they all joined in singing the poignant lyrics

When the lights go on again, all over the world

And the boys are home again all over the world

And rain or snow is all that may fall from the skies above

A kiss won't mean "goodbye", but "Hello to love".

When the lights go on again all over the world

And the ships will sail again all over the world

Then we'll have time for things like wedding rings and free hearts will sing

When the lights go on again all over the world.

When the lights go on again all over the world

And the ships will sail again all over the world

Then we'll have time for things like wedding rings and free hearts will sing

When the lights go on again all over the world.

Handkerchiefs appeared to dab away tears as they remembered loved ones, reminisced, prayed and wished for an end to the war and a brighter future.

Then the strains of *In the Mood* filled the room, creating smiles with each note played until the ambiance returned to one of fellowship and hope.

Suitably sated by the magnificent feast, everyone helped to clear the table and carry plates and dishes to the kitchen. Chrissy and Vera packed up the leftovers while Mima and Katie washed and dried the dishes.

'Where is Meggie tonight, Katie?' Mima asked.

'She is back at Mum and Dad's with Grannie Bella. We thought that it would be the easiest option. Alan's mum loves being with her, and she will be able to choose what to listen to on the wireless. We'll go and see her soon after the bells. She's quite happy – it's *me* who's struggling. This is the first time I have left Meggie on her own.'

'She isn't on her own, though. I'm sure Alan's mum is more than capable. She raised a big strapping lad after all, and a night out together will do you the world of good.'

'Aye, I suppose so, but I can't wait to give her a cuddle when we get back.'

'Let sleeping dogs and babies lie is good advice. Don't forget it. You go through, we've almost finished here.'

'Thanks, Mima, I will. I'll see if Great-grannie Maggie needs anything ... she looks really tired.'

Martin had been overjoyed at being invited into the sitting room with the men and wasted no time in asking Bob what would be expected of him on the farm. He was excited to start work, but it seemed like such a big step from school. He also made the odd enquiry about the Land Girls, much to Bob's amusement.

Charles busied himself by retrieving glasses from the back of the large oak sideboard, setting them out on a tray with the bottle of port and the bottle of sherry. He was keeping the whisky until the bells chimed the end of 1944 and the beginning of 1945.

Alice was sleeping soundly in her pram near the range; Vera had decided that it would be easier than running up and down stairs to check on her. She was cosy, covered by her crocheted blankets, her hand-knitted pink teddy bear propped up by her side. Vera allowed herself a few precious minutes to drink in her daughter's delicious aroma and to watch as she made various facial expressions, often a half-smile, the corner of her mouth twitching slightly.

'The red tin has shortbread in it, and the blue one has my make do and pretend version of black bun,' said Maggie.

'Right, you are, Mrs Barnes, I'll put them on plates nearer the time. Why don't you go and rest your legs?' Vera had noticed that Maggie's ankles were badly swollen. 'We can manage here now, so go and listen to the wireless for a wee while.'

'I think I will, lass. I've been on my feet all day, it's been worth it, though, to see that table tonight with everyone's contributions. It was a sight to behold! I just wish Billy had managed to get enough time off to visit us. Hopefully he will make it in the new year,' Maggie said sadly.

The chatter continued over the next few hours, stories of Hogmanays past, absent friends and family, hopes and dreams, fears and apprehensions. Rex had taken it upon himself to lie beside Alice's pram, coincidently the warmest spot in the house, his little tummy full to brimming after he had worked the room with his cute head tilts and doleful eyes, each person feeling that they had been singled out especially as they tried to hide the fact that they were sharing a bit of this and that.

'I can't stop yawning, Uncle Charles. What time is it now?' asked Martin.

Charles was standing in front of the fireplace and turned around to look at the clock.

'Just a half-hour to go and then we can toast each other and bring in the new year, and then you can go off to bed.'

'Will I be allowed a sip of Aunt Mima's wine?'

'I don't see why not; after all, it *is* a special occasion, your last year as a schoolboy. You'll be a working man in 1945!'

'What do you think Mum and Dad will think about me working on the farm? Do you think they will approve?'

'In my opinion, they will think that you are a very sensible young man. With teachers so thin on the ground, night school isn't an option, and you can't get into medical school until you are 18. I'm not saying you'll be working on the farm all that time – maybe you will find a placement somewhere – but you must use the time to study. I've still got my old text books: Latin, maths, biology, chemistry and physics amongst others. Chrissy's daughter works at Scottish Aviation in Prestwick and she's going to find out if there is something you can do there.'

'That would be ace! I've always enjoyed helping on the farm and I have learned a lot during the holidays, but something a bit different would be a good thing too, especially if I get to see Spitfires and Hurricanes up close.'

'Right, Charles,' said Vera, 'I will leave you to fill the glasses. Chrissy, if you pop the plates onto the side tables for now, we can hand them round later, and Charles, when you light the fire, I have some juniper branches you can add.'

'I would like to say a few words if I may?' Charles addressed the assembly of friends.

'As we gather tonight, listening for the chiming of Big Ben on the wireless, we will remember the five long years behind us now. The blackouts and the rationing. I have to mention the people of London, my brother included, who will never forget May 1941 when they were bombed relentlessly by the Luftwaffe. We've held our breath with every news report.

'As we stand on the threshold of 1945, we can for the first time in years, see a faint but definite light on the horizon. Our armies are advancing, and Hitler is being pushed back.

'But tonight, let us not only think of the future, but also remember the immense courage of every soldier who pushed forward, every sailor who braved the Atlantic, and every pilot who took to the sky. We thank you. And think too of every woman who worked in a factory, every Land Girl who tilled the soil, and every child who did their bit. We thank you.

'Let us raise a glass, not just to 1945, but to those who won't be joining us tonight, and to those still far from home.

'Let us look forward to the day when the blackouts are a memory and our streets are bright again. To a final victory, and to a lasting peace.'

'Hear, hear! But you forgot to mention doctors and nurses!' Maggie chortled.

'Quickly, turn the wireless up, Mima, the countdown has started!'

Five, four, three, two, one ... Happy New Year!

As Big Ben chimed the first stroke of midnight, the assembled friends raised their glasses and wished each other a happy new year with murmurs of appreciation as they sipped the whisky and wine.

'Happy new year, Mum!' Chrissy said and hugged her mother tightly.

'Happy new year, my pet lamb, and here's to John returning to us soon, eh?'

'I'll drink to that! I wonder what he's doing. Will they celebrate in any way, do you think?'

'I hope so. I'm sure the men will find a way; it won't be like this, but they will find a way.'

As the fire caught in the grate, a warm glow caressed the room, the flickering flames reflected in the newly polished furniture, the brass and silver ornaments creating a cosy mood even though there wasn't much heat as yet.

There was a lull in conversation as the cluster of friends became submerged in their own thoughts and prayers until Charles asked: 'Now, who needs a top-up? These are very small glasses!'

'I'll have a nice cuppa, please, if there's one going?'

'Of course, Maggie, coming right up,' said Vera. 'Chrissy, would you do the honours, please?'

'I think I'll go to bed now. I didn't like the wine much. It's made be a bit dizzy,' said Martin.

'Take a glass of water with you, Martin, and I'll look in on you later when I come up.' Vera stroked his head and pulled him in for a hug, and he squirmed. 'You'll never be too big for a hug, don't forget that!'

Donald, a shy man, had been noticeably quiet all evening, but now, armed with Dutch courage, he walked over to Charles and raised his glass.

'Thank you for inviting me, Dr Durnie. Jemima talks about your family all the time. She is so grateful to you and the difference you have made to her life.'

'You're welcome, Donald, as is Mima; she has been a great help to us. I don't know what we would have done without her. She is a good woman.'

'She certainly is. She has brought new meaning to my life, too. I have been living very quietly since my wife died, but to have someone to go to the pictures with or even just for a walk has made such a difference to me.'

'Did I feel my ears burning?' Mima approached them with a plate of black bun.

'Indeed you did. We have been talking about you, but it was all good!'

Mima beamed. Her cheeks were flushed and her eyes were slightly glazed, unaccustomed as she was to alcohol.

'Katie, before you go, have you managed to find out who I can contact about getting work for Martin?'

'Funny you should ask that, my friend called round yesterday. She is working in the transport office and ...'

'Oh, no, my God no! Mum, can you hear me?' Chrissy was on her knees by her mother's chair. Maggie was still sitting uptight, but her eyes were fixed and unmoving, her teacup and saucer lying on the floor, the tea soaking into the rug.

Charles was by her side in an instant. Within a minute or two he shook his head.

'I'm afraid she has gone,' he said quietly. 'She has gone peacefully in her sleep, surrounded by family and friends. I'm sure that is how she would have wanted it to be.'

CHAPTER FORTY-SEVEN

Chrissy, 1945

As the last of the guests left the house, Chrissy kicked off her shoes and almost fell onto the couch.

'Let me get you a cup of tea, hen, you look done in. It's been quite a day.'

'That would be great, Bob, thanks. Is that you ready to go, Katie?'

'Aye, it is, Mum. I would like to get this one home in the daylight. Alan is so sorry that he couldn't come, but there was no one to cover his shift.'

'I told you to tell him not to worry. Now, you get going, and keep that wean warm, it's bitter out there!'

'Look at her, Mum, she's dressed for the North Pole! I've only got cardboard lining my boots, so I expect my feet will be soaked with slush by the time I get home ... Are you sure you will be alright, Mum? I feel I should stay...'

'I will be fine, lass, now get going or you will miss your bus. Just let me have one last cuddle.' She lifted Meggie onto her knee. 'Cheerio, my pet lamb, you be a good girl for your mammy. Shut those peepers when you are in your cot and sleep until the morning, do you hear me?'

Meggie was sleeping soundly, oblivious to her grandmother's tears splashing onto her shawl.

'Here's your tea,' Bob said. 'I'll walk Katie to the bus stop'

'There's no need, Dad, it's a hop, skip and a jump away, and I don't have much to carry. You stay with Mum. Cheerio, we will see you soon!'

And with that she was gone, leaving Chrissy and Bob alone.

Chrissy reached over to a small side table and picked up her mother's precious biscuit tin, the tin that had reunited her with Uncle Billy, the tin that had been filled and emptied on countless occasions, the very old and bashed tin that Chrissy knew she would cherish above everything else. It radiated with her mother's character – just a tin to anyone else, but to her it exuded Maggie's spirit.

'I can't believe how full the church was today. I haven't seen it like that for a while – just goes to prove how highly thought of your mum was. Even Mrs Todd was there, bless her.'

'The minister's wee sermon was just right. I think Ma would have loved it.'

'She would, especially when he mentioned that she was one of the best bakers in the village. I noticed a few noses being put out of joint. It's just you and me again, hen, at least until John comes home. Oh, I wish this bloody war was over!'

'It's bound to end soon. The news on the wireless gets better all the time, and in the papers too. Every other day another town is liberated.'

'Aye, and those pictures of our boys crossing the Rhine … and the Russians closing in on Berlin from the other side. The Nazis are crumbling.'

'There's still Japan, though, Bob. The boys will be on ships headed for the Pacific soon. It's not going to end all at once for everyone, is it?'

'No lass, I don't think it is. All we can do here is to carry on carrying on, I suppose, make sure that when the boys do come back that they have communities, homes and jobs to come back to.'

'You know, Bob, I'm glad my mum is at peace, no more worrying about rationing. She never could accept that one for the pot became none for the pot – she liked her tea strong. And look what she went through in the Great War, working in a munitions factory, losing two of her boys while the other was blown to smithereens! I often wonder how she kept going. Dad, too.'

'Well, they had you at home for a start, and anyway, what was the alternative? They kept going in the same way as we do, hoping for a brighter future, not one under the Nazi regime.'

'There weren't Nazis back then.'

'You know what I mean. Without hope, what is there? We have to believe this is for our wee granddaughter, and all the other weans oot there. We're doing it for them. Anyway, hen, have you finished your tea? How about a walk before dinner?'

'That's a good idea. It's not often I get the chance to step out wi ma man.' She gave him a watery smile, but a smile nonetheless and it pleased him. 'Are you sure you won't be needed? What about the milking?'

'Tom is taking young Martin under his wing, showing him the ropes. He's a strong laddie and a quick learner, I'm sure they can manage without me for once.'

They walked along Irvine Road towards the shops and crossed the road to look over the bridge at the burn that was bubbling merrily on its way. They could see a group of children further up the hill, paddling and screeching with glee as they splashed each other.

'I bet at least one of them will get a skelpin' when they get home with soaking wet clothes,' Bob laughed. 'I know I always did.'

'I was a goody-two-shoes. My head was always full of stories. I loved reading about Anne Shirley – her life seemed to be so glamorous compared to mine, and the three Florence Nightingale books in the library that I borrowed over and over again ...I never got tired of reading them.'

They passed the post office and turned left to walk up the Boo'in.

'How did it get its name, Chrissy? There must be a story attached to it?'

'You know, I have no idea. It's always been the Boo'in and always will be in my book.'

As they meandered through the wooded area, Chrissy pointed to a thicket.

'That's where Mum used to pick the nettles for her nettle soup. It was lovely. She kept an old pair of gloves specially for the job.'

When they emerged into Annandale Crescent, they could see Mr Boles tending to his vegetable plot.

'Still digging for victory, Mr Boles?'

'I am that. Come over, I have some smashing beetroot and a spare cabbage going if you fancy it. It's a bit frozen, but it's a guid size.'

Chrissy and Bob walked over.

'Just a minute, I'll run in and get some newspaper to wrap them in.'

He struggled to come down the steps; he still suffered from a shrapnel wound received in the Great War.

'My, that was a lovely service the day, Chrissy. Your mum would have loved it. She'll be missed around the village. I remember her when she was a lassie. I fancied her ma self, but Jim Barnes got there first!' He laughed, causing him to choke and splutter.

'Damn gas all those years ago, you'd think it would have loosened its hold by now!'

'Thank you for these, Mr Boles, they will be put to very good use.'

They walked back towards the shops. Chrissy stood opposite the church and gazed at it.

'When I was small, I dreamt about being a bride in there. This is my favourite view; you can really grasp the beauty of it from here. It is so quiet now, it's hard to imagine that just a few hours ago it was packed with people. I expect they have gone back to work, or they are at home keeping busy. So many people coming together to support each other – we are all in exactly the same boat.'

'Come on, hen, it's getting really chilly now. Looks like we might get some snow. Let's get home and settled in.'

As they walked towards home, Chrissy looked along Gatehead Road towards the Co-op.

'Bob, look, there's a queue. I wonder what it's for. Should I tag on the back? It might be fruit.'

'No, lass, our loss will be someone else's gain, and you look worn out, so let's just get home.'

'You're right ... let's go back to the empty house.'

Bob stopped and looked at her.

'It's not empty – it's full of memories and full of love, and we have many *many* more memories to make, Chrissy, just you wait and see!'

CHAPTER FORTY-EIGHT

Vera, 1st May 1945

'Don't study too late, Martin, you have a busy day ahead of you. Springtime on the farm is hard work, remember.'

'I know that, Aunt Vera, I won't be too long.'

'I've just put Alice in her cot. Give me a shout if you hear her, won't you?'

Back in the kitchen, Vera got back to making her potato bread. The Home Service on the wireless had just announced that the allied forces were continuing with their advance into northern Germany, British troops had entered Lubeck and that in Italy, German resistance was collapsing, but now the BBC Variety Orchestra were playing upbeat tunes.

Vera swayed as she kneaded the dough.

She had received a letter telling her that Mima and Donald were now engaged and planning a very quiet wedding in the summer. She was overjoyed for her friend and read the letter to Chrissy, who was equally pleased. It was heartening to have something to look forward to.

She glanced at the clock; it was almost time for *Tommy Tinder and Workers' Playtime* to begin on the wireless.

Where is Charles? Surely, he must be finished for the night? she thought.

Charles and Chrissy were working late, autoclaving cotton wool ball and bandages, stocking the drug cupboard and cleaning. A much-needed delivery of supplies had arrived at last, but Charles had been working at Kilmarnock Infirmary all day and then had to deal with a fishing accident when he got back. She decided that if they weren't in here for a cocoa by the time *Lift up your Hearts* began, she would go in there and *insist* that they finish for the night. Just then the door swung open.

'I'm sorry, Vera, it took us a long time, but it looks as good as new through there now. We'll be able to cope with anything tomorrow. Chrissy, thank you for staying on. Bob will be wondering where you are.'

'He won't even have noticed I'm not there. I left him a cold plate for dinner. He works until the last glimmer of daylight is nothing but a memory.'

'True, and I expect Martin will need to get used to that too. It will stand him in good stead for his medical training. What was that saying I heard from Bob? "Remember, Doctor, I get up before the sparrow's first fart"!'

Chrissy flushed with embarrassment. 'You need to excuse my man, he has a peculiar turn of phrase!'

'Am I too late for a cup of cocoa?' asked Martin as he rushed in through the door.

'Grab a chair, there's plenty in the pot, we were just saying you'll need to get used to late nights soon!'

Martin smiled. 'I'm looking forward to it. Some of those Land Girls are very pretty!'

'Oh, here we go, that's all I need – a lovestruck nephew moping about after some girl ...'

'Shh, the news is starting. They said earlier that developments have been made.' Vera walked over to the wireless and turned up the volume.

This is the BBC Home Service. Here is the news.

From Germany this evening, it has been announced that Adolf Hitler is dead. A broadcast from Hamburg, now under Nazi control, stated that the Führer fell at his command post in Berlin, fighting to the last against Bolshevism.

The exact circumstances of his death remain uncertain. The German announcement, delivered by Admiral Dönitz, claims Hitler died a hero's death. British officials have yet to confirm the details.

In London and across the country, the news has been met with cautious relief. Crowds have gathered in public squares, and church bells have rung in some towns.

The Prime Minister is expected to address the nation in the coming days.

Meanwhile, Allied forces continue their advance into Germany. The war in Europe is not yet over, but tonight, one chapter has closed.

They sat quite still and stared at each other over steaming cups of watery hot chocolate.

Martin was first to speak.

'What happens now, Uncle Charles?'

'I'm not sure, Martin. It's hard to believe, but if the BBC are broadcasting it, we can only presume that it's true.'

'Does it mean the war is over?'

'Not yet, but it certainly is the beginning of the end.'

'I expect there will be dancing in some streets tonight. I wonder if the church bells will ring in the village?'

'I can't help thinking about all the souls who didn't get to hear this news. I wonder if John knows. I don't suppose they will have told the prisoners of war, will they?'

'I doubt it, but I can't help thinking you will be seeing your boy sooner rather than later.'

'I pray to God that you are right.'

CHAPTER FORTY-NINE

Chrissy, 3rd May 1945

The sun was shining through the open window. At the far end of the field, Chrissy watched the burn. from this distance it looked like a sparkling blue ribbon, strewn here and there with greens and browns.

Rex was sitting by her feet. Now that Martin was at the farm from morning until night it seemed sensible for the little dog to spend more time in his old abode.

'What do you want? I need to go to work soon. I know, you want a sun bath next to the pig pail for a smelly-scented snooze, don't you?'

She opened the back door just as Bob called out to her.

'Chrissy, come and listen to this!' He started to read aloud from his morning paper. '"Hitler is dead."'

'Well, we already know that, don't we? Why is that news?'

'Haud yer wheesht, wummin, and listen,' he said and then continued to read. '"Not in battle. Not dragged to trial. But by his own cowardly hand, in a bunker beneath a burning Berlin."'

Chrissy gasped. 'Never! The coward, the evil bloody coward!' She held her hand over her mouth, every nerve in her body prickling with anger.

'"The man who brought Blitz to our cities, who sent our boys to die in deserts and forests, who filled Europe with graves, chose a bullet over justice. Let no one mourn him. Let no one speak of honour or bravery. He was a tyrant, and he died as tyrants do, alone, afraid, and defeated.

In the pubs of Manchester, the streets of Glasgow, the kitchens of Brixton, people are raising a quiet toast, not to his death, but to the hope that peace is near.

We've waited six long years for this. We've buried our dead, rationed our food, and blacked out our windows. Now, the light begins to return. Hitler is gone. And Britain stands tall."'

'The bastard has evaded trial, he deserved to be publicly and painfully brought to justice! You are right, Chrissy, he was a coward, nothing but a bloody coward!'

'Surely it can't be long now before Germany surrenders! How can they go on after this?'

'I don't know, hen, but I need to get back, lots to do today. See you later.' Bob rose and pulled his wife into his arms.

'The end is in sight, hen, and our boy should be home soon. Imagine, no more blackouts! I expect rationing will go on for a while yet. We might not be digging for victory anymore, but digging we shall do, I have no doubt about that.' He pulled her close and kissed her, a long passionate kiss that took her breath away.

'Bob Ramsay, what has got into you?' she giggled. 'What was in that tea?'

'A bloody good splash of hope for the future, hen, that's what.'

CHAPTER FIFTY

7th May, 1945

The mood was light and the chatter was loud as the village women queued for soap. Word had spread like wild fire that the Co-op had some in stock.

'I'm so glad I had this morning off. I'd have missed this otherwise. I heard they had some tinned fruit yesterday. I wonder if there will be any left?'

'I doubt that very much, Chrissy, but fingers crossed there might be.'

'Have you had any word about your William recently, Mrs Fraser?'

'The last letter came in March. He said the heat was unbearable, the jungle is as thick as his grannie's potato and leek soup, and the mosquitoes are nippier than the Japs. He wrote, "Don't worry, Mum. We're pushing forward. I'll be home before the tatties are up." I've read that line a dozen times. Folded it back into the envelope like it might keep him safe.'

Chrissy saw tears starting to form in the woman's eyes.

'The papers say Rangoon's been taken. That's good, isn't it? Maybe it means the end is near.'

'Aye, but there's no word from the War Office, no telegram, no new post. Just silence. I can't stand not knowing. They hardly ever mention Burma on the wireless, it's all about Europe.'

Chrissy noted the bitterness in the distraught mother's voice and couldn't blame her for it one bit.

'What's going on up there, who is shouting?'

'It's Mr Fulton. I saw him coming out of the post office like a rocket a few minutes ago.'

'It's just been oan the wireless – the Nazis are surrendering!'

A collective gasp rose and hung in cloud-like anticipation above them.

'They said General Eisenhower's got the papers signed. And Churchill's going to speak tomorrow. It's going to be Victory Day!'

The reaction was restrained at first, followed by an eruption of pent-up emotions, relief, frustration and grim satisfaction; smiles and tears mingled with the fresh new spring air and sunshine.

Chrissy gripped Mrs Fraser's hand tightly. When Mr Fulton noticed Mrs Fraser's distress, he spoke up.

'We'll ring the church bell, Mrs Fraser. For William.

For all of them. I'm heading for the church hall now. We will need to dig oot the buntin' for the morrow.'

The women, including Mrs Fraser, started to disperse, heading to their homes to spread the news.

With the soap safely tucked into the bottom of her bag, Chrissy headed home. At the last minute, she decided to pop in to see Mrs Fraser; she knew how the woman felt, but at least she now knew that her son was safe and would hopefully be coming home soon.

She walked along Kilmarnock Road and stopped at the sandstone cottage which stood not far from the church. She knocked on the door; there was no answer, but she could hear the sound of someone crying softly through the open window.

'Mrs Fraser, it's me, Chrissy. Can I come in? I managed to get a wee packet of biscuits.'

The door opened and Mrs Fraser fell into her arms and sobbed.

'Come and sit down. I'll put the kettle on.'

'Please don't think I'm being selfish. I am glad the war is over, of course I am, but I won't be celebrating tonight or tomorrow.'

'I can't say I blame you. Here, take this.' Chrissy handed over a cup of tea. 'And I will open these,' she said as she set the bag of biscuits on the table.

'I've decided to light a candle in my front window tonight for all the mothers like me who are still counting days and letters. I will keep the bunting in the loft until William walks through that door.'

CHAPTER FIFTY-ONE

8th May, 1945

Churchill's voice on the wireless put the rubber stamp on the news that the war was well and truly over.

"Germany has surrendered unconditionally."

Chrissy looked over to the pram; Alice was munching on a crust of bread, her blonde curls peeping out from under her cotton bonnet. She was clutching onto a red, white and blue teddy bear.

'My goodness, Alice, you have your very own VE Day teddy! How patriotic!'

Alice scrunched up her nose and snorted.

'It's her new party trick. She did it once and we laughed; there's no stopping her now,' Vera apologised.

'I knitted it for her,' said Mima. 'It only took a couple of days. I needed something to keep me occupied, and maybe I was jumping the gun a bit, but it has paid off.'

'It certainly did, Mima, every child in the village will want one now.'

'I asked Alice to say thank you to her auntie Mima, but she shouted "Daddy" very loudly and then snorted again. I expect she will grow out of it.'

'Katie, Alan and Meggie will be arriving soon. They'll meet us outside the church.'

'Ah, I thought that might be the case. I knitted a teddy for Meggie, too.'

'Mima, you are too kind, thank you, she'll love it.'

'It has given me peace to finish my jigsaw. She doesn't natter quite so much when she's busy,' Donald quipped.

'Do you have a date for the wedding yet?'

Mima and Donald looked sheepishly at each other.

'Well, actually, we *are* married. We had a very quiet ceremony last week, just two witnesses: Donald's sister and my niece. I hope you aren't offended, but we thought that under the circumstances this way was best.'

'Congratulations to you both! I couldn't be happier for you!' said Vera.

'Same here!' said Chrissy. 'You make the perfect couple! Congratulations!'

'I hardly think two old biddies getting wed is quite the same as the end of a war but thank you for the sentiment,' Mima laughed, and reached for Donald's hand in an unusual display of affection.

'Let's go,' said Charles, 'the festivities await. I've checked the waiting room, and, as I expected, no one is there. I'll lock the door now. I'm sure people will find me if they need me.'

'That they will, Charles. There's bunting hanging up all over the village – I don't think anyone will be looking for you tonight unless it's an absolute emergency. Let's go.'

They headed along Irvine Road towards the village.

'Dr Durnie, come over here a minute.'

Mrs Gibson was standing by her garden fence.

'Here's a bottle of my ginger wine and a bag of barley scones. Maybe you could share them with Mrs Ramsay?'

'That's very kind of you, Mrs Gibson, I'll do that, and thank you.' His expression acknowledged that this was much more than a VE day gift; it was also a peace offering. 'Mrs Ramsay will be delighted, too, I'm sure.'

*

Home Guard lads were outside the Co-op playing accordions, and some of the Land Girls had escaped duties and were dancing fit to burst along with the villagers. Bobbing heads and happy faces were everywhere as people hugged each other, let their hair down and embraced this new era of peace.

A huge crowd gathered in the church grounds. When the bells stopped ringing, they packed themselves into the pews. Some Land Girls and farmers stood at the back, muddy boots and soil under their fingernails, while villagers sat in pews wearing their Sunday best.

Chrissy noticed Mrs Fraser sitting in a side pew and was pleased to see that her daughter was beside her, as was her brother.

'Mum, any room for a small one?'

*

'Katie!' Chrissy wanted to jump up and give her daughter a hug but that could wait for now.

'I'll shuffle up a bit. Bob, take Meggie, will you? Where's Alan?'

'He got the short straw – with this being a national holiday, folk are travelling all over the place to visit family and friends. someone has to keep the buses running.'

'Will we see him later?'

'I hope so. Meggie and I might even stay over if that is fine with you?'

Chrissy beamed. 'I can't think of anything better! Shush ... listen! The minister is speaking.'

'My dear friends, today we gather not in mourning, but in gratitude. The war in Europe is over. The bells have rung, the flags have flown, and our hearts, although heavy with sad memories, are lifted with hope.

'We give thanks for the courage of our soldiers, sailors and airmen. For the quiet strength of our women, who kept homes warm and fields sown. For the children who grew up in the shadow of sirens and ration books yet never lost their laughter.

'But let us also remember peace is not the absence of war, but the presence of justice, mercy and neighbourly love.

'Many of our loved ones are still serving in the East. The war is not yet done. And many will not return. So, we light our candles today not only for victory, but for remembrance.

'Let this church be a place of healing. Let our village be a place of rebuilding. And let our lives be a testament to the resilience of the human spirit.

'May the Lord bless this day, and all the days to come.

'Now, let us sing together *O God Our Help in Ages Past.*'

The contrast between the day and night celebrations was marked and welcome. Everyone needed to let off steam, let their hair down and have a good time.

A huge bonfire blazed and crackled in the park; there seemed to be a never-ending queue of people waiting to throw on black-out boards and curtains on top of it.

On the main street, wireless sets sat by wide open windows, and music played well into the night.

Everyone stopped to listen to Churchill's speech before accordion and fiddle music drenched the night sky with Scottish country songs.

Tables had been dragged outside, and every scrap and morsel of food that could be spared, from spam sandwiches, mock cream-cakes and bottles of homemade ginger beer, were laid out to share with one and all.

The Women's Rural handed out victory buns and paper hats to all the children who whooped and jumped with sheer joy; even the youngest could sense the change of mood and ambience.

Smile muscles were working overtime and would ache in the morning.

'When the war began, we hardly knew each other!' said Charles who had gathered with Vera and their friends. 'Who could have imagined this night back then? I propose a toast to Mima and Donald – thank you for all you have done for us. Bob, and Martin too, of course, we thank you for keeping us fed. I know your workload isn't about to get lighter anytime soon but thank you for all you have done. Vera, you have given me a beautiful daughter; I had given up hope of ever becoming a father. You are an amazing woman, and I love you very much. Last, but not least, Chrissy. At the start of the war, you were not only heartbroken but totally broken. You were challenged and you rose to it with dedication and professionalism. We just couldn't have coped without you, and I want you to know that I will fight to keep you working at the surgery. Quite frankly, I can't imagine who could take your place, except Mima, of course, but she's going to be enjoying her retirement with her new husband. Here's to each one of you!'

They raised cups and glasses filled with ginger beer, homemade wine and toasted each other.

'And here's to you, Charles, and to the impending National Health Service! Who knows, we may have Martin as the village doctor one day!' said Bob.

'Here's to an exciting future!'

'To an exciting future, cheers to one and all!'

PROLOGUE

July, 1954

'Grannie, tell me again about what you did in the war.'

'Meggie, I've told you a million times. Now come over here and help me with these vegetables or there will be no television later.'

'Coming. I like hearing about it, Grannie, about how you and my great-grannie were there when I was born.'

Chrissy watched her granddaughter. She was wearing an apron over her grey pinafore, her pigtails falling over her shoulders like thick, shimmering ropes, each tied with a blue ribbon.

She getting to be so tall, and only ten years old.

'Will there be a coronation this year too? I loved watching that with all the neighbours. My friend Cara says they don't have a television, but they don't care; she says they're common. What does that mean, Grannie?'

'No and there won't be another one for a while yet, and it means you are chattering too much. Much more of this and you will miss *Children's Hour*; remember, it starts at five.'

'Look, I'm nearly finished.' Meggie pointed to the bowl of scraped carrots and peeled potatoes.

'Can I go through now, Grannie? Otherwise I'll have time to read another chapter of your favourite book before it starts.'

'*Anne of Green Gables*? I'm glad you're enjoying it.'

'No, Grannie, I finished that ages ago. I've started the one about Florence Nightingale.'

'Off you go, then, wash your hands first, though, you don't want to get the pages dirty.'

'What time will Grandpa be home?'

'About six o'clock I should think, and he will be hungry. Off you go and let me get on.'

Chrissy was thankful that Bob was now working in a greengrocer shop in Kilmarnock. It was situated just by The Cross, so very handy for the buses to and from Crosshouse. He was still in constant agony from all his "digging for victory" years, but it was at least more manageable now.

Plus, it had the advantage that he could go into the fishmongers a few doors down and pick up some bargains at the end of the day.

'Ah, here he is now.'

He took off his coat and hat, hung them up in the hall, and gave Chrissy a peck in the cheek.

'Wait until you see what I've got the night, hen.'

'Let me guess ... vegetables and fish?'

'That's enough. Rationing has only just ended, and you are getting awfy picky all of a sudden.'

'Sorry, Bob, we are having fish pie tonight, it will go off if I don't cook it soon.'

'It's not fish, look at this.'

He opened the package in his hand while simulating a drum roll. 'Ta da!' he looked like the cat that got the cream; meanwhile, Chrissy looked on perplexed.

'Are they rissoles?'

'Are they rissoles? No, Chrissy, they are hamburgers!'

'Hamburgers! But that looks like minced beef to me.'

'Do you remember we read about that place opening in London, the Wimpy I think it's called? They serve these hamburgers in a bread roll. The idea came from the Yanks, and they're meant to be really tasty. The butcher is trying to keep up with the cafés in town. They are selling them there. I'll see if I can find some Heinz tomato ketchup, as well. That's what you put on top, and you serve them with chips.'

'I'll certainly give it a go. Meggie is next door, probably with her eyes glued to the television.'

'How is my wee flower the night?' Bob said as he approached his granddaughter.

'Grandpa!' Meggie flew into his arms, nearly knocking him over. 'Can we watch this together until dinner is ready?'

'Aye, we certainly can.'

'Perfect!' This was her new favourite word, and she used it all the time.

'That's the word, hen, perfect.'

*

'How long will I be staying here, Grannie?' Meggie asked as she snuggled down into her bed, pulling the blankets up around her shoulders.

'Just until your mummy comes out of hospital. It won't be long now, and you will get to meet your new baby brother.'

'I wanted a sister, Grannie, someone to play skipping ropes, collect scraps, and play at houses with dollies. Boys are stupid, they don't like any of those things, they just like football and playing at being soldiers.'

'Well, Meggie, when it comes to brothers and sisters, we need to take what we get and be thankful.'

'I promise to be thankful if you tell me a story about the war,' Meggie grinned, exposing the gap in her front teeth.

'What do you want to hear?'

'I want to hear about your brother Billy, Great-grannie, Martin and Uncle John. Why is he so grumpy? Sometimes he's as nice as pie, and sometimes he won't talk to me.'

'Uncle John was a prisoner of war for many years; he didn't get home until the war ended. He doesn't like to talk about it, but if we look after him and are kind to him, he will get better.'

'What about Martin?'

'He will be a doctor soon, just like his uncle, Dr Durnie. His parents lived in

London. The ship they were on was sunk and he never saw them again. He hoped for a while that they had survived, but they didn't. It's very sad, but he was so lucky to have his uncle and his aunt Vera, Mrs Durnie to you, of course.'

'Their little girl is about the same age as me, isn't she?'

'Yes, Alice is just a little bit older than you. She says she wants to be a nurse like her mummy.'

Meggie opened her eyes wide and gasped.

'That's what I want to do, Grannie; I want to be a nurse just like you were during the war!'

'You have a long time to think about it, Meggie. Now it's time to sleep.'

'Do you think Uncle Billy was happy having only one arm and one leg?'

'Not at first; it was very hard for him, but I know he was happy once he came to terms with his injuries. He helped so many people and he won an award. He had a good life in the end with his wife and stepchildren. Enough now, you need to get some sleep. Night night, sweetheart.'

'Night, Grannie.'

Chrissy switched off the light and started to close the door.

'I really mean it, Grannie; I'm going to be a nurse one day.'

PART 3

Crosshouse, The Battle of Loos, and True Stories

While researching The Great War – World War One – for this book, the Battle of Loos caught my attention.

A video called *Stand To, Crosshouse Loos*, has been posted on YouTube by Living Tradition. The video is accompanied by Bob Fox singing *Stand To*. It is highly emotive. I watched it with tears streaming down my face.

Dr Derek Patrick of St Andrews University said that "the disproportionate number of Scots who went over the top at 06:30 on September 25th, 1915, ensured Loos would be remembered as a Scottish battle."

I wish we had been taught about it in school. I studied WWI history. We were taught about the Marne, Gallipoli, Verdun, the Somme and Passchendaele, but not about the Battle of Loos.

I understand the men who fought and survived WWI did not talk about it. They did not want to re-live or disclose the horror. They did not want to talk about the slaughter and carnage. Then, in 1963, some of the men did speak about it to the BBC, for the first time ever.

I am grateful that they did, and that their stories have been told and will not be forgotten. Even in my own family, it was not talked about.

More about the Village of Crosshouse

I was incredibly fortunate to receive some fascinating documents from Crosshouse resident Sadie McHarg a few years ago.

She knew I was writing a novel set in Crosshouse during World War I and World War II.

Among the documents were ten pages penned by Charlie Hannah in collaboration with Sadie's father, Jimmy Stewart.

They exquisitely captured the essence of childhood exploration, taking the reader on a walking tour around the village of Crosshouse while describing its layout, shops, businesses and people.

I eventually managed to alter the format and conducted, hopefully, thoughtful editing.

My goal was to retain the heart of the author's narrative while making it relatable to today's readers. This was a delicate balance. The original words had an unmistakable charm, yet some explanations and contexts were necessary for readers unfamiliar with certain references, hence, explanatory brackets were added.

One part of the memoir mentions the construction of Crosshouse Hospital. Building began in 1972, and it opened its doors in 1984, suggesting the memoir was penned sometime in the 70s and 80s.

I hope you enjoy reading and reminiscing as much as I did. Charlie and Jimmy truly brought Crosshouse in the early 20th century to life in a way only locals could.

The memories captured by Charlie and Jimmy serve as a time capsule. They transport readers to an era filled with vivid experiences. Their writing emphasises the communal spirit that characterised Crosshouse, marked by belonging, mutual respect and shared experiences.

Additionally, the wartime memories added at the end create a striking contrast. They underscore the resilience of Crosshouse residents who lived amid the uncertainty of World War II.

Weaving Through the History of Crosshouse

by Charles Hannah and Jimmy Stewart

The old name of the village was Corshouse. Originally known as Corsehouse Muir, Crosshouse is part of the parish of Kilmaurs. The church was built in 1882, but before this, residents trekked to various churches – some to Kilmarnock, others to Kilmaurs, and a few to Dreghorn.

Those who attended the parish church in Kilmaurs walked up through Knockentiber and then halfway to Kilmaurs, where a path branches off to the right, trails under the railway, and meanders through fields to Kilmaurs Church. This path was the right-of-way.

From 1870 until the church's opening in 1882, Crosshouse was served by a missionary probationer, appointed jointly by Dreghorn and Kilmaurs. He conducted services alternately in the outlying areas of both parishes. The church, originally costing £6,000, was built in 1882. In 1887, a manse was constructed, costing £1,400, raised through public subscription. Mr. Pollock Morris of Craig contributed £500 towards the pipe organ.

The Struggles for Education

In October 1704, members of the Kilmaurs Kirk Session, all residing in the Crosshouse area, petitioned for a school in Crosshouse. The entire Session, after careful consideration, promised the sum of 11 shillings and 8 pence (58p) per annum to support the school. This must have strained their resources because, from 1739 to 1765, the allocation was reduced to 5 shillings (25p) annually.

By 1804, the heritors of Crosshouse agreed to pay one hundred merks (13 shillings and four pence, exactly two-thirds of a Scottish pound) per year as a salary for the schoolteacher. A school and schoolhouse appear to have been constructed by subscription around 1808, with a small debt still lingering at an 1820 meeting.

In 1887, a new school and schoolhouse were built, taking the place of the original school, facilitated under the School Board. This structure underwent extensions between 1901 to 1911 to address the burgeoning population. Below is a list of schoolmasters:

Schoolmaster/Year

Allan Orr 1705

Mr Gilbey 1750

Thos Brunton 1753-1762

Arthur Smith 1755-1757

Thos Walker 1757

Andrew McTire 1758-1759

John Duff 1759

Arch Gillies 1761

Robt Boxentoor 1761

Daniel Thomson 1763-1765

James Johnstone 1765

Arthur Smith received his appointment from the Secession Church of Kilmaurs' Session. Mr Smyton, the minister, took a keen interest in Crosshouse School during this period. The teacher received a gratuity from the Poor Box to support him on the meagre income from his role!

The 'Brig' and its History

Before the bridge was built, the road dipped down the brae (hill) towards Hunter's Garage and crossed a ford. The riverbanks were built up, with steps installed down both sides leading to the burn. Large stones were placed to facilitate crossing the water.

In one of the houses on the burn side, Andrew Fisher, Labour Prime

Minister of Australia, was born. If you observe closely at the end of the bridge near the laundromat, you can see steps on both sides leading down to the burn, allowing villagers to collect water for washing.

Next to the laundromat stood a slew of cottages, which were in ruins by the early 1920s. A shed used to house Will Stewart's horse and wagonette, which ferried passengers to and from Kilmarnock before the advent of motorbuses.

Murdoch's Smiddy, a bustling hub for shoeing horses and repairing farm implements, played an important role in the community.

Next, we arrive at Carmel View, owned by the Keast family, who also managed the butcher shop at the Cross – now owned by the Co-operative. A field behind the butcher shop served as a grazing area for sheep.

Connecting with the Co-ops and Community Services

Behind Carmel View were sheds for keeping pigs which were slaughtered on-site. Moving forward, we reach the Co-operative Buildings containing multiple dwellings alongside the tailor, cobbler and drapery departments. Subsequently, the dairy relocated to new premises, occupying the previous drapery space.

This marked the end of the village proper, with an open field beyond it and two nurseries, one owned by Michael Brown and the other by George Brown.

A large house, Craufurd Hill, served as the home and surgery for Dr McLaren. During Dr McLaren's tenure, a waiting room for patients didn't exist; patients waited outside, sheltered against the gable end of the house. Fortunate patients found refuge in the garage during their wait. Ultimately, Dr McLaren moved his practice to an old shop, now an open area between the Cross Garage and the petrol pumps, later constructing a clinic after demolishing a cottage.

The Evolution of Community Spaces

What is now the post office was once Montgomery's Buildings. The post office was situated on a small triangular patch of land at the end of this establishment. The road currently known as Annandale Lane was once referred to as the Boo'in, with some houses occupied by workers from Annandale Farm.

The village concluded at the Manse, behind which was the original Crosshouse Waverley football pitch. Across the road, housing resumed, starting with the residence of the village constable. Next was a structure that eventually morphed into a hosiery factory –Blackwood's Building.

The building adjacent was Douglas Cottage, Number 38 Kilmarnock Road, the first in Crosshouse to be fitted with electric lighting. I recall the crowd that gathered to witness the lights being turned on!

We have now reached McChristie's Buildings, home to the Portland Arms. Behind the pub were numerous houses, accommodating no fewer than sixteen families. Passing by the school brought us to the Co-operative grocery shop.

Behind it were stables and offices. Several cottages ended opposite the Toll House situated at the Gatehead Road corner. On the Portland Arms Street side, each garden used to have a well to supply water for household needs before public water installation.

I remember witnessing the demolition of old houses behind the Portland Arms. When a lorry dislodged a large slab, it revealed a deep well, previously unknown to residents, that has since been filled.

Replies to my call for help!

I had a chat with my mum. She can remember some of the shops in the village: the chip shop, run by a Tam Walker; Lyons, a grocery across from the bridge; the baker's and bake house (Co-op), where the chemist is now, where you got your bread wrapped in white tissue paper! She said it was a Mr Ross who ran the grocers where the Spar is today.

She remembers there being an air raid shelter at Playing Field Road, which was in the school playground. They stayed in Playing Field Crescent. Mum says they used to play on the air raid roofs as they were like hills, and they jumped from one to another!

Rationing – they got a jar or tin of jam once a month, ¼ lb butter per person weekly and 2oz margarine weekly. She can't remember sugar as she says that they always ran out of it.

Gordon Walker

Just checked with my mum who has lived in Irvine Road all her life and is now 91. She can't remember an air raid shelter in Irvine Road but does remember walking down from her gran's house in Playing Field Crescent with her dad during the bombing of Clydebank and remembers the sky being all lit up with the fires.

She remembers the old hosiery in Irvine Road which later became a bed shop. The Tory hut and the Labour hut was where the launderette is now. There was also a canteen built for the miners where the fisher restaurant was.

The library was at the back of the old school building next to the janitor's house. Upstairs in the old school was a large community hall where weddings etcetera were held.

The Co-op on Gatehead Road was originally a house which she thinks was demolished and the building that is there now was built to replace it.

Finally, the shop in Irvine Road, May Orr's old shop, now the barber shop, was originally a chip shop, as was the small building where the bookies was on the corner of Gatehead Road.

Stephen Crawford

My mum told me there was an air raid shelter in Playing Field Road where the school playground meets the houses straight across from where she lived.

Matt Dorrans

Ayrshire in general was counted as a safe area, with coal mining counted as a reserved occupation. Miners joined up at the start of the war before the UK Government had chance to act on the drop of man power in the mines. RAF Dundonald (where Monsanto was) was possibly the largest military base near Crosshouse, with the exception of Annanhill Army Camp for D-Day preparations.

There were also some top-secret activities carried out on the Ayrshire coast on route to Loch Striven: SAS, SBS, 618 Squadron, X-craft.

Look up the following:

- RAF Dundonald and 516 Squadron combined operations (D-Day and Commando beach training)
- Annanhill Camp – a Canadian base in the run-up to D-Day
- Secret Scotland website
- Galston/Darvel – British SAS, French and Belgian SAS based and trained there, visited by FM Montgomery in run up to D-Day (on video)
- HMS Dasher disaster – see John Melville as the potential "the man that never was" in Operation Mincemeat
- Luftwaffe fighter plane crash-landed in Kilmarnock.
- RCAF Halifax bomber crashed at Bunton Hill Farm, Kilmaurs.
- Arran – Special Boat Service (SBS) formed at Sannox.
- 618 Squadron flew from RAF Turnberry to Loch Striven Argyll testing highball bouncing bombs.
- Dankeith House was used for D-Day planning.

Enjoy checking these out. Ayrshire was full of secrets during WWII!

Another interesting story: pilots Douglas and Margaret Fairweather were buried together in Dunure. They were based at RAF Prestwick. She was an Air Transport Auxiliary pilot and the first female to fly a Spitfire.

The following story was told to East Ayrshire Library Staff by Jeanette McGinty (now Diamond) during a People's War Workshop at the Crosshouse Library on 4th May 2005:

Jeanette recalls VE Day vividly, despite being only six years old. The village of Crosshouse in Ayrshire was adorned with flags hanging from every window, a testament to the widespread jubilation. She distinctly remembers heading to the public park, where a massive bonfire had been lit, and everyone danced around it in joyous celebration. Her dad and uncles, home from the war, were part of this cheerful gathering.

The celebrations continued at her house later that evening, where a grand party took place. Neighbours gathered, singing and dancing, creating an atmosphere akin to that of a street party. One of her friends even remembered young women dancing in the streets in their pyjamas, swept up in the excitement of the moment.

Situated in the village was The Craig House, a significant residence where soldiers from across the country were stationed. These soldiers were warmly welcomed into the village to join in the festivities. Crosshouse also played host to evacuees from Glasgow and Wales, who found refuge there for a significant part of the war.

Jeanette's memories extend beyond VE Day. She recalls soldiers marching to the railway station at Gatehead, singing songs as they went. She also remembers being at Kilmarnock station, waving to soldiers as they departed for war. Her father was away for six long years, and his infrequent visits meant that she scarcely recognised him, having been very young when he left.

One of the more harrowing memories from her childhood was witnessing the bombing of Clydebank from Crosshouse, despite the considerable distance. The sky lit up with the explosions, a sight that left a lasting impression on her young mind.

Jeanette's uncle, a sailor, brought back bananas – a rare treat and the first she had ever seen. This same uncle earned a DSM medal in the Navy for his bravery in rescuing people, likely from a sinking ship. Her mother contributed to the war effort as well, working as a riveter at the Barassie Works, where she made parts for aeroplanes. The blackout conditions necessitated the use of torches to navigate their way to work.

Jeanette's recollections paint a vivid picture of VE Day and the wartime experiences of Crosshouse, capturing both the joy of victory and the enduring hardships of war.

My War Memories by Martha Law

The war started when I was six. It didn't mean much to me and my friends until my two uncles were called up. Everyone was crying at the station when we went to see them off on the train. When they came home on leave after about six weeks training, we were so proud of them in their uniforms. After the first leave was over, they were posted overseas, and we didn't get any news for a long time. One uncle was in France, and we didn't know where the other one was for quite some time. We then received news that our other uncle was in Egypt, a prisoner of war for four years!

My grannie started doing work for the Red Cross and she got all the family enrolled into making scarves, socks and blankets. They then started making things to sell. The children would all go down to the beach and gather shells. My grannie bought special cord, and my uncle John would decorate the shells and fix them onto the cord to make bracelets, necklaces and brooches.

Just after the war started, the boys in our street were all called up to go into the Services. We lived in a circle of houses which had a big, round grassed area in the middle where we all played. One by one they were all called away, some to the Army, others to the Navy or Airforce. Five in our circle never came home.

Everyone started doing things to help the war effort, so our circle decided to have a concert. Our mothers gave us old curtains, hats and shoes to dress up in and everyone came along and paid their penny, and a penny for the raffle. We danced, sang and recited poetry and then raffled the things our mothers had given us. The concert was enjoyed by all and the Red Cross got 13s and 6d! There was no holding us back after that! The "circle kids" had a concert every other week from then on.

When food got scarce, we were issued with ration books. Babies got green, schoolchildren got blue, and adults got beige-coloured books. If you had a green book, you could get bananas, oranges and orange juice.

The books had coupons in them, and these showed what you were entitled to. When you went to the Co-op grocery and handed over the books, they would cut out the coupons and give you your rations. You could then go to the butchers and wait in the queue for meat. We often got fed up waiting and went to play hide and seek which meant we'd lose our place in the queue! Then when we got served there would be no steak or links left, and we'd get a row when we got home!

We were luckier than some families. I had an aunt in Canada and my mother's friend lived in America. They would send parcels, great big boxes with tins of sweets, sugar, jam, nylons and clothes. My mother used to share them out with the neighbours. The sweets came in long strips, and I used to take them out and break them off for my pals. I remember the first time we got cranberry sauce. My mother thought it was a new kind of jam or jelly, so we all had a "piece and jeely" that night!

We had our own home guard in the village. My brother was in it as he had tuberculosis and couldn't go into service. We also had wardens who would go round the village at night to check that all the windows were blacked out. This meant that all houses had to have black blinds or very thick curtains so that no light would shine through.

All downstairs houses had to have a shelter; ours was under the stairs and my mother had blankets and seats in it. When the sirens went to tell us there was a raid, the people upstairs would come down and go into the shelter with us. Our upstairs neighbours were deaf and dumb and when the sirens went, the wee man, Sammy, was first down the stairs. My father always had the door open for him, and he wouldn't come out for hours.

When there was no sugar left, we had to use saccharin, which was also scarce. There was one family, however, who could get it on the black market (whatever that was!), so everybody went to their door and got a packet for 1/-.

One day, the head teacher came into our class and told us that because there had been a lot of bombing in Glasgow, children from there were being brought to our school. They were hoping that our parents would take in some of these children to live in our homes. I was first to put my hand up and said, 'I'll take two!'

When I got home and told my mother, she nearly took a fit! However, she came along the next week and took two boys home. They stayed for two years and were just part of the family.

Archie Johnstone told the following stories to East Ayrshire library staff at their tea party on 11th June 2004

I was eight years old when war broke out and it didn't mean much to me. I remember that sweets weren't around, and they were something I missed. Sweets were a treat. I remember food parcels being sent from Australia where I had an aunt and three cousins, with whom I have just got back in touch via the internet.

The Grand Hall in Kilmarnock was used to incarcerate Italian prisoners of war. My parents befriended them and, when they had to get rid of their dog, they gave it to me and my sister. I can remember one of the Italians was called Mario Motto; he had twin sons, and he was a butcher from Palermo. I can't remember the names of any of the others. The Italians from Kilmarnock were interred at Mauchline. I especially remember the Incentti (?) family from Valley Restaurant, 6 Green Street, as I had to go and collect pig trotters for their restaurant.

The three air raid centres next to the water's edge on Green Street were underground and I wonder now if they were filled in when they redeveloped the area (it is now part of the one-way-system in Kilmarnock – does anyone know?).

My main memory of the War was going to the cinema to see the *Movietone News* and the white cockerel in the middle of the screen. We went to the Plaza Cinema that was built in Mill Lane in 1939.

I have a vague memory of a bomb dropping on, I think, the Kilmarnock Cemetery (the Strawberry Bank area).

To celebrate VJ Day, I remember a big party in the big car park in Waterloo Street. The police chased someone for setting a flare off.

The following story was told to East Ayrshire library staff during their tea party on 11th June 2004 by Mary Niven who is nearly 97 (maiden name McGivern). She tells her husband Jack's story.

Jack Niven was an engineer; before that he was a footballer at Bonnyton Square. He played for Queen of the South and Chester, and teams in Wales and Ireland. He gave it up at 30 when he and Mary married and he went back to the railway works for his engineering, and, because he had a reserved occupation, he didn't go to war.

Mary had four children altogether, and had to look after her mother: no home helps in those days. Mary calls the war her "blank years" as it seemed to be all work. They had to live with her mother for most of the war as they couldn't get a house, but eventually they got a house in Armour Street, Kilmarnock. Her children went to Bentinck School in Kilmarnock.

Rationing was a nightmare, but folk managed somehow. Mary even got a holiday in Saltcoats, going by train. She went to the quietest part of the shore to get some peace and quiet with the children.

Billy Arnott

My mum was waiting for a train at Kilmarnock Railway Station when she noticed a large crowd of people standing there.

A man wearing a very smart American uniform began walking along the platform towards her. He was apparently very nice, and he shook her hand.

It was none other than General Eisenhower, who went on to become the President of the United States of America. He flew into Prestwick in January 1944 to assume command as Supreme Allied Commander for the invasion of Europe, known as Operation Overlord. He visited again in April 1944. This trip was part of his preparations for D-Day

In 1945, the 5th Marquess of Ailsa gifted the top floor of Culzean Castle to him for his personal use during his lifetime. This gesture was a tribute from the people of Scotland for his leadership during the war.

Unknown author, Kilmarnock

There was a surprise and shock in Kilmarnock in the early hours of Tuesday, 6th May 1941, when it was realised that the Luftwaffe was dropping bombs on the town. The people of Kilmarnock knew exactly what to do and where to go. They had rehearsed the same procedure on several other occasions when the Luftwaffe had flown over Kilmarnock, but they had never dropped bombs on the town before. In truth, Kilmarnock folk felt quite safe. Kilmarnock was not a prime target. Any German raid in the west of Scotland was likely to be on more important targets such as the shipyards of Clydebank and the explosive works at Ardeer. Apart from that, the west of Scotland was a long way for Luftwaffe crews to fly, and they had to spend a lot of time in British airspace. It is now known that a single aircraft dropped 14 bombs. Their weight and the precise location that they landed have all been logged and charted on documents held in the National Archives of Scotland. Only one of the bombs caused casualties. That was the one that destroyed a block of flats in Culzean Crescent at the time there were wartime restrictions on reporting such things, and while the *Kilmarnock Standard* could report that four people had been killed "as a result of enemy action", the paper could not give the street name and could not even say that bombs had fallen on Kilmarnock.

When the raid started, there was work to be done. It was the responsibility of the ARP to find out the extent of the damage caused by the bombs and try to allocate resources to where they were needed most. First reports were confused, but it soon became clear that urgent help was required in Culzean Crescent. A block of flats had been hit. People were injured. Some were possibly trapped. The rescue squad arrived quickly. Neighbours were already on the scene. Half of the block of four flats was gone; it turned in a few moments from two homes into one pile of rubble.

One of the rescue workers eyed the buildings in the street and was astonished to see that several windows in the part of the block that had been hit remained intact and not a single pane of glass was broken in the buildings on either side of the one that been hit. On the other side of the street, however, several windows were shattered. But the rescue workers had no time to ponder on such odd matters. From the part of the building that was left standing, rescue workers helped lead two women and two young children to the safety of the street. The planes had gone, and the all-clear had sounded. The two ladies were a Mrs Robertson and a Mrs Cree, and the children were Jim Robertson and Shona Cree. Moments later, Mr Robertson was also accounted for. He had been at the back door of the house when the bomb fell, and he had thrown himself full length close to the gable of the building. It astonished the rescue party that none of the five of them had the slightest scratch or injury.

But it was quickly established that four other people from the two demolished flats were still not accounted for. They were a Mrs McGeachie, an elderly woman; her middle-aged daughter, Alice; and John Bissett and his housekeeper, Dorothy Armour. To add to the complications of the rescue, neighbours told the ARP men that Mr Bissett was a deaf mute. If he had survived the blast, he would have been unable to shout for help and he would not have heard the rescuers calling to him.

Rescue workers tore at the pile of rubble. Soon they found a body, then another. The other two bodies were found several hours later when demolition squads were removing the debris. Before the day was out, the survivors had all been rehoused by the town, and work had started on clearing the site.

Nancy Fleming

Mum told us that village signposts had been removed; she was always amazed when the bus conductress called out the names of the stops correctly! She remembers air raid drills at school and taking her gas mask to school with her.

Pete Heywood

I can't help you directly but I have some audio recordings of Andrew Macindoo talking about his time in the army. He served in Burma.

http://www.secretscotland.org.uk – Secrets, Annanhill Camp

JHW

Dad remembers catching eels to take to the Italian prisoners of war in Knockentiber. He would go walking with his aunt Agnes to watch the Spitfires at RAF Dundonald. Agnes worked in Ardeer explosives factory, a major producer of explosives during World War II.

Dad also remembers rationing, and being found out after his mother discovered an empty can of condensed milk she had been saving for Christmas. He had bored a hole in the base and taken all the contents, then placed the empty can back in its place in the pantry.

My grandfather was unable to join the armed forces, but worked as a long-distance lorry driver, often visiting London during the Blitz. He was also a bus driver and remembers finding a dead body in the middle of the road when he was driving from Crosshouse to Springside. It was very dark, and the headlights on the bus were covered or painted over to comply with blackout regulations, so it was lucky that he spotted it.

All his brothers joined up. Billy served with The Chindits, special operations units of the British and Indian Armies.

Mum, although not originally from Crosshouse, remembered receiving dresses and sweets from a neighbour's daughter who was working as a nanny in New York for the Colgate family. She was the envy of all her friends at parties when she was wearing her pretty American dresses. She always shared the sweets.

Loos

Loos-en-Gohelle, was a coalmining village near to the town of Lens.

Crosshouse was also predominantly a coal mining village, situated near to the town of Kilmarnock.

Both villages are linked by the men and families who suffered the worst the Great War could throw at them.

The Battle of Loos was where, for the first time, the British used chlorine gas as a weapon against the enemy and the first battle using Lord Horatio Kitchener's so-called New Army, consisting mostly of volunteers, who had only been training since August 1914.

Loos, as it is more commonly known, is situated in French Flanders, an industrial area of coal mines and mining villages.

In 1915, the village was attacked and held by German troops. The terrain was flat, apart from slag heaps and colliery towers.

One famous landmark, lifting gear by the main pit, stood about 150-feet tall. It was referred to as Tower Bridge by British soldiers, and it could be seen clearly in the distance as they awaited battle instructions. I have listened to *Voices of the First World War*, and many men recalled seeing this tower.

British troops were deployed to attack the strong German defences to support French offensives in the south. Half of the 72 battalions in the Battle of Loos belonged to Scottish regiments. Apologies to all of the other regiments who were involved in this bloody battle, but I have chosen to focus on the Scottish regiments.

"The scene of the coming conflict was not a picturesque one... the open plain was dotted with squalid little red brick villages and ugly mine works."

Newman Flower, 1916

Battle of Loos, 1915

A great deal of nonsense has been written about Loos. The real tragedy of that battle was its nearness to complete success. Most of us who reached the crest of Hill 70, and survived, were firmly convinced that we had broken through on that Sunday, 26th September 1915. There seemed to be nothing ahead of us, but an unoccupied and incomplete trench system. The only two things that prevented our advancing into the suburbs of Lens were, firstly, the exhaustion of the "Jocks" themselves (for they had undergone a bellyful of marching and fighting that day) and, secondly, the flanking fire of numerous German machine-guns, which swept that bare hill from some factory buildings in Cite St. Auguste to the south of us. All that we needed was more artillery ammunition to blast those clearly located machine guns, plus some fresh infantry to take over from the weary and depleted "Jocks". But, alas, neither ammunition nor reinforcements were immediately available, and the great opportunity passed."

Major-General Richard Hilton, Forward Observation Officer

Out of almost 10,000 British soldiers, 8,246 were killed or wounded in three hours during the Battle of Loos.

The Forgotten Battle by Patrick Macgill

The Unwanted Battle: Loos 1915 by Gordon Corrigan (2018, Sharpe Books)

"The disproportionate number of Scots who went over the top at 6.30 am on September 25, 1915, ensured Loos would be remembered as a Scottish battle."

Dr Derek Patrick, University of St Andrews

1914 - 1918

PTE	CUMMIMNGS McMILLAN
PTE	JOHN MILLIGAN
PTE	JOHN MONTAGUE
PTE	DAVID IGGS NEWLANDS
PTE	JAMES OWENS

PTE	ROBERT ROSS
PTE	ROBERT SHEARER
PTE	DAVID STEWART
PTE	JAMES STEWART
PTE	DAVID STEVENSON
PTE	ANDREW STRUTHERS
PTE	JOHN TAIT
PTE	WILLIAM WARDROPE
LIET	GEORGE CARLYLE
LIET	ANDREW Y YOUNG
SERGT	WILLIAM HUNTER
SERGT	GEORGE SHIELDS
SERGT	THOMAS WALKER
SERGT	ROBERT WHITE
CORP	ROBERT BURLEIGH
CORP	CHARLES HANNAH – military medal
CORP	WILLIAM LAMONT
CORP	ROBERT OWENS
LANC/CORP	JAMES COWAN
LANC/CORP	F CUMMINGS
LANC/CORP	JOHN HUNTER
LANC/CORP	A LIVINGSTONE
LANC/CORP	JAMES ROSS
LANC/CORP	GEORGE STEWART

1939 - 1945

ABLE SEAMAN	WILLIM CANDLISH
STOKER	FRANCIS FREW
PTE	DAVID SPROTT
PTE	ROBERT W LUNDIE
GUARDSMAN	ALEX ALLARDYCE
GUARDSMAN	ALEX SPEIRS
GUARDSMAN	JOHN R WILSON
GUARDSMAN	CHARLES HOWIE
GUNNER	JOHN A COLE
TROOPER	ROBERT T MILLAR
FUSILIER	JOHN WILSON
LANC/CORP	DAVID FLETCHER
LANC/CORP	ALEX ELLIOTT
LANC/SERG	JOHN ANDERSON
AIRCRAFTSMAN	WILLIAM S GOODMAN
SERG	JOHN HILLHOUSE
SERG	SIMPSONN ADAIR
FUSILIER	JOHN ORR
SAPPER	JAMES McDOUGALL
CORP	WILLIAM TODD

How it all began in 1914

What follows is my understanding of events in simple terms. Apologies to any historians who are expecting a more detailed account.

On 28th June 1914, Archduke Franz Ferdinand went to inspect Austrian troops in Bosnia. He was assassinated by a 19-year-old Bosnian Serb called Gavrilo Princip. This act of terrorism was described as "the spark that would set light to a continent that was riddled by tensions."

Reports in the *Times* newspaper said that the assassination "produced horror and consternation throughout Europe".

On 5th July, Germany promised total support for Austria-Hungary.

On 28th July, Austria-Hungary enraged Russia by declaring war on Serbia.

On 30th July, Russia mobilised her army which alarmed Germany.

On 3rd August, Germany implemented the Schlieffen Plan by invading France through neutral Belgium. Germany planned to attack and defeat France first by travelling through Belgium, capturing Paris, and finally going on to attack Russia.

On 4th August, Britain declared war on Germany because of the 1839 Treaty of London which bound Britain to guard the neutrality of Belgium.

Compared with the small-scale British attacks in spring 1915, the Battle of Loos was a mighty offensive, referred to as The Big Push. The Germans were deeply entrenched in France.

Allies had begun a new joint attack on the Western Front. The British were to launch an attack on Loos, and the French were ready to attack in Artois and Champagne. Champagne was to be a wholly French offensive, and Artois a joint French and British attack, with the British providing a diversionary attack on Loos from the La Bassee Canal to the north of the village, while the French would attack from south of Lieven to Arras.

Lord Kitchener went to the Western Front on 16th August and saw for himself that the ground over which the British were expected to traverse was incompatible with success. He is quoted as saying, "We must act with all energy and do our utmost to help France in their offensive, even though by doing so we may suffer heavy losses."

The British did not want to fight the Battle of Loos. General Douglas Haig felt that it was too soon, that Britain was not ready. He thought that July 1916 would be better which, of course, was when the Battle of the Somme took place.

General Douglas Haig was overseeing the attack on Loos, under Field Marshall Sir John French, commander of the British Expeditionary Force on the Western Front, but Haig had serious reservations and fears. He knew that the advancing British infantry would have almost no cover or protection as they traversed the flat terrain. They would be in full view of the German Army. British stocks of artillery and ammunition were insufficient.

At that time, Germany was producing 250,000 shells a week, France was producing 100,000, but Britain was only producing 22,000 per week.

Loos, situated in French Flanders, was an industrial area consisting of coal mines and mining villages. But by 1915, the village had been attacked and was being held by German troops. Miners' cottages provided shelter for the German troops since most had basements.

The muddy, treeless terrain was flat but had a gentle incline towards the German front line. It was dotted with slag heaps and colliery towers. In short, the British troops were at the bottom of the incline with no cover whatsoever. German soldiers had positioned themselves in the prime locations on top of the slag heaps. They had machine guns as well as heavy artillery; in short, the British Army with no cover would be in full view of the enemy as they advanced towards Loos. No man's land stretched ominously out towards enemy lines, varying from one hundred yards to six hundred yards away, heavily peppered with a maze of crisscrossed wire, mainly barbed, about one hundred feet in depth and two to four feet in height. The British had tried to cut through with artillery but the volunteer soldiers in charge of the guns lacked experience and precision. Wiring parties had done what they could to cut through under cover of darkness, but it had been observed from ariel photographs that much of it remained in situ.

One landmark for the British, which they had tried and failed to destroy, was a tower that housed lifting gear next to the main pit in Loos. The structure was about 150 feet tall and was referred to as Tower Bridge by British soldiers. Crucially, from Tower Bridge, the German Army could see at least two miles beyond the British forward positions. The tower could be seen clearly in the distance by the British as they waited for zero hour and orders to advance. Some British soldiers were to depend on this landmark for direction as they advanced through the bloodbath of confusion, smoke and gas.

Field of Corpses

"Never had the machine-gunners such straightforward work to do nor done it so unceasingly. The men stood on the fire step, some even on the parapets, and fired exultantly into the mass of men advancing across the open grassland. As the entire field of fire was covered with the enemy's infantry, the effect was devastating, and they could be seen falling in hundreds."

German Regimental Diarist, after the Battle of Loos

Chemical Warfare

The Battle of Loos was the first battle of WWI in which the British would use demoralising and deadly gas as a weapon.

Four months before the Battle of Loos took place, Germany had used gas as a weapon, causing the Allies to complain bitterly, and declaring that it was banned. The Hague Convention of 1907 did ban using artillery shells to dispense gas, but it did not mention or ban the use of gas cylinders.

Sir John French called the use of gas "a cynical and barbarous disregard of the well-known usages of civilised war".

The British went on to develop more effective and horrid gases and ways to deliver them, going on to launch almost twice as many gas attacks as Germany.

When chlorine contacts moisture in the nose, eyes and lungs, it turns into an acid that burns, blinds and blisters. It destroys the lungs, and victims drown in their own body fluids. Those who did not die went on to suffer lifelong lung problems.

In the early days before gas masks, soldiers had to make do with socks or rags soaked in their own urine to protect themselves against the effects of the gas. A Canadian artillery officer was horrified to see men "literally coughing their lungs out" and later to "roll about like mad dogs in their death". A Canadian medical officer suggested using fabric soaked with water, baking soda and urine. The ammonia in the urine reacted with chlorine to reduce the effects. By 6th June, British and Canadian soldiers were issued with the first gas mask designed by Captain Cluny Macpherson of the 1st Newfoundland Regiment. His next mask, which had eyepieces and an exhalation valve, was nick-named "the goggle-eyed bugger with the tit" by Captains Robert Graves and JC Dunn of the Royal Welsh Fusiliers.

If a whiff of gas you smell,

Bang your gong like bloody hell,

On with your googly, up with your gun –

Ready to meet the bloody Hun.

The British smoke helmet, also known as the hypo helmet, became available in July 1915. It was not popular. It covered the head and neck, and was tucked into the collar of the soldier's tunic. The material was impregnated with hyposulphite which removed chlorine from the air in the helmet. It was effective, but it was hot difficult to see and hear.

It was determined by the British that 9,000 cylinders would be required but there were only 4,000 available, and so it was decided that smoke and gas would be released intermittently.

Canisters of chlorine gas, provided by special units of the Royal Engineers, were stacked up at the ready in the British trenches. The plan was for the gas and smoke to be released at zero-hour before the men were sent over the top in two columns leaving reserves to follow on later. The time of zero-hour would depend on the wind direction. A gas attack could only be successful if there was a wind blowing in the direction of the German trenches.

Sir Douglas Haig felt that if the wind were against them and gas could not be used, the attack should be postponed. However, the French were determined to go ahead come what may on 25th September, and General Haig did not receive support from Sir John French, although Sir John agreed to an abridged plan if it was not possible to use gas.

At 5 am on 25th September, General Haig checked the wind direction himself and gave the go-ahead to continue with the original plan.

Many soldiers were carrying pickaxes, shovels and sandbags as well as guns so that they could alter the direction of enemy trenches once they had captured them. The men were told that once the order to advance was given, anyone retreating or caught being a shirker would be shot.

The battalions consisted of regular soldiers, the Territorial Army, and an army of volunteers and reservists which became known as Kitchener's Army, named after the Secretary of State for War, Lord Kitchener, who planned to use the mostly untrained and unprepared men in a major battle for the first time during the war.

Throughout the country, men had volunteered in large numbers; patriotism was running high, and Kitchener's face stared out of posters declaring *Your Country needs You.* Almost every town and village in Scotland was affected by the battle of Loos. Seventy-two battalions, half of which belonged to Scottish regiments, were involved. Scottish divisions made the main attacks, with battalions from every Scottish regiment fighting in the battle. Dundee's 4th Black Watch, also known as "Dundee's Own", suffered one of the highest casualty rates in the country, but the heavy losses affected families and loved ones not only in Dundee but also in Aberdeenshire, Lanarkshire, Perthshire, Fife, Stirlingshire and Ayrshire.

Sir John French resigned "under pressure" in late 1915 and was succeeded by General Douglas Haig who went on to become Field Marshall.

> *"I saw some rats running from under the dead men's greatcoats, enormous rats, fat with human flesh. My heart pounded as we edged towards one of the bodies. His helmet had rolled off. The man displayed a grimacing face, stripped of flesh; the skull bare, the eyes devoured and from the yawning mouth leaped a rat."*
>
> Author unknown

Sources

Voices of World War One, BBC Documentaries, Dan Snow

www.thelonglongtrail.co.uk by Chris Baker

Loos 1915 podcast by Dr Nick Lloyd

Loos 1915, The Unwanted Battle by Gordon Corrigan

The Trench Warfare Department, 1914-15,

www.thewesternfrontassociation.com

Battle of Loos: Landscape and Gas by Professor Peter Doyle

15th Scottish Division at The Battle of Loos 1915 by Stuart Roxburgh (You Tube)

Stand To Crosshouse-Loos, 1915 (You Tube)

Over There by Sadie Stein, 19th June 2014

"The trench was a horrible sight. The dead were stretched out on one side, one on top of each other six feet high. I thought at the time I should never get the peculiar disgusting smell of the vapour of warm human blood heated by the sun out of my nostrils. I would rather have smelt gas a hundred times. I can never describe that faint sickening, horrible smell which several times nearly knocked me up altogether."

British Captain Leeham

https://www.bbc.co.uk/bitesize/guides/z4n4jxs/revision/4

25th September 2025

I read the following article online on 25th September 2025 (*Daily Express*). It touched me so deeply, I can't find the words to describe it.

I must mention that more than half a million soldiers are still missing from World War One, and over a third are thought to be buried as unknown. More are being discovered all the time through agricultural work and building development.

"Relatives of two Scottish soldiers killed in the First World War gathered in France on Thursday to witness their burial with full military honours.

Lieutenant James Grant Allan, 9th Battalion, Gordon Highlanders, and Lance Corporal Gordon McPherson, 7th Battalion, Cameron Highlanders, were laid to rest alongside their comrades exactly 110 years after they were killed in action.

Lt Allan, from Melrose, left Edinburgh University to join the Gordons when war was declared in 1914. He joined at the same time as his brother Nimmo, and they both went to fight in France.

He was killed on September 25, 1915, the first day of the Battle of Loos. A friend and fellow officer wrote 'Jim's men thought the world of him,' and continued, 'I have gained from his friendship... He may have left this world but only to go to a freer one... I have been strengthened by the thought of him, or his presence.'

He was identified after artefacts found with the casualties suggested one was an officer, which narrowed the search by the Ministry of Defence's team of War Detectives. The families of the battalion's 14 missing officers were traced and tested, with Lt Allan's family proving a positive match.

LCpl McPherson was working as a tobacconist in Newcastle when he joined the Cameron Highlanders in November 1914 alongside his two brothers and their father, James. Born in Portsmouth where his father was serving in the Royal Marines, he grew up in Aberdeen.

He too was killed on 25 September 1915. A fellow soldier of his machine-gun section described him as 'the life and soul of the section. His imitations of Charles Chaplin were enjoyed very much by his comrades. His favourite song, Trumpeter, What are you Sounding Now?, grew to be the most popular song in the section... It was Gordon's song. We can't sing it now.'

LCpl McPherson was identified by a small set of buttons from the Newcastle Corporation Tramway that he had in his pocket at the time of his death. After studying the 1911 census, the War Detectives discovered that his father worked for the Tramway after leaving the Marines, so a DNA test was sent to the next of kin, which came back positive.

Six more Scottish soldiers whose identities remain unknown were buried today. All were discovered during construction work for a new hospital on the outskirts of Loos. The service was organised by the MOD's Joint Casualty and Compassionate Centre (JCCC), also known as the MOD War Detectives."

ABOUT THE AUTHOR

Jacqueline Heron Wray was born in Kilmarnock and grew up in the village of Crosshouse. She completed her General Nurse training in 1981, and her Midwifery training in 1982.

Work and marriage took her to Thurso in Caithness, North Berwick in East Lothian, Illinois in the USA, the Cotswolds, and Hertfordshire. She returned to Ayrshire, with her retired Metropolitan Police Officer husband, Mike, in 2017. They live in a farmhouse in the countryside where they enjoy a quiet life with their Newfoundland, Layla, the local wildlife, and beaches.

As well as writing, Jacqueline is an avid reader, enjoys painting, crafting and spending as much time as she can with her daughters.

Jacqueline's first book, *King Street to King's Road*, a memoir, was published in 2019.

Printed in Dunstable, United Kingdom

01004907R00101